CHRISTOPHER BUSH
THE CASE OF THE SILKEN PETTICOAT

CHRISTOPHER BUSH was born Charlie Christmas Bush in Norfolk in 1885. His father was a farm labourer and his mother a milliner. In the early years of his childhood he lived with his aunt and uncle in London before returning to Norfolk aged seven, later winning a scholarship to Thetford Grammar School.

As an adult, Bush worked as a schoolmaster for 27 years, pausing only to fight in World War One, until retiring aged 46 in 1931 to be a full-time novelist. His first novel featuring the eccentric Ludovic Travers was published in 1926, and was followed by 62 additional Travers mysteries. These are all to be republished by Dean Street Press.

Christopher Bush fought again in World War Two, and was elected a member of the prestigious Detection Club. He died in 1973.

CHRISTOPHER BUSH

THE CASE OF THE SILKEN PETTICOAT

With an introduction
by Curtis Evans

DEAN STREET PRESS

Published by Dean Street Press 2020

Copyright © 1953 Christopher Bush

Introduction copyright © 2020 Curtis Evans

All Rights Reserved

The right of Christopher Bush to be identified as the Author of
the Work has been asserted by his estate in accordance with the
Copyright, Designs and Patents Act 1988.

First published in 1953 by MacDonald & Co.

Cover by DSP

ISBN 978 1 913527 05 1

www.deanstreetpress.co.uk

To

BARBARA McILWAINE

with love

INTRODUCTION

Ring out the Old, Ring in the New
Christopher Bush and Mystery Fiction in the Fifties

"Mr. Bush has an urbane and intelligent way of dealing with mystery which makes his work much more attractive than the stampeding sensationalism of some of his rivals."
—Rupert Crofts-Cooke (acclaimed author of the Leo Bruce detective novels)

New fashions in mystery fiction were decidedly afoot in the 1950s, as authors increasingly turned to sensationalistic tales of international espionage, hard-boiled sex and violence, and psychological suspense. Yet there indubitably remained, seemingly imperishable and eternal, what Anthony Boucher, dean of American mystery reviewers, dubbed the "conventional type of British detective story." This more modestly decorous but still intriguing and enticing mystery fare was most famously and lucratively embodied by Crime Queen Agatha Christie, who rang in the new decade and her Golden Jubilee as a published author with the classic detective novel that was promoted as her fiftieth mystery: *A Murder Is Announced* (although this was in fact a misleading claim, as this tally also included her short story collections). Also representing the traditional British detective story during the 1950s were such crime fiction stalwarts (all of them Christie contemporaries and, like the Queen of Crime, longtime members of the Detection Club) as Edith Caroline Rivett (E.C.R Lorac and Carol Carnac), E.R. Punshon, Cecil John Charles Street (John Rhode and Miles Burton) and Christopher Bush. Punshon and Rivett passed away in the Fifties, pens still brandished in their hands, if you will, but Street and Bush, apparently indefatigable, kept at crime throughout the decade, typically publishing in both the United Kingdom and the United States two books a year (Street with both of his pseudonyms).

Not to be outdone even by Agatha Christie, Bush would celebrate his own Golden Jubilee with his fiftieth mystery, *The Case of the Russian Cross*, in 1957—and this was done, in contrast with Christie, without his publishers having to resort to any creative accounting. *Cross* is the fiftieth Christopher Bush Ludovic Travers detective novel reprinted by Dean Street Press in this, the Spring of 2020, the hundredth anniversary of the dawning of the Golden Age of detective fiction, following, in this latest installment, *The Case of the Counterfeit Colonel* (1952), *The Case of the Burnt Bohemian* (1953), *The Case of The Silken Petticoat* (1953), *The Case of the Red Brunette* (1954), *The Case of the Three Lost Letters* (1954), *The Case of the Benevolent Bookie* (1955), *The Case of the Amateur Actor* (1955), *The Case of the Extra Man* (1956) and *The Case of the Flowery Corpse* (1956).

Not surprisingly, given its being the occasion of Christopher Bush's Golden Jubilee, *The Case of the Russian Cross* met with a favorable reception from reviewers, who found the author's wry dedication especially ingratiating: "The author, having discovered that this is his fiftieth novel of detection, dedicates it in sheer astonishment to HIMSELF." Writing as Francis Iles, the name under which he reviewed crime fiction, Bush's Detection Club colleague Anthony Berkeley, himself one of the great Golden Age innovators in the genre, commented, "I share Mr. Bush's own surprise that *The Case of the Russian Cross* should be his fiftieth book; not so much at the fact itself as at the freshness both of plot and writing which is still as notable with fifty up as it was in in his opening overs. There must be many readers who still enjoy a straightforward, honest-to-goodness puzzle, and here it is." The late crime writer Anthony Lejeune, who would be admitted to the Detection Club in 1963, for his part cheered, "Hats off to Christopher Bush....[L]ike his detective, [he] is unostentatious but always absolutely reliable." Alan Hunter, who recently had published his first George Gently mystery and at the time was being lauded as the "British Simenon," offered similarly praiseful words, pronouncing of *The*

Case of the Russian Cross that Bush's sleuth Ludovic Travers "continues to be a wholly satisfying creation, the characters are intriguing and the plot full of virility. . . . the only trace of long-service lies in the maturity of the treatment."

The high praise for Bush's fiftieth detective novel only confirmed (if resoundingly) what had become clear from reviews of earlier novels from the decade: that in Britain Christopher Bush, who had turned sixty-five in 1950, had become a Grand Old Man of Mystery, an Elder Statesman of Murder. Bush's *The Case of the Three Lost Letters*, for example, was praised by Anthony Berkeley as "a model detective story on classical lines: an original central idea, with a complicated plot to clothe it, plenty of sound, straightforward detection by a mellowed Ludovic Travers and never a word that is not strictly relevant to the story"; while reviewer "Christopher Pym" (English journalist and author Cyril Rotenberg) found the same novel a "beautifully quiet, close-knit problem in deduction very fairly presented and impeccably solved." Berkeley also highly praised Bush's *The Case of the Burnt Bohemian*, pronouncing it "yet another sound piece of work . . . in that, alas!, almost extinct genre, the real detective story, with Ludovic Travers in his very best form."

In the United States Bush was especially praised in smaller newspapers across the country, where, one suspects, traditional detection most strongly still held sway. "Bush is one of the soundest of the English craftsmen in this field," declared Ben B. Johnston, an editor at the *Richmond Times Dispatch*, in his review of *The Case of the Burnt Bohemian*, while Lucy Templeton, doyenne of the *Knoxville Sentinel* (the first female staffer at that Tennessee newspaper, Templeton, a freshly minted graduate of the University of Tennessee, had been hired as a proofreader back in 1904), enthusiastically avowed, in her review of *The Case of the Flowery Corpse*, that the novel was "the best mystery novel I have read in the last six months." Bush "has always told a good story with interesting backgrounds and rich characterization," she added admiringly. Another southern reviewer, one "M." of the *Montgomery Advertiser*, deemed *The Case of the Amateur Actor* "another Travers mystery to delight the most critical of a reader audience," concluding in inimitable American lingo, "it's a swell story." Even Anthony Boucher, who in the Fifties hardly could be termed an unalloyed admirer of conventional British detection, from his prestigious post at the *New York Times Books Review* afforded words of praise to a number of Christopher Bush mysteries from the decade, including the cases of the *Benevolent Bookie* ("a provocative puzzle"), the *Amateur Actor* ("solid detective interest"), the *Flowery Corpse* ("many small ingenuities of detection") and, but naturally, the *Russian Cross* ("a pretty puzzle"). In his own self-effacing fashion, it seems that Ludovic Travers had entered the pantheon of Great Detectives, as another American commentator suggested in a review of Bush's *The Case of The Silken Petticoat*:

> Although Ludovic Travers does not possess the esoteric learning of Van Dine's Philo Vance, the rough and ready punch of Mickey Spillane's Mike Hammer, the Parisian [sic!] touch of Agatha Christie's Hercule Poirot, the appetite and orchids of Rex Stout's Nero Wolfe, the suave coolness of The Falcon or the eerie laugh and invisibility of The Shadow, he does have good qualities—especially the ability to note and interpret clues and a dogged persistence in remembering and following up an episode he could not understand. These paid off in his solution of *The Case of The Silken Petticoat*.

In some ways Christopher Bush, his traditionalism notwithstanding, attempted with his Fifties Ludovic Travers mysteries to keep up with the tenor of rapidly changing times. As owner of the controlling interest in the Broad Street Detective Agency, Ludovic Travers increasingly comes to resemble an American private investigator rather than the gentleman amateur detective he had been in the 1930s; and the novels in which he appears reflect some of the jaded cynicism of post-World War Two American hard-boiled crime fiction. *The Case of the Red Brunette*, one of my favorite examples from this batch of Bushes, looks at civic corruption in provincial England in a case concerning a town counsellor who dies in an apparent "badger game" or "honey trap" gone fatally wrong ("a web of mystery skillfully spun" noted Pat McDermott of Iowa's *Quad City Times*), while in *The Case of the Three Lost Letters*, Travers finds himself having to explain to his phlegmatic wife Bernice the pink lipstick strains on his collar (incurred strictly in the line of duty, of course). Travers also pays homage to the popular, genre altering Inspector Maigret novels of Georges Simenon in *The Case of Red Brunette*, when he decides that he will "try to get a feel of the city [of Mainford]: make a Maigret-like tour and achieve some kind of background. . . ."

Christopher Bush finally decided that Travers could manage entirely without his longtime partner in crime solving, the wily and calculatingly avuncular Chief Superintendent George Wharton, whom at times Travers, in the tradition of American hard-boiled crime fiction, appears positively to dislike. "I generally admire and respect Wharton, but there are times when he annoys me almost beyond measure," Travers confides in *The Case of the Amateur Actor*. "There are even moments, as when he assumes that cheap and leering superiority, when I can suddenly hate him." George Wharton appropriately makes his final, brief appearance in the Bush oeuvre in *The Case of the Russian Cross*, where Travers allows that despite their differences, the "Old General" is "the man who'd become in most ways my oldest friend."

"Ring out the old, ring in the new" may have been the motto of many when it came to mid-century mystery fiction, but as another saying goes, what once was old eventually becomes sparklingly new again. The truth of the latter adage is proven by this shining new set of Christopher Bush reissues. "Just like old crimes," vintage mystery fans may sigh contentedly, as once again they peruse the pages of a Bush, pursuing murderous malefactors in the ever pleasant company of Ludovic Travers, all the while armed with the happy knowledge that a butcher's dozen of thirteen of Travers' investigations yet remains to be reissued.

Curtis Evans

PART I
DEATH BY DROWNING

1
THE CRITIC AND THE BLONDE

Dɪᴅ you ever see anybody step up publicly to the late George Bernard Shaw and give a contemptuous tug to his beard? Or watch some indignant Picasso-addict crash down a Constable canvas on the head of Munnings? Or a disgruntled concert-goer make his way to the rostrum and take a swing at Beecham? I doubt if you did. But I saw something almost as good. I was there when a beautiful blonde kicked the shin of the one and only Clement Foorde, and that's a story, believe me, which I could one day tell to the more sophisticated of my children—if I had any.

I wasn't six feet away. A grandstand seat, as they say. I actually saw—

But maybe I'm getting too far ahead. Maybe, too, you haven't any use for flashbacks: those moments when you're just getting comfortably into the story and then there's a fade-out and you're suddenly back heaven-knows-where and among heaven-knows-whom. Not that that famous episode in the Café Rond—which, by the way, isn't its real name—is in the nature of a cinematographic flashback. It was plumb in the middle of a murder, if I may put it like that. For murders—the planned and tricky kind—don't just happen. There's what I might call a period of growth: that interval which Shakespeare speaks of as

> Between the acting of a dreadful thing
> And the first motion. . . .

There is, in fact, that moment when a murder first comes to the murderer's mind, or it may not even be that. It may be the beginnings of circumstances which will ultimately make murder seem the only way out. Between the first circumstance and the actual murder is an interval which may be weeks or months or even years. In the case to which I refer, it was a matter of months, and that affair in the Café Rond came in the middle of those months. And after that unconscionable deal of self-defence, permit me to tell you what actually did happen that early evening of March in the bar—commonly known as the Stoke-hole—on the ground floor of the Café Rond.

You will pardon, I hope, a brief repetition if you are already aware that some few years ago I was lucky enough to acquire an old-established detective agency in Broad Street. I'm entitled also to call it a high-class concern, but in any case it's something for my own spare time when I don't happen to be employed by the Yard as what they call an unofficial expert. Norris is my manager, but he had suddenly gone down with a bad chill, and for the whole of a week I had virtually lived in Broad Street directing things generally and lending a hand on an arson enquiry for one of our best clients—an important insurance company.

By the Monday evening everything was in hand and Norris arrived to relieve me. A client had been in the office, and he and I shared a taxi to Swan and Edgar's Corner. I was feeling mentally tired, and, although it's not four hundred yards to my flat at St. Martin's Chambers, I decided that I badly needed a drink, so I made my way across to the Café Rond.

It was almost half-past six and the bar was pretty full. There was plenty of chatter and so much of a smoke haze that I had to give my hornrims a polish before I could see clearly to the far end. Behind the bar, and against a long background of multi-coloured bottles, a cocktail-wallah and a couple of barmen were busy as beavers. A fat man slid off a stool and put on his hat, and I was on that one vacant bar stool before its temperature had sunk by half a degree and ordering a treble whisky and splash. Then I had a good look to my right, and there was Clement Foorde.

I won't say I was surprised, even if I knew that he was rarely at the Café Rond. There was a time when he was a frequent visitor of the Café Royal, which is almost next door, but for the last year or two, someone had told me, his visits even there had been very few. Nor was I gratified to be in the presence of so public a figure. After all, he and I are members of the same club, and so, for that matter, is Ashman, about whom you have yet to hear. Perhaps I was just mildly titillated, and in the vaguest of ways, at being so near. Had I leaned forward I could have stroked the voluminous cape or the silky head of swept-back white hair. I could almost have counted each hair in the moustache and the little imperial that barely reached the bottom of his chin, and I could see each detail of the setting of the handsome antique ring that flashed as he gently waved a white, gesticulating hand.

He was in one of the deep leather chairs with a low table between him and his listener, a donnish-looking man whom I did not know. And though I should have been capable of unashamedly listening, I could hear nothing of what was being said; the chatter of the room was too noisy for that. My drink had come, and as I took the first heartening pull at it my elbow jogged my neighbour on my left, and I turned to see Howard Breck, one of the star writers on the *Sentinel*. I grinned by way of apology and gave a little nod.

"Don't often see you here, Mr. Travers?" he said.

"I stray occasionally," I told him.

He leaned forward till his lips almost brushed my ear.

"Honoured tonight, aren't we?"

I felt a bit self-conscious as I whispered back that apparently we were.

"The old maestro looks in good fettle," he said. "Know who the cove is with him?"

"Never saw him before," I said. "But isn't that Tom Latimer over there in the corner?"

"Why not?" he told me, and shrugged his shoulders as he finished his drink.

I asked him to have another, and I was wondering why two newspaper men of the standing of himself and Latimer of the *Record* should happen to be in the Café Rond at the same time.

"I suppose it isn't in order to ask if you and Latimer happen to be here just because Foorde is here?" I asked him as the waiter produced his Martini.

"Good God, no!" he told me blasphemously. And that was the moment when things began to happen.

I admit that I ran only a casual eye over the girl—or should I say woman?—as she came past us, for at that moment I couldn't possibly have conceived that she was anything different as a customer from, say, myself. My mind, I believe, registered the fact that she was what is known as an uncommonly good-looker, that she was a blonde, and that the fur cape she wore was probably nutria.

"Pardon me, but aren't you Clement Foorde?"

Her voice had a hardness of timbre and was curiously penetrating. The chatter was suddenly less noisy as I swivelled round on my stool.

"Yes, my dear lady."

Foorde was hoisting himself to his feet. The voice was suave and almost unctuous.

"It was you who wrote that letter to the Press about Bobby Ashman's book?"

"Did I?" he said slowly, and with a pose of trying to remember. The rather full lips had a faint, ironical smile.

"You know what I'm talking about," she told him fiercely. "You're a filthy-minded old swine—that's what you are!"

And with that she kicked him hard on the shin. Foorde staggered back, tripped against the chair and fell. She stood above him for a moment, face flaring and breasts heaving, and then she turned and went. No one stopped her as, head high, she went quickly along that room. I felt a movement at my elbow as I turned. Breck had gulped his drink and was hard on her heels. He was not two yards behind her as she went through the swing-doors. And it was then, I think, that I realised that Latimer had gone too.

I turned round to look at Clement Foorde, but he was back on his feet and the man with him was handing him his hat. Foorde had said never a word. One might have expected some epigram:

some *a propos* remark on the impetuosity of youth or a word of bland apology for that brief fraças, but Foorde was moving off unruffled, and his friend—an even taller man—was holding him gently by the arm as the room made way for the two of them. Ripples of chatter followed their wake and burst to a babel as the swing-doors closed. I remember staring for a moment at my empty glass, and then I slid from my stool and made my own way to the doors.

I think now that things had happened even more quickly than I have told them. I know that I stood for a minute when I was outside, and the first thing I was thinking of was the girl who had attacked Foorde. Her back had been to me, but I remembered the blonde hair as it curled back above the fur cape. I remembered the high cheekbones and the poise of her, and the level, bitter clearness of her voice, and how that voice had had just a hint of the vulgar. And then my mind went to Foorde himself, and it was of him I was thinking as I slowly walked towards home: of a man who had become something of a legend; of the veritable sacrilege of that scene in the Café Rond.

Clement Foorde, I said slowly to myself. There must have been few moments when he was unselfconscious: a poseur by what must have long become second nature and who probably struck an attitude in his bath. A brilliant brain, mind you: a many-faceted man, even if the brilliance shone best in a light where fine quality paste can pass for the real thing. About the theatre he could write with affection and insight, and his memory—or his volumes of cuttings—must have been prodigious. As the leading dramatic critic of his age he wielded an enormous power. A play damned by him stayed damned, and his praise was a passport to popularity. But, as I said, there was a hard brilliance about his writing and too deft a scattering of epigrams which, one maliciously felt, were taken as needed from a notebook carried on his person and in which he recorded his own ephemeridae and, more surreptitiously, the cynicisms and witticisms of his friends.

There were facets, as I said. In the *Clarion* he regularly reviewed selected books, and an excellent summary of that side of him was provided by a cartoon of Harold Wadsworth's showing the great man in malicious enjoyment, with the caption—

CLEMENT FOORDE REVIEWING CLEMENT FOORDE
REVIEWING A WORK BY MR. X.

As an author himself—I refer particularly to *Decadence and the Drama* and *Fin de Siècle*—he wrote of what he would call his beloved theatre. That writing had the grand manner: the certainty of one who has much to say and has no difficulty in giving an impression of unique experience and authority. In his autobiographical *First Curtain*—it was to be followed by at least two sequels—he was, to me at least, the poseur who endeavours with his tongue in cheek to prove he is no such thing. In it, too, his passion for the epigram was as irritating as, say, the alliteration of Swinburne or Chesterton's prepossession with paradox.

But a great figure nevertheless: flamboyant; the Cyrano of critics, flaunting his panache, and flaunting at his own selected times a personality he had polished and perfected. But not too much of a public figure: nothing common-hackneyed in the eyes of men. At racing, which was one of his passions, I've been told that the popular meetings never saw him, but Ascot he never missed, nor Goodwood. Those small dinners at his town flat were extremely rare, but the last word in the *recherché*. And he had also a kind of anchoritic pose at a small place in some Surrey village or other where he would retire for long periods for the purpose of what he might have called creative art, and where a married couple looked after his wants.

His income I can't possibly assess, but it must have been large if only for the reason that he spent enormously. I would not say extravagantly or lavishly, but fine and fastidious tastes can never be gratified at a cheap rate. I did once hear a rumour—not too long before this story opens—that he was financially embarrassed, but it was a rumour in which there was apparently no vestige of truth. In any case it never prejudiced me in any way against him, and maybe because I had never felt either liking or aversion. I saw him from time to time at my club, but I never wished to make his acquaintance, because, perhaps, I hate a poseur and a snob. But, as I would wish to repeat, the indifference of someone so utterly unimportant as myself could not detract in any way from the fact that he was a great, and in many ways an important, public figure.

And it was this man whose shin I had just seen kicked by a blonde in the Stoke-hole of the Café Rond! There had been mention of a book and a Bobby Ashman—I saw at that moment no connection between that Ashman and the Ashman with whom I was vaguely acquainted at my club—and something that had been written by Foorde himself. Something stirred tenuously in my mind—something my wife had said: something, surely, about Foorde and a certain book. But I couldn't remember, and perhaps because I did remember something else. Breck must have done some polite lying in the Café Rond. He and Latimer couldn't surely have been there by chance, and it couldn't possibly have been by chance that something so sensational had happened while both were there. And both had left the room on the heels of that blonde.

I'm a curious person. It's partly my nature and partly because of my job. I hate an unsolved puzzle, and a mystery can gnaw at me like a bad tooth. That was why, as soon as I had drawn up a chair to the fire, I told Bernice about that evening's happening.

"But you knew!" she said, with that emphatic kind of raillery which wives can adopt at times.

I told her I knew nothing, except perhaps that for eight days I'd lived at Broad Street and come home to a belated bite and a bed. I'd forgotten everything I previously knew; and if there was anything new, then I hadn't heard it.

"I did tell you," she insisted, "but now I've destroyed the paper. It was about a book, a novel: *The Silken Petticoat*, by someone called Ashman. Clement Foorde wrote to the Press about it. He called it every kind of disgrace: to the people who published it and the libraries who might take it and the people who might be tempted to read it."

"Why? Was it obscene, or what?"

"I think he called it just unadulterated filth," Bernice said with a *moue*. "If it wasn't that, it was something equally direct. Oh yes. He ended by inviting all concerned to bring a libel action."

"Good," I said. "*The Silken Petticoat*, by somebody—probably Robert—Ashman. I'll buy a copy tomorrow."

"Ludovic!"

That full length name is a sign of many things, but my withers for once were unwrung.

"Look, my dear," I said, and I think it was said charmingly, "let's keep a sense of proportion. I'm not interested in pornography, but I *am* interested in what happened tonight. I want to see just what it was that Foorde was so indignant about. I'd like to judge if he was in any way wrong and if that girl was right. In fact I'd like the inside story."

"But if those two reporters were there, won't everything be in their papers tomorrow morning?"

I said that was an excellent point. I didn't add that both were rather more than reporters or that she had a touching belief in the truthfulness of the popular Press, or, shall we say, its unbiased presentation. But in any case that's where things were left, at least till the following morning.

Maybe you're wondering why I should have taken such an interest in an affair which was no real concern of mine: why I should have been, in fact, such a busybody and possessed of so shameless a curiosity. But when, for over twenty years, you've been engaged in various sorts of detection, it is second nature to look in even the most commonplace happenings for clues and motives. Besides, I'm a student of humanity. It just happens to be my hobby, and it's not without its uses. In public conveyances or hotel bars or where you will, I like to try the old Sherlock Holmes technique of deducing the occupations and general milieu, so to speak, of the ordinary run of people with whom I happen to be then in contact, and I as shamelessly try, by getting into conversation or otherwise, to check up on what I may have happened to deduce. Through the years I must have acquired a certain tact, for I've never yet been actually rebuffed.

But that affair in the Café Rond was, to my thinking, far from ordinary. It was something that, to someone like myself, shrieked for a little enquiry. Clement Foorde, for instance, was not an ordinary man, nor was it normal to have found two first-class newspaper men on the scene when the event occurred. And that girl had interested me. I really did want to know, as I had told Bernice, whether or not she had a certain amount of reason on her side. That was why I rang the newspaper office to ask about Breck. But he, as I'd anticipated, would not be there till round about eleven.

I had done Breck one rather important favour and he had the right to expect that in future I might put him in the way of more than one good story, so I got out my car and made my way to Muswell Hill. Breck, I judged, ought to be at or finishing his breakfast by ten o'clock and there'd be time for a quarter of an hour's chat.

Mrs. Breck came to the door. I had been only once to the house, but she remembered me. When you're six foot three and decidedly lean and have bat eyes demanding horn-rimmed glasses, you're probably something that when once seen is never forgotten. She seemed uncommonly friendly as she showed me into the little workroom study. Breck had finished breakfast and was running an eye over an array of papers. His look was somewhat quizzical.

"Funny," he said in his dry way, "but I told Freda I wouldn't be surprised if you turned up. Have some coffee."

I said I'd breakfasted long since and I wasn't proposing to take up a lot of his time.

"Seen the papers?" he said.

I said I'd seen both the *Sentinel* and the *Record*. His eyebrows lifted.

"Quite a good job you two made of it," I said. "Everything just as it happened. No overwriting, no hysteria. So tell me something. I'm willing to believe that neither you nor Latimer was there because of Foorde. But why *were* you there?"

He made play with filling his pipe.

"You tell *me* something. Why were you there?"

I told him.

"Then that affair was nothing to do with any private business of your own?"

I said it definitely wasn't.

He took his time over lighting the pipe.

"If I tell you something, you'll keep it well under your hat? . . . Well, it's this. A phone call came about three o'clock to the paper. A woman's voice—"

"Just a minute. The same woman who kicked our friend's shin?"

"You didn't expect that I took the call?" he asked me dryly. "I didn't hear the voice, so how could I compare it? All I know was this. It was a woman's voice and described as belonging to someone educated, but—well, not quite on the upper shelf. It asked most urgently that someone important should be in the bar of the Rond at six-thirty. It said whoever went would not be disappointed."

"The same thing happened at the *Record* office?"

"Uh-huh."

I thought that over.

"It's easy to theorise," I said. "But doesn't this strike you as a publicity stunt? An effort to boost the book?"

"That stood out a mile—after it happened," he said. "But there's just one snag. Still in strict confidence, it depends on whether or not you can believe Ashman."

"That's the author?"

"That's the author. We've been in touch and he disclaims all knowledge. In fact he was highly indignant."

"And you believe him?"

He made a wry face.

"I had some dealings with Ashman before and he's a tricky customer. I may be wrong, but that's the opinion I formed of him."

I thought that over. I asked what sort of a fellow he was. A pretty thorough chap, Breck. He came across almost at once with virtually a biography.

Robert Ashman was about thirty. His father, a manufacturer up North, had left him a tidy slab of money. That was after the son had served in the war and reached the rank of major. Public school and Cambridge, by the way, Breck told me, and then apologised unnecessarily because he remembered I was much the same myself.

"My information is that he did the old man a dirty trick," Breck went on. "He was left the business with no contingencies and then sold it, which was what the old boy never anticipated. Came to town with the money and began backing shows. He also wrote a play that had a bit of a run at the Maryland—*The Twisted Dial*: a psychological thriller."

"Just a minute," I said. "He's a tall chap, broad, dark-haired?"

"You know him?"

"Only as a member of my club," I said. "And that's intriguing, in a way. Foorde's a member too. A member of the Garrick as well, of course."

There was a pile of odd papers on his desk. He reached out as if to find something among them, then changed his mind.

"I've been into some of that," he said. "You mightn't believe it, but I wasn't in bed till four this morning and I was up again at seven. And I think I know all about Foorde and Ashman. Foorde bestowed his gracious benediction on *The Twisted Dial*. If you like to make some judicious enquiries at the club I think you'll find that Foorde was on reasonably friendly terms with Ashman. The old maestro and the young beginner, if you know what I mean. Foorde liked to be regarded as a patron, provided one didn't take liberties. And I think Ashman did do something of the sort, or else he didn't pay sufficient homage. My information is that for some time they haven't been on speaking terms."

I gave a grunt. He was certainly giving me something to chew over. I also knew he was hoping—and why not—to pick my brains.

"One of those rather too cheerful chaps, Ashman," I said. "Or that's how he struck me. Not that I mind being addressed straight away as *old boy*, if it's by the right person."

"To get back to a possible stunt," he reminded me. "My information is that Ashman isn't too well fixed for money. He's a spender—his type always is."

"Is that why you didn't trust him when he disclaimed all knowledge of what happened last night?"

"Well,"—the same old dry smile came again—"you're a sleuth. How do you work it out yourself?"

"Foorde's always news," I said. "That'll make last night talked about. Whether it can boost a book into a best-seller I very much doubt. But something else in the same context. Would you people be interested in seeing the book a bestseller?"

"Why not? News is news. If it did turn out to be a bestseller, there'd be another story in it. A flashback and a follow-up."

I shifted ground slightly.

"But the girl herself," I said. "Who is she? If you can tie her up in any way with Ashman, then you know it was a stunt. You followed her up last night?"

"Yes," he said. "As far as the pavement. A taxi was there with the engine running and she was off—pouf!—like that. I got the number and, later on, the driver. He dropped her at Hyde Park Corner. And where's that get us?"

He got to his feet. I offered him a lift to Fleet Street and he said it'd be a change from the Tube. We did a little more talking when the traffic was reasonably clear.

"The girl's disappeared in the blue," was one of the things I said. "But there's a way to find out if she's connected with Ashman. I know you can deduce it from the fact that she alluded to him last night as *Bobby* Ashman, but that could have been the hysteria or hero-worship of a fan. So why don't you get someone on Ashman's tail and see if he leads you back to the blonde."

"The voice is the voice of Ludovic Travers," he told me cynically, "but the hands are Scotland Yard's. You don't think for even a moment my paper would go for anything like that?"

"Just a suggestion," I told him mildly. "Trying to drum up a little business for the Broad Street Detective Agency. Not that I don't think your paper *capable de tout*."

He let that pass.

"What about the book itself?" he said. "You read it?"

I said I hadn't. He'd read it immediately after Foorde's letter. He said he wouldn't even call it pornographic and he named half a dozen books published over the last few years which were far more objectionable.

"It's a bit bawdy and saucily suggestive," he said, "but surprisingly well written. I passed it on to Freda and she pretended to be shocked, but I'm dam' sure she enjoyed it. I'd fifty times rather have it than all this morbid stuff the modern critic raves about."

I wanted his opinion about Foorde's attitude.

"He's refusing to talk," he said, "and I think he's quite right. All he would say was that he didn't retract one word of what he'd written about the book."

"Maybe," I said, "he felt very strongly on the subject and was really annoyed. I felt quite a sympathy for him last night. I still think he took the whole thing very well."

"What I can't forget is that look on his face when she kicked him," he said. "I don't know if you were watching him, but it was a look of absolute incredulity. Just like Jove might have looked if Ganymede had suddenly kicked him in the pants. I beg his pardon—the toga. Or am I still wrong?"

All that had brought us well into the Strand. I assured him that everything would be confidential, that I had no business axe to grind, and that I had no intention of approaching Latimer. He promised that if any new development occurred he'd give me a ring. I told him to make it my private number. I'd earned a holiday and I was going to have one. And with that we were drawing up outside the *Sentinel* building.

I went on to Ludgate Hill, drove round, and back into the Strand. At a bookshop I bought a copy of *The Silken Petticoat*.

2

CLIMAX AND END

THE spring sales had begun. Bernice had a rendezvous with a friend and I had the flat to myself, which was just as well, for I stretched myself at full length on the chesterfield before the fire and settled to a reading of *The Silken Petticoat*. It was a filthy day outside: not actually raining but chill and overcast: the sort of day, in fact, when reading is a necessity as well as a pleasure.

At midday I rang down for a service lunch, did *The Times* crossword while I ate it, then got my pipe going and went on with the novel. I admit a certain amount of quick scanning, which is why I finished that book at three o'clock. Then I shook up the cushion, got my pipe going again and did some assessing.

The Silken Petticoat was a clever book, there wasn't a doubt about that, and it was based on what seemed to me an uncommonly clever idea. The story ran for exactly a hundred years, beginning in 1852. It was a series of episodes connected by family ties and, particularly, by the petticoat itself. At least it began as a petticoat; a marvellous silken affair, handsomely embroidered, but through the years and with each change of ownership it underwent drastic changes. One lady made it into part of a dress—you'll pardon me if, as nothing of an expert, my technical terms are inexact—and the next owner fashioned it into a species of blouse. From that it deteriorated into an ornate scarf and its final owner made it into a brassiere.

The novel consisted of the love affairs of each of those five owners. The petticoat itself was not obtruded, though at each climax one saw the discarding of the particular garment that it happened to be at the time. That, in my judgment, was extremely cleverly done. Each love affair had a different treatment—in the sense that while the first was almost flagrantly described, the next had a witty kind of reticence, and that sort of sandwich went on till the final episode. The wit had a Gallic flavour, though it lacked—while being far more outspoken—the rare quality of, say, *Clochemerle*. There was plenty to which a prude could take strong exception, but was Foorde—a bachelor—any kind of prude?

But when I put the vital question, I had only one answer. Was it a book I should like to see Bernice enjoying? The answer was an emphatic no! Here and there were certain touches of nastiness. One felt that various experiences must have been autobiographical—the one in Germany, for instance—and that, for me at least, actually destroyed all verisimilitude and left in the mouth a highly unpleasant taste.

Then I looked at it from another angle. What did the publishers think when they received the manuscript? It depended, of course, on who those publishers were, and with that I had another look at the jacket of the book. Lanyer and Pope. I said the names to myself and thought back a bit. If I remembered rightly, they used to specialise in what I called exotic stuff: translations of French novels that were, to say the best about them, uncommonly spicy. Things, too, that were remarkably near the knuckle. And, in any case, theirs was an imprint that I definitely avoided when I was entrusted by Bernice with the changing of library books.

And so Lanyer and Pope would probably have hailed the arrival of the manuscript of *The Silken Petticoat* with something more than enthusiasm. They would have thought it a winner.

But always provided—provided what? That it could be sufficiently boosted? Even to the extent of that affair at the Café Rond? And that brought me slap up against another question. Had that blonde been employed by Lanyer and Pope? Had the whole thing really been an organised stunt?

Scope there, as you see, for an attractive bit of sleuthing had I been prepared to spend either the time or the money. Neither worried me too much, but I did retain a sense of proportion. I could send a man to those publishers to worm out something about a smart-looking blonde. Another man could be put on Ashman's tail with the hope that he might lead to the same blonde, but, as I said, I had a sense of proportion. There was, in fact, such a thing as carrying curiosity too far. And just as I'd made up my mind to that, the telephone bell rang. It was Breck.

He spoke very guardedly.

"Thought you might like to know that a certain author has written a letter absolutely dissociating himself from a certain affair. Read tomorrow's paper."

"Thanks," I said. "That rather queers a certain theory. You interested in another?"

"Depends what it is."

"Well, suppose everything was publisher-inspired?"

I caught his little incredulous sort of grunt.

"My dear fellow, you don't think there's a publisher still in business who'd risk a thing like that?"

"Takes all sorts to make a publishing world," I told him. "Suppose this silk undergarment business simply had to be a financial life-saver, what then?"

"Uh-huh."

"It's up to you people, of course."

"We've covered it—partly," he said. "I saw one of the partners. The whole business horrified him—so he said."

"With his tongue in his cheek?"

"Maybe. All the same, we're letting the whole thing peter out, unless, of course, something sensational flares up."

That was what I did myself, even if it was with a certain regret. And I did realise that there was one very possible and simple answer to the whole thing. Neither Ashman nor his publishers had been behind it. Each was genuine in his protestations. What had happened had been engineered by the blonde herself, even though she might be only one of Ashman's lady friends. That he would guess who the lady was I myself was pretty sure, though I doubted if Breck would be prepared to ask him that particular question.

And yet, as I said, it was with a definite regret that I put the whole thing personally aside. Spread gratuitously in front of me had been a first-class puzzle that gave infinite scope for a bit of amusing if unprofitable detection. It was true that I had arrived at three possible solutions, but about none of them was I particularly happy. And I don't like solutions that leave me restless and undecided, and I hate loose ends. All the same, I could pat myself on the back a day or two later when I found that I really was forgetting the whole thing. Strength of mind and the gift of proportion are admirable things, especially when one is pleased to recognise one's self as their possessor.

Months afterwards I was to remember that there was one question about that Café Rond affair which I had never asked myself. It was a question so obvious that I winced when I thought back to the incredible woolliness of thought that had made me overlook it. It was a question which would have immediately produced only one possible answer, *and that answer was to be the one which would solve a murder case.*

Did that question occur to you? If so, did you see the answer? If you did, then you won't wish to go on reading this book. But if, like myself, you missed it altogether, then let's get on with the story.

The Café Rond affair ceased to be news. The big drums no longer beat, but from time to time there were faint echoes and reverberations as far as I myself was concerned.

I ran into Breck again, and he told me that a little judicious enquiry had given him the news that Ashman had no real lady friends who were straw-coloured blondes. The lady with whom he had occasionally been seen, and then not in the brightest lights, was a brunette, and nobody knew her name.

Then at the club I happened to see a man who was talking at the time to Robert Ashman, and as that man was a fairly close acquaintance of mine I managed to insinuate myself into their company. I noticed several things about Ashman that I had never noticed on that other occasion when I had been near him. He was, for one thing, very good-looking, though already in a rakish kind of way. I suppose it was a kind of theatre pallor, if I may call it so: the sort of thing that may come from too many late nights and too few sleeping hours, and, maybe, just a too-frequent lifting of the elbow.

But he was much more subdued on this occasion than on the last, with no boisterousness about his manner. Maybe a hint had reached him, as it had me, that certain older members of the club had been horrified both at the Café Rond publicity and *The Silken Petticoat* itself. Now he was being an author of maturity, so to speak: the creative artist who had been forced, maybe regretfully, to write the truth because he wholeheartedly believed it to be such. I rather cunningly played up to the idea, even if what I said was also the truth.

"I liked that book of yours," I said. "Things, of course, that might have been toned down, but I thought it a very clever bit of work."

Was he gratified? His very deprecation was the answer.

"I don't know," he said. "If I wrote it again I certainly would do as you say. There's always a certain immaturity about a first novel."

"It's going well?"

The deprecating smile was there again.

"As a matter of fact it's selling very well. Perhaps you won't believe me, but I really do feel that it's in some way unfortunate. There *are* people who might ascribe it to certain regrettable— well, to unfortunate publicity."

"Don't let it worry you," I told him paternally. "Count the cash and let the scandals go."

He asked me to have a drink, which I refused, and he also called me *sir*. A remarkable step, forward or back, from the *old boy* of our other meeting. But, like Breck, I didn't trust him somehow. That far too curious and suspicious mind of mine would keep wondering about that sudden and drastic sobering down of what had been a playboy. And then all that again went out of my mind.

I did happen one day—and I don't really know why—to ask the hall-porter if Clement Foorde had been in the club lately. He looked rather surprised, as if it should have been the duty of members merely tolerated, like myself, to keep themselves informed of the whereabouts and immediate activities of those whose every movement and act, whose mere names, in fact, gave the club a cachet and distinction.

"Mr. Foorde is in the country, sir," he told me reprovingly. "He comes to town when necessary, sir, but we understand he's engaged in writing."

And then, as yet another reverberation, I happened to glance at the advertisements on the book page of a Sunday paper, and there, in huge black letters, was *The Silken Petticoat*.

60,000, AND STILL SELLING!
EIGHTH LARGE IMPRESSION NOW PRINTING!!

Beneath was a long list of quotes. Miss A. had hailed it as her fortnightly masterpiece. B. simply couldn't lay it down. C. spoke of Gallic wit. D. complained that it had kept him from his bed for far too long. E. said it was a book that would live. F. made a comparison with *Clochemerle*, to that book's detriment. G. managed to drag in Congreve and Restoration wit. H. had never chuckled so much in his life.

Ashman, in fact, seemed to be on the way to a small fortune, even after taxes had taken the inevitable and clutching toll. Where Lanyer and Pope were finding all the paper was something that rather intrigued me, but I supposed that, as with most things in life, there were ways and means. And they, too, must be making a very nice penny to be able to afford so large an advertisement.

After that Sunday I kept an eye out for the advertisements of Lanyer and Pope, till at last their megaphonics began to bore me. By August *The Silken Petticoat* has passed the 100,000 and was said to be still in enormous demand. It was also said to be sweeping America. Every European country outside the Iron Curtain had got it or was after it, and even Stalin, one gathered, had his surreptitious copy. The film rights were about to be sold in America.

Happy Robert Ashman and happy Lanyer and Pope! All that was needed as a final laurel wreath was that article at which Breck had hinted—

ROMANCE OF A BEST-SELLER

with an our-readers-may-recall reference to that little affair in the Stoke-hole of the Café Rond. Not that I was in the least degree jealous of anyone's financial success. I wasn't worrying a lot about anything when I read that last advertisement in the Sunday *Clarion*, for I was on holiday and, as far as an age of maturity permits, having an excellent time.

When I returned, Norris took his holiday and I was in harness again. It was the last week in August, and on a Monday, that I read some astounding news.

I had noticed nothing in *The Times* when I glanced through it after breakfast. It was a hurried look and a hurried meal, for I was rather late and I liked to be at Broad Street by at least half-past eight. In the office we always have every important daily, and that as a matter of business, and it was a headline in the *Sentinel* that caught my eye.

FAMOUS AUTHOR MISSING
CLOTHES FOUND BY A SUSSEX STREAM

Take away the padding and there was not much information, but there was quite a good photograph of Robert Ashman. I rather gathered that the news had come in late and that the front page had been hastily reset.

The news was this. On the Sunday morning a Mr. Morgan Brown, farmer, of Wenhurst, Sussex, fetched his horse from a meadow which runs alongside the Nelder, and on the river bank he saw a pile of clothes. It was nearly eleven o'clock, but they were in the shade and the dew was still on them, which showed they had been there all night. He mentioned the matter to his wife and later they decided to ring the local police.

From the contents of the pockets the clothes were identified as belonging to a Mr. Robert Ashman. In the lane which skirted the meadow, on the grass verge beneath the trees, was Ashman's car, the ignition key of which was in his trouser pocket. On the face of it, it looked as if Ashman had been going further south—the car was headed that way—and had been tempted by the uncommonly sultry evening to take a swim. The fact that the car was two hundred yards from the clothes seemed to show that he had walked along the river looking for a suitable place. What he had chosen was a wide space between the rushes, and the river there was quite deep.

In the car was what might be called a week-end bag, and it had been opened as if a bathing costume had been removed. What was feared was that the bather had been overtaken by cramp or had become entangled with the rushes. The police were already exploring the river.

That, except for a brief biography and much about *The Silken Petticoat*, was virtually all, but, as far as I was concerned, it was enough. I had had no liking for Ashman, but at least I knew him, and while there was no personal blow I could feel something of the tragedy and futility. That Ashman was dead seemed almost a certainty, and at the age of thirty-one. He had had the gift of writing, though he had discovered and utilised it rather late, and he might have produced in time things that were really worth while, but vaguely at the back of my mind was the knowledge that he had always had money. Not that the enormous success of *The Silken Petticoat* couldn't have been gratifying in the extreme. But had he been some indigent, hard-working young author who had suddenly made good, I think I should have let what I had read overcloud my mind far more than it actually did.

Late that afternoon I sent out for an evening paper and found more news. A Mr. Albert Keeper, landlord of the Foxhounds, Pettiforth, Sussex, had come forward to state that Mr. Ashman had rung him on the Saturday afternoon to ask for a single room to be reserved for the week-end. Keeper's daughter Rose had taken the message and had consulted her father. There was a room available and Ashman had stayed there before, so everything was arranged. Finally Ashman said he might be rather late and he was quite prepared to pay extra for any little meal that might be found for him on arrival. When Ashman hadn't turned up after all, Keeper naturally expected a telephone call on the Sunday morning, and even though none came he couldn't possibly regard the matter as one for the police. What he did think was that the Monday might bring a letter. What happened was that he saw his newspaper instead.

A still later edition of the *Evening Sentinel* had an interview with Keeper. He said he did a high-class week-end trade. Right up to the war he used to have fishermen, but now he got younger people who liked to be near Seahurst though not actually in it. Seahurst, one of the most chic of the southern seaside resorts, happens, by the way, to be otherwise named.

Mr. Ashman, Keeper said, had stayed once or twice at the Foxhounds and he had found him a very nice gentleman indeed: very good company and—well, the right kind of person to have in the house. Keeper had always thought him someone connected with the theatre, and when Mr. Ashman once gave him two seats for a show in town he had been thrilled to find that Ashman himself was its author.

Then, at nine o'clock that night, I turned on the news. I listened to the headlines and was just about to switch off when, at the end and just before the weather summary, the voice of the announcer suddenly fell in that hushed theatrical and irritating way that so often precedes the announcement of a death.

"The body of Me. Robert Ashman, the well-known author, was found about an hour ago in the River Nelder."

I guessed at the time when details would be given, switched off and later switched on. In a minute or so I was hearing all about it—at least the little there was. The body had been dragged to the surface about four hundred yards downstream from where the clothes had been left on the bank. A quick, potted biography and that was all.

Bernice and I had been talking about Ashman while the News was off. When I'd finally switched the set off she suddenly asked a question.

"Didn't Grace Haverford once live at that Pettiforth place?"

I said I didn't know. I thought it was somewhere else. But I got out a road map and found the place, which was about two miles off the main London-Seahurst road and about seven miles from Seahurst itself. I picked up the Nelder where, about two miles north, it makes a violent swerve toward the Arun, and found the tiny village of Wenhurst, where Ashman's body had been found. From Wenhurst to Pettiforth was about fifteen miles.

Then I hunted for the reason why Ashman had been to so out-of-the-way a place as Wenhurst at all, and I thought I had the answer. If you want to avoid traffic, there's a good second-class road that goes to Pettiforth, but on the far side of the Nelder and about a mile away. Ashman, on Keeper's showing, knew that district. He'd suddenly thought he'd like a swim, so he took that side lane. A mile from where he left his car that lane rejoins the secondary road and goes right on to Pettiforth.

There is an abrupt and chilling finality about death. Ashman was dead, and the whole episode which had so intrigued me a few months before was now as dead as he. I admit that I read the inquest report in a paper that gave it at some length. The verdict was, of course, accidental death by drowning, and that verdict seemed the only possible one to bring in. There was just one interesting thing. I don't know why I should have been surprised to read that Ashman had a brother, but he had, and that brother made the formal identification of the body. It was also interesting to read that Keeper stated that it was he who, on a previous stay of Ashman's at the Foxhounds, advised him when he was going back to town to avoid traffic by taking that secondary road. That seemed to confirm my own theory.

That was definitely the end of what had scarcely been an episode, or so I thought. In a week's time the whole thing had gone from my mind. Then came a Saturday morning, exactly a fortnight after that Saturday when Ashman had set out for Pettiforth and had never reached it. Norris was due back on the Monday, so I was just ending another spell of duty.

I had a look through the correspondence and came to a letter with a London W.1. postmark. It was good quality, grey parchment paper and in the left-hand corner of the envelope was *Urgent*. When I saw the signature at the letter's foot, my eyes popped a bit.

—Hotel,
London
W.1

To the Broad Street
Detective Agency.

Dear Sirs,

I should like to consult you and, I hope, make use of your services on a matter of extreme privacy. You will pardon me if I say that I saw your advertisement and then made various enquiries which convinced me that you would handle the matter with the tact I am sure it needs.

I am staying until Monday morning at the—Hotel and I should be glad if on receipt of this letter you would give me a ring.

Very many thanks,

Yours sincerely,

MAURICE ASHMAN.

Maurice Ashman! I don't quite know why, but, as I said, the name hit me like a blow. I read that letter a second time and then reached for the telephone.

3
SHADOW OF DOUBT

AT ELEVEN o'clock he was in my room. I don't say I would have seen a likeness if I had met him casually in the street, but as soon as I clapped eyes on him I did see a close likeness to his dead brother. But he was older by quite four or five years and his face was more finely moulded and thinner. He looked, in fact, infinitely more mature.

"Glad to see you personally, Mr. Ashman."

He gave me quite a nice smile.

"Glad to see you, Mr. Travers. I hope I'm not going to take up too much of your time."

"A client's privilege," I told him. "But, as a matter of fact, I have all the time in the world."

He had the faintest trace of a northern accent. Like myself, he preferred a pipe to a cigarette, and he showed that kind of northern independence by refusing to fill up from my pouch and using his own.

"A bad business about your brother," I said. "I knew him personally; that is, to speak to. He happened to be a member of my club."

"That may make it easier," he said. "I hope you weren't in any way annoyed when I told you on the telephone that I'd rather not mention business, but I can tell you now that it's to do with my brother."

I gave a non-committal nod.

"If I'm not going to bother you," he went on, "I'd like to get round to things gradually. You know anything about him personally?"

I told him frankly everything I knew, and it was from what Breck had told me and what I'd read in the newspapers.

"That's about right," he said. "Both Bob and I were intended for the business. Not a big business, but doing quite well. Sort of freelance engineering, to be exact. I cut loose first. I wanted to paint."

"You're an artist?"

"Of sorts," he said. "I still make a living."

He had a dry, likeable sort of smile.

"My wife happened to have money, but I still make my own living. Don't suppose you've ever heard of me, but I had a couple of things in this year's Academy."

I tried a smile of my own.

"You're not trying to tell me that if we work for you we'll be sure of our money?"

"I'm not so sure that I'm not," he said. "What's more import-ant is that you should know that I'd still cut loose from the old man if I had to choose all over again. He was my father, but he was a tough one. Bob played his cards better. He had a year or two in the business, but the war came just in time to stop him cutting loose too, and just when it ended the old man died and Bob sold the business. There wasn't an awful lot after everything had been settled. Somewhere about forty thousand pounds."

"Sounds useful to me."

"But it's not worth selling your soul for," he told me. "Bob always wanted to be in the theatrical business, and that's what he did, as you said. The trouble was, he backed the wrong shows. He was down to his last thousand when he wrote that book of his."

I raised incredulous eyebrows.

"I wasn't worried," he said. "He had it in him to make good one way or another. But the point I want to make is this. If he'd been a success he might have made enemies—before he wrote that book, of course."

I nodded again. I had a vague idea of what was in his mind, but I wanted him to bring it into the open in his own time and way.

"I did let him have a loan just before he finished writing that book," he told me, and then that dour smile came again. "I wasn't bothering if I never saw it back, but now I've got it back—with interest."

"You're not his heir? I mean you'll recover it from the estate?"

"I *am* the heir," he said. "That's what I meant. It's going to be a tidy sum of money. Been going through things with the publishers and so on. The film rights have been sold for fifteen thousand."

"A lot of money. But there'll be taxes."

"There'll still be plenty. You can always arrange a certain amount of what they call spread. Or so they tell me."

He leaned forward in his chair, the cold pipe in his hand.

"I didn't want that money. Believe me, Mr. Travers, I'd not only give back that money but every personal penny I have if he could be alive. That's why I'm here this morning."

What else could I do but once more nod.

"I think it's going to be tricky," he said. "And it's about time I came to the point. Frankly I don't believe my brother was drowned."

I couldn't help staring.

"But the evidence! You were at the inquest. You heard medical evidence and everything?"

"I know," he told me dourly. "But you can't get away from a hunch. And you can't get away from what keeps coming into your mind. What sticks in your mind till you can't eat or sleep."

I leaned back for a moment. It was going to be tricky, as he'd said.

"Let me be frank," I said. "Or let me ask you to be frank. Everything said here is as confidential as the grave, so speak your mind. Are you here to ask us to try to prove that your brother didn't die an accidental death?"

"That's what it amounts to."

"And the evidence?" I hastily added a rider. "Your own evidence."

"Practically none," he said. "Only this, that I don't believe Bob did any swimming for over fifteen years."

He told me about it. Some schoolboy horseplay or other when Bob was home from Hepley. A ducking in the public swimming-pool which nearly ended in tragedy and as a result of which he completely lost his nerve for water. Maurice had since been in his company many times at the seaside, but his brother had never bathed. He had, in fact, a horror of it.

"He couldn't have overcome it quite recently?" I asked him. "Mightn't his war experiences have made a difference?"

"When I was glad to make him that loan a year or so ago we were at Scarborough," he said, "and he still had the same aversion."

"Right," I said. "Let's take it as fact, which brings us to a highly important point. Did you pass on that information at the inquest? Or to the police?"

"I wasn't asked at the inquest," he said, "but I did tell the police afterwards. The only answer I got was that he *did* bathe in that river, and that's that."

"On the face of it, a good answer," I said. "A bit abrupt, but it followed on the inquest evidence. And that's the only reason you have for not crediting that evidence?"

"That's all," he said. "That, and the hunch."

I leaned back in my chair again. It was going to be even trickier than I'd thought, and finally I told him so. In the States, as I thought it as well to explain to him, an agency had to have a licence; and for interference, real or supposed, with the work of the police or unorthodox conduct that licence might be revoked. But not here. We had to have no licence, but in the event of stepping beyond any legal bounds we brought ourselves, like any private citizen, within the law.

"What I've got to be sure of," I said, "is that you made that point very emphatic about your brother and swimming. Who were the actual police?"

It turned out that Wenhurst, for all its remoteness, came within the police jurisdiction of Seahurst. I looked it up and Grainger was still Chief Constable. That made it easier. He and I knew each other pretty well. And looking up things had given me time to make up my mind.

"May we leave it like this," I said. "You go back to your hotel, or preferably you ring from here with me as witness. You try to get the Chief Constable and you tell him you still can't help being worried about what you told him. Be perfectly natural. I'll listen in in another room."

He was quite agreeable. And we were lucky enough to get hold of Grainger. Grainger was perfectly sympathetic and courteous. He said, and rightly, that there was never a shred of evidence likely to upset that inquest verdict. Robert Ashman might have had that horror of water, but there's no accounting for a man's suddenly getting over such an aversion. And every shred of evidence showed that he did get over it. He said he was sorry and he could only hope that that little talk would ease Maurice Ashman's mind.

"This afternoon," I told Ashman, "I'll speak to the Chief Constable myself and follow it up with a letter for his files. At six o'clock I'll ring you at your hotel and tell you if we will or will not undertake the case. Is that agreeable to you?"

He said it was. Then he pulled a list of names out of his wallet.

"If you want to make any enquiries about my bona fides, here are some people you can ask."

I said, and truthfully, that I didn't think it would be necessary. As soon as we weren't reasonable judges of character, then
we'd be out of business. Then he insisted on talking over terms.
I said they'd come pretty high, but he didn't object. He even
insisted there and then on paying down—in fivers—a substan-
tial retainer. I gave him a temporary receipt till a contract
should be signed.

Five minutes later he had gone and I was a man in two minds.
Something was urging me to take that case and something far
more matter-of-fact was telling me that with so little to work on
we'd be taking money for virtually nothing. And an unsatisfied
client is the last thing one wants on the books.

Perhaps it was to bring some end to my indecision that I rang
Grainger's office at once, and I'd hoped, too, that he might still be
in. He seemed delighted to hear me, even if he did freeze somewhat when I told him frankly what Maurice Ashman wanted, I
said I myself wanted everything open and above-board. I'd send
a man down, and what he'd do I didn't at the moment know, but
I could promise that he'd be a good man and discreet.

"All I want is your blessing," I told him.

"You'll hand over to us anything he's lucky enough to find?"

"Most decidedly. I'll mention it in the covering letter."

He promptly unfroze.

"That'll be fine," he said. "You're within your rights in any
case, but I'd rather have it the friendly way."

And that, virtually, was that. At six o'clock I rang Maurice
Ashman. At seven o'clock I was putting the contract away in
the safe.

I liked Maurice Ashman. We were sympathetic, as the
French say: people who understood each other without lengthy
explanations. He had never said as much, for instance, in so
many words, but it was plain enough that he had had a tremendous affection for his younger brother. But that didn't alter the
fact that we had taken a case, and a man's money, with very little
hope of giving satisfaction. There was nothing unethical, mind

you. We were asked to do what I might call a perfectly legitimate job and the client himself had been told the difficulties.

What had we to go on in an attempt to break that inquest verdict? The answer was, one apparent fact and one hunch. As to the fact, Maurice knew his brother. He had accepted as a part of that brother's make-up a positive dislike of bathing—even sea-bathing, which has to be regarded as much more enjoyable than bathing in a river. As to the hunch, I knew sufficiently well the tenacity with which a hunch can take control of one's mind. I didn't regard it as fantastic when he spoke of being unable to eat or sleep. In the first place, he didn't intend those expressions to be taken absolutely literally, and also one had to take into account the shock of his brother's death and that deep affection.

But when I found myself wishing to get to work on the Ashman case and being momentarily sanguine about upsetting that inquest verdict, I was ignoring the fact that such feelings were really a belated backwash of that other Ashman affair of months before: that little fraças in the Café Rond which also, at the time, had struck me as highly intriguing and on which I should have been extraordinarily happy to work. That it and the present case had any connection was remote from my thoughts. It's too far a cry from the summer evening quiet of a little Sussex river to the sophistication of a Regent Street bar.

But I did get things going practically at once and Hallows came to see me at my flat on the Sunday morning. He's our best man: in fact he's the best man at his job that I've ever run across. I, for example, have a certain nimbleness of mind, but the trouble is that it's often too nimble. Mine is the multi-informed crossword kind of brain: Hallows has the brain of a man who can really play chess. Like myself, he would never be taken for a detective; but whereas I am far too indicative of everything no detective could be, Hallows has the gift of being practically everybody, which means no one at all.

The previous evening, and before he arrived that morning, I had spent a lot of time in typing out every possible thing I knew about Robert Ashman, and I had a couple of reports of the inquest. When he'd read everything and had asked me a few explanatory questions, I wanted to know if he had any ideas.

"Let's put aside that aversion to bathing," he said. "What I'd like to know is why he bathed in that particular spot. As I see, that's our best starting-point."

I asked him to elaborate.

"Well, he couldn't have bathed there at the request of someone else," he said. "He'd booked a single room at Pettiforth and presumably he was travelling alone. If he had had a passenger, then what became of him or her? If they were together at the water, what was done when he got into difficulties? The passenger didn't take the ignition key and leave it by the car. Admittedly Ashman might have had a rendezvous at Wenhurst with a local girl who might have been too scared to tell the police what had happened, but that seems a bit too far-fetched. Not that I shan't have a look into it.

"But this is the main point. The reason assumed for the bathe was that it was a sultry night. But you needn't be too sticky when driving a car. Besides, he had only fifteen miles to go to get a bath at the pub—say twenty-five minutes. And there's something else. He'd said he might be late. He knew he'd be putting the Foxhounds to some trouble, so he offered to pay extra. And yet he made himself still more late by going off the road and round by that lane and having a swim. It doesn't seem to fit in."

"I see all that," I said, "but I ought to tell you he was the inconsiderate type. Anything else?"

"Yes," he said. "Since it's the brother's main plank, we ought to get as bang up to date as we can about that bathing phobia."

"How?"

"Well, presumably he had a holiday this summer. We might find where he spent it and, if it was at the seaside, whether or not he bathed. If he didn't bathe, we ought to clinch the thing by finding someone at the same hotel, say, to whom he spoke about the matter."

This was all he had at the moment. In the morning he'd be going to Sussex and he'd stay there till he'd squeezed the last small driblet of juice out of every possible source of information. I should be getting to work at once about that not unlikely summer holiday, and if I had anything before he left I'd give him a ring.

Had it not been a Sunday I should have gone to the offices of Lanyer and Pope, for it was a certainty that they would have had his holiday address. As it was, I got out the car and drove to Everdale Court, a handsome block of flats in the neighbourhood of the Tate, where Robert Ashman had lived.

At the desk in the main hall I asked for a word with the manager and handed over one of the business cards. Five minutes later I was being shown into the manager's room.

He looked rather bellicose and was twiddling my card in his hand. The expression subtly changed at the sight of me. I don't know what he'd expected, but he wasn't seeing it.

"Mr. Travers?"

"Yes," I said. "It's very good of you to see me. I'm positive I shan't keep you more than five minutes."

"Take a seat," he said, and laid the card down. "My name's Cobell. I see that you're the chairman of a detective agency. Nothing wrong as far as concerns us, I hope?"

I assured him most affably that there wasn't. I said my firm were working on behalf of Maurice Ashman in connection with his late brother's affairs. I gave him Maurice's telephone number in case he wished to confirm.

"A dreadful business, that, about the brother," he said. "I knew him well, of course. And what're you doing particularly? Straightening out his affairs?"

"Yes," I said. "That's what it amounts to."

"Funny," he said, and the smile wasn't quite so nice. "I'd have thought he'd have wanted a firm of accountants."

I shrugged my shoulders.

"You'll keep it confidential?" I said.

His look was both complacent and pitying.

"My dear sir, that sort of thing is my chief asset. You'd be surprised the things I know."

I said I could well believe it. But what I would tell him in strict confidence was that a rather unpleasant claim was being made against the estate.

"Find the lady, eh?"

"Well"—I gave my man-of-the-world smile—"you're not too far wrong. But we think it arose from a recent holiday he took, and we don't know whether he was stationary or went from place to place in his car. What I'm mainly here for, in fact, is to ask if he gave a forwarding address before he left."

"That's easy," he said. "I ought to have it right here." He opened a drawer of the desk and flipped over the pages of a kind of ledger.

"Here we are. He left here very early on the morning of the 7th July and came back on the evening of the 6th August. Forwarding address—Hotel Bon Accueil, Bandol."

"That's fine," I said, and got to my feet. But it wasn't fine at all. As I saw it, it was damnably complicated.

"He went with his car?"

"That's right. Folkestone-Calais, I believe. I think he was taking four days each way on the road, so he had about three weeks at the hotel."

"Lucky fellow," I said. "I suppose he told you about it?"

"He did say he had a dam' good time."

"The bathing good down there?"

"I don't know that he mentioned it. I know he was pretty brown."

I thanked him again and held out a hand.

"You know your way out," he said, and then when I was at the door he cleared his throat.

"Rather interesting what you've been telling me. Suppose you couldn't pass on anything you happen to pick up?"

"I might," I said, and turned back. "After all, we're both aware of the facts of life. And he was that way inclined, was he?"

"Not here," he told me hastily. "He used to drop a hint occasionally. My own idea was he had a nice little private nest somewhere."

That last remark was almost a hopeful question.

"Yes," I said slowly. "There was, I believe, a highly attractive brunette. Still, there we are. Thanks for the information. Perhaps I'll be seeing you."

But I hadn't intended to go. I wanted to use his telephone before he had time to ring Maurice Ashman. But I didn't want to make it too obvious. I'd practically closed the door before I turned back once again.

"Oh, just one little favour you could do me. Might I ring my client from here?"

He as good as told me to help myself. He even made a pretence of leaving the room, but I asked him to stay. So he heard me ask for the hotel and for Maurice Ashman, and I gave my name. I suppose I had a three-minute wait before my man was on the line.

"Travers speaking, Mr. Ashman," I said. "That business we're working on for you. It appears that your brother spent three weeks or so at a hotel at Bandol: that's a little seaside resort between Marseilles and Toulon. . . . Of course you didn't know, but the point is that enquiries ought to be made there. It'll be quicker and cheaper on the whole to fly to Marseilles. I shall probably go myself, but I want you to sanction the expenses. . . . Yes, it's rather out of the ordinary. . . . Good, I'm sure it's something that has to be done."

That was the gist of it. I offered to pay for the call, but Cobell waved an indifferent hand.

"Wish to God I was going with you."

"Why don't you?" I said with something that must have been remarkably like a leer.

"You know how it is. And the wife wants to go to Scotland."

He actually accompanied me to the door, and in the corridor I had again to shake that pudgy hand.

From that moment that Sunday was hectic. I drove on and round to the flat, collected our available money, saw that my papers were in order and then went to the airport building and got a seat on a late Monday morning plane to Paris and a connection to Marseilles. Then I had to go on to Norris's place and spend a long session breaking the news. I had to get in touch with Hallows again, and by then it was late in the evening.

In the morning I managed to get travellers' cheques and the statutory French currency from my bank and had barely time to catch the plane. At Paris I had a longish wait and it was about six o'clock when we touched down at Marseilles. It was just after seven o'clock when I reached Bandol, and I'd managed to get a room for two nights at the Hotel Bon Accueil.

4

THE HORSE'S MOUTH

I HAD come a long way: too long a way, you may think—as far as concerned the pocket of a client—merely to find out if a man, after all, had bathed in the Mediterranean. But I had more in mind than that.

It was strange to be back in Bandol. I'd spent an afternoon there twenty years before when we'd been staying at Sanary, which is a few kilometres nearer Toulon. Then both Sanary and Bandol had been little more than fishing villages: now Bandol had been commercialised out of recognition. New hotels were everywhere and the Bon Accueil was newest of the new. It was a huge affair within a few yards of the harbour, and the beach—which lies at the back of the town—was hardly a stone's throw away.

I had a bath and was in ample time for dinner. The place was as full as they'd hinted over the telephone and more than half the guests were English. After the meal I didn't hurry things. I wanted to get the feel of the town and absorb its new atmosphere as Ashman must have done. I wanted a background against which to frame my enquiries, so I took an evening stroll along the kilometre or so of front. It had been a blistering day, but the night was perfection, with just a faint breeze that rustled the fronds of the palms. Everywhere was gaiety. Coloured lights were strung between the trees, and the red light of the break-water end was reflected in the still water. Cafés were doing a trade and even shops were open. People were making for the casino, a monstrosity of a building as garish and out of place as a Fair Isle jumper at a funeral.

It was nearly ten o'clock when I got back to the hotel, and at once I approached the manager. We went to his office, and I was wishing I had been able to flourish my Yard warrant card. But the firm's card with its photograph and stamp seemed impressive enough. As for my French, it was far better than his English. It ought to be after the money that was spent on it in my youth when there were vague ideas about my entering the Diplomatic Service.

I oughtn't to have been surprised when M. Bourgues revealed at once that he knew about Ashman's death.

"But he was a famous author," he said. "All the English here were excited about him. That made us interested."

"And what was he like with everybody?"

"Most charming," he said. "Agreeable with everybody. The English are always nice to have, but he was particularly nice."

"He was alone?"

That was the jackpot question.

"Yes, and no," he said. He was dramatic even for a French-man, and his hands as eloquent as any I've seen. His gestures more than his words conveyed the slight disapproval of English proverbial moral hypocrisy and his approval of liberty, equality and the pursuit of happiness.

Ashman, it appeared, had written from London a fortnight or so before his arrival to book rooms—two singles. He would have preferred rooms with a communicating door, but none were available, and he was given adjoining rooms; one for himself and one for the charming brunette—a fiancée possibly—who arrived with him in his car. The two were inseparable during their stay, and they left together. Her name was Miss D. Malone and his book merely showed her as from London.

"They filled in the usual forms for the police authorities?"

"But of course," he said. "Some hotels elsewhere ignore it, but here we have to insist."

I said that was all I wanted to know, but I was going to ask him to supply me with certain information. The reason for it I wrapped up in a considerable amount of verbiage about the Ashman estate, but what I wanted were the names of English people who had been at the Bon Accueil during Ashman's stay, with their possible addresses. Above all, I wanted that information only about those who had been specially friendly with Ashman and the fiancée: people with whom they went out—to bathe, say, or for the evening apéritif or for a night at the casino. I said that if he could give me the information by lunch next day it would be time enough.

"Just one other little thing," I said. "Did M. Ashman bathe?"

The hands registered incredulity. Everyone bathed, from babies just out of arms to grandmothers.

"What I want is direct evidence that M. Ashman bathed," I had to tell him. "Perhaps the waiter at his table could tell you. One of the house or kitchen staff, perhaps, who saw him hanging up his bathing trunks after a morning bathe."

He promised to do what he could. Had he been an Englishman I'd have asked him to have a drink with me. As it was, the *Merci, monsieur, vous êtes bien agréable* seemed uncommonly inadequate.

An excellent *petit déjeuner* was brought up as usual to the room. I took my time about dressing and then had a look at the little town by daylight. It was a superb morning with a promise of heat, and at half-past ten I made my way down some steps near the back of the hotel and found myself on the semi-circle of beach. There was little sand; only very fine shingle which worked its way into one's shoe tops and made walking uncomfortable, and when at last I sat down with my back against a wall I was glad to take the shoes off. Only a couple of hundred yards of the way by which I had come had been in shade: the rest of the beach was in the full sun and already it was slightly hot. In a few minutes I was taking off my coat.

By eleven o'clock the beach was filling up. On the calm waters of the bay were a pedalog or two and a few canoes, but the beach itself—with never more than six or seven paces of it between sea and wall—seemed almost too full, and newcomers were having to pick a way over the bodies of the sun-bathers. My nostrils caught an aromatic whiff, and I turned to see a couple rubbing their bodies with *huile solaire*. Children, grandparents, everyone was sea- or sun-bathing, as M. Bourgues had said. There were the experts who trudgeoned or crawled spectacularly, and the plodders who breast-stroked just within their depth.

That was what I had wanted to know. The bottom shelved quite gradually, so that at ten yards out the average man would still have had his shoulders clear. The water was warm and it was buoyant, so that if Ashman was ever going to take up swimming again the beach of Bandol was ideal. There was a certain amount of oil in the water, so I was told by a Frenchman with whom I got into conversation, and due, so he said, to the sunken battleships of Toulon, but it wasn't enough to be more than occasionally annoying.

I went right along the beach and up some steeper steps and back to the hotel through the town. M. Bourgues motioned me to join him in his office. He had learned nothing about Ashman's bathing, but he did have the list of English guests. And he had the people with whom Ashman had been particularly friendly and whose stay had virtually coincided with his own. They were the Leishmans—father, mother and small son—of Sevenoaks, and the Pantlings—father, mother and small daughter—of London. I gathered they were all spenders and that they had come together in a big American car.

I had an excellent and distending lunch and after it dozed off for an hour in a deck-chair on the terrace under an acacia. The town in any case would be almost dead till three o'clock, and it was about half-past when I went to one of the two banks and cashed my two travellers' cheques. Then I went on along a narrowish hemmed-in street and found the unpretentious, almost dingy building that housed the *Police d'État*.

The office was on the ground floor. A civilian in shirt sleeves—he turned out to be the secretary—was working at a table in that ground-floor office, a *cendrier* at his elbow half-filled with cigarette butts. If Bourgues had been easy, then never had a man been so difficult. It took me a quarter of an hour to produce a smile, and then I didn't feel certain that it wasn't a sneer. Finally, just when I was ready to admit that I was endangering the republic, he went to a filing cabinet and produced what I wanted.

The Miss D. Malone was Dallas Malone, address given as merely London.

The Leishmans were Ernest, Pamela and Tony, of Sevenoaks.

The Pantlings were Claud, Irene and Jill, of Briarwood, Enfield, Middlesex.

The grown-ups were in the late twenties or thirties, which made them of an age with the Ashman pair. The age of Dallas Malone was put down as twenty-seven. And, as I had learned from Bourgues, she was a brunette, and chic.

I thanked that secretary and left at speed, and on a seat in the little market by the church I assessed the value of what I had learned. Those forms which one fills in for the police vary throughout France, and, as Bourgues had said, there are hotels which do not demand them at all. Useless information is demanded—that mainstay of bureaucracy—but there seems considerable laxity about the alien's home address: to state it as London, for instance, which is really no address at all. But the Leishmans had put down Sevenoaks, which was reasonable enough, and the Pantlings had given their full address. Ashman had added his postal area to his London, but Dallas Malone had put merely the London: the bare minimum statement the authorities were likely to accept. And that seemed to show that she had been none too anxious to reveal what her full address was.

It was she I'd have preferred to question on my return, but unless I could get that full address from the others, then I'd have to rely on what I could glean from the Pantlings and, if necessary, reinforce and check with what I might manage to get from the Leishmans. But on the whole I was feeling quite happy about things, even if I did have to wonder why that lady friend of Ashman had never come forward in any way after his death. I had to wonder, too, whether or not he had mentioned her in his will, but that was something I could learn from his brother.

I had tea and a cake at an excellent shop on the farther front, and when the first cool was in the air, I had a look at the men playing *boule* and then went back to my room and wrote a full report for Maurice Ashman. By then it was time for dinner. I did myself well for the good of the house, and I learned from an Englishman at the next table that there was a café where most of the English took a post-prandial coffee and liqueur. I waited for a time and then made my way there.

The outside tables were almost all occupied, but I found one at the back and ordered a filtre and a kümmel. A couple of waiters were operating outdoors, and one of them—a spry little chap called Max—seemed to specialise with the English. He had an English of his own, which alone seemed to be some kind of joke, and he was practically on nudging terms with the clientèle. I nobbled him when I went to the bar to buy some cigarettes and beneath his eyes I transferred some thousand-franc notes from wallet to a handy pocket. He told me he'd be comparatively free in an hour, and I finally killed the time with yet another walk along the front.

I described Ashman and he recognised him. He recognised him enthusiastically. He even looked genuinely upset when he heard of his death. Ashman had apparently been the life and soul of that café for an hour every evening. And Max remembered Dallas Malone. With vivid hands he indicated her outlines. She was *charmante* and *tout ce qu'il y a de plus chic*. She didn't speak French, but Ashman could at least make himself understood.

"M. Ashman, did he bathe?"

He didn't know, but he knew that before he left he was remarkably brown. When he first came to the café he had had a pallor.

He had heard no discussions about the bathing, and even if he had I doubted if his vocabulary was sufficient to understand the normal chatter of the English. He had no ideas as to whether or not the Malone girl was Ashman's fiancée. Everyone, he said, was friendly.

"Plenty money. Plenty drink. Make joke. Plenty fun. Go to casino. Lose plenty money."

That was his one lapse into English, if I may call it so. And I was at the end of my likely questions, so I tipped him the equivalent of a pound and then made my own way to the casino. But I was too early. At ten o'clock the place, but for its cinema, was dead, and it wouldn't come to life, so I was told, till well towards midnight. To stay that while wasn't worth the boredom.

Next morning I settled a fairly stiff bill, said goodbye to M. Bourgues, and caught the local autobus to Marseilles. It fitted reasonably with my return plane, and at six o'clock that evening I was back home, and on all that last part of the journey I'd been wondering how Hallows had fared in Sussex.

While Bernice saw to a belated tea I rang the office, but Norris happened to be out. After the meal I found the telephone number of the Pantlings. It was a woman's voice at the end of the line.

"Mrs. Pantling, is it?"

"Yes?"

"Mrs. Pantling, my name is Travers, and I'm speaking on behalf of Mr. Maurice Ashman, the brother of the late Mr. Robert Ashman, whom you met, I believe, at Bandol. I wonder if I might call on you this evening?"

"Well, yes," she told me nervously. "But what's it all about? I mean, it's such a surprise."

"Nothing unpleasant, I assure you, Mrs. Pantling. Merely something to do with clearing up his estate. Your husband will be in?"

"Well, yes."

"Then what time would suit you both?"

"I hardly know," she said. "Perhaps after dinner. Say at half-past eight."

"That'll be fine," I said. "I'm very grateful to you, Mrs. Pantling. May I repeat that it's nothing serious at all."

She'd had every reason to be nervous. An utter stranger had rung her out of the blue and had mentioned Bandol and Robert Ashman. Ashman's death must have been something of a shock to her, and to hear his name suddenly mentioned by someone whom she didn't know from Adam, and in connection with Bandol, must have been very much of a startler. As for trying to visualise her before I saw her that night, that was far too difficult. My preoccupation with my fellow-men hasn't brought me to such perfection that I can be even half-sure of a reconstruction from the brief sound of a voice. Her voice, I did think, was just a bit hard. In normal conversation it would probably have had a stridency or aggressiveness, and there had been about it that elusive something that placed her as just a little below the top shelf.

It was just before half-past eight when I at last found Briarwood. The gate had been left open for me and I had to get out of the car to verify the name, and then there was a drive of about fifty yards to negotiate. As I drew up before the largish house a light went on over the porch. The door opened before I could reach it.

"Mr. Travers, is it?"

That was Claud Pantling: a shortish, thick-set man who looked older than his official thirty-six. My first guess made him a stockbroker. His voice was rather the blurting type.

We shook hands and he took my hat.

"You're a lawyer?" he asked me.

"Afraid not," I said. "As a matter of fact I'm chairman of a highly reputable detective agency. This is the firm's card."

He gave the card the most casual scrutiny: I was the one who was under his startled look.

"Do you know, I thought as soon as I clapped eyes on you that I'd seen you somewhere. Didn't you give evidence at the Old Bailey when they were trying Valbury?"

"I believe I did."

"I was there," he said. "Keeping an eye on the interests of one of our clients. You were working for the Yard then, weren't you?"

I told him I still occasionally did.

"Let's get in," he said, and actually took me by the arm, and I was ushered through a door and into a lounge. At first glance it was all chintzes and cushions, and I also saw a television set and a cocktail cabinet. No sooner were we in that room than Pantling was telling his wife of that coincidence. He was so full of it that he seemed to assume we'd actually met.

Irene Pantling was tallish and slim. Everything about her was smart and streamlined—the dress, the make-up, the sleek set of the bronze-coloured hair.

"You surely can't be Mrs. Pantling," I told her gallantly.

"Why on earth not?"

"Well, to be the mother of a growing-up daughter."

She laughed.

"Jill's only seven. You're married yourself?"

"Oh yes," I said. "No children, unhappily."

I had helped myself to a chair. Pantling asked me what I'd drink. He and I had whisky and the wife had a small glass of port.

"Do you know, you quite scared me, Mr. Travers," she told me, and if I'd have guessed for a thousand years I'd never have arrived at the extraordinary thing she was about to add.

"Hearing Bob Ashman's name mentioned like that. Do you know that in a way I was responsible for his death?"

My eyes must have bulged.

"No, no, no, my dear," Pantling told her. "We were all in it. Besides, it couldn't have had anything to do with his death. It was like this, Mr. Travers."

I'll make his story compact and try to show you the picture as I saw it myself. Irene Pantling and Pamela Leishman were sisters: Pantling and Leishman were partners in a Mincing Lane firm of importers, and the two families were accustomed to taking their summer holidays together. The Pantlings had only the one child: the Leishmans had Tony, who was eight, and a daughter, Betty, aged four, who had been left with a grannie.

Ashman and Dallas Malone had come over on the same boat and had happened to get into conversation with the other party because Pantling and his wife had been to Bandol before and Ashman had seen a Bandol hotel label on a case which had been brought on board. The bigger and much faster car had beaten Ashman to Bandol by a day, but as soon as Ashman arrived the six grown-ups had become almost inseparable and the two children were soon to regard Ashman and Miss Malone as an aunt and uncle. Every morning at about eleven o'clock they would go to the beach together, and again in the afternoon at about half-past three. At about half-past five they would drive their cars along the front to that tea-shop, and after dinner they would have coffee and liqueurs at that café and then go on to the cinema or casino.

It was not till that first day together at Bandol that the party—as I conveniently call them—learned that Ashman was the famous author of *The Silken Petticoat*. The party was very impressed, though later the men would pull Ashman's leg about it. Ashman himself was quite modest about the whole thing.

But about that morning visit to the beach. Ashman had actually arrived without a bathing costume, but he bought himself one at a little shop next door to the *librairie* where the party bought their English papers. It was a pale-blue pair of trunks with a dark-blue decorative stripe at the sides, but to everyone's surprise that costume was only for the purpose of sun-bathing, and for three or four days the party had great fun at the expense of a hefty fellow like Ashman who'd come seven hundred miles merely to flop on the sand. And then Dallas Malone let them into the secret of that phobia.

"I was ever so ashamed," Irene Pantling told me. "We all were. And then the most extraordinary thing happened. We were just in the sea one morning and swimming well out when Claud said, 'My God, look what's happening!'"

What had happened was that the two children had grasped Ashman by the arm—he was sitting in his trunks reading his paper—with a "Come on, Uncle Bob." He hadn't minded getting his feet wet, and he went with them almost up to his knees. But that bottom was stony in places and he tripped and fell forward, and before he knew what he was doing he was swimming. Almost at once he touched the bottom and quickly made his way out. Dallas had swum back, and she told the others he was shaking like a leaf.

Nobody said a thing to him, but in the afternoon Dallas told the others that she'd been talking to him, whatever that might mean. And that afternoon, when the others were again well out, Ashman walked into the sea and began swimming parallel to the beach, always well in his depth. He didn't stay in long, but the great thing was that he had swum at all. Again no one said anything, but later at Jean-Jacques—the tea-shop—he had suddenly opened out, as Irene Pantling called it. He had insisted on everyone having a special tea with ices, and he was as pleased as Punch because he'd mastered that phobia. But he hadn't mastered it entirely. He wouldn't swim out of his depth, and every few yards he'd touch bottom to make sure. And he made no bones about admitting that if he had found himself out of his depth he'd have gone down like a stone. And he would never go out in a pedalog or canoe.

"But, my dear lady, you can't possibly blame yourself for his death," I said.

"But I do," she said. "I just can't help it. I suppose because I'm made that way. If I hadn't laughed at him about not swimming he might never have swum at all, and then he wouldn't have wanted to bathe that night in that river and he might have been alive now."

"Sheer morbidity, don't you think so, Mr. Travers?"

I agreed, less abruptly, with Pantling. And I thought it was time I brought the conversation round to myself and why I was at Briarwood. The reason I gave was Dallas Malone. I said she was wanted in connection with the winding up of Ashman's estate, but we couldn't get hold of her. She seemed, in fact, to have gone into thin air. That was why enquiries had been made at Bandol, where she had last been seen.

Husband and wife both began to talk. He gave way to her.

"I can explain it," she said. "You see, we all wanted to keep in touch after we got back. We'd had such jolly times together. But Dallas was going out to Hollywood at once—something to do with the filming of the book—and she hadn't any permanent address. She was going to be there for some months, but she promised to write."

"Yes," I said. "That's certainly an explanation. But it's curious, don't you think? She must have heard of his death. Even the French papers carried the story. M. Bourgues knew about it at the Bon Accueil. You'd have expected there'd have been at least a letter to his brother."

"It *is* a bit curious," Pantling said. "But perhaps she didn't know the brother."

I suddenly knew I ought to leave things like that.

"That's probably it," I said. "There'll be a letter to the solicitors or someone in due course." I turned to Irene Pantling. "What sort of a girl was she?"

She frowned slightly.

"Well, she was not quite the social class he was. He was public school, like my husband, and had been to Cambridge, but she was very nice. Very good company. Always ready for fun."

I don't know why that word always makes me wince. Maybe it's because of the B.B.C. There's no more frightening word in the English language than when in some ballyhoo or other they suggest you listen to some coming programme or other and have fun.

"She was his fiancée?" I said.

"No one ever knew," she said. "And naturally we couldn't ask."

"The idea was that she was part fiancée and part secretary," Pantling said. "They were pretty affectionate."

I'd happened to be looking straight at him, and he'd given me the most flagrant wink.

"Good-looking, was she?"

"Oh, very," Irene said. "Something rather French about her, don't you think so, Claud? A beautiful complexion, and the way she did her hair—a sort of pompadour or upsweep."

I chuckled. I might be a married man, I said, but that was Chinese to me.

"Well, brought up from the back to the top of the head. She'd very dark-brown hair—almost black—and very dark eyes, just as if she used mascara, but she didn't. Dressed very well too. She had the loveliest clothes."

"Something just a bit hard about her at times," Pantling said frowningly. "Probably that secretary side of her. And I must say she had no sex appeal for me, though she might have had for quite a lot of men. Not that I didn't like her. She was very good fun."

"And Ashman?"

"A great chap," he said, and smiled. "Out to get the most out of life and didn't care who knew it. The kids adored him."

"You saw him when you got back?"

"No," he said, and his face suddenly straightened. "He was drowned on that Saturday when he was coming out to dinner here the following Wednesday."

Then he suddenly thought of something.

"I remember now. When we were fixing things up I mentioned Dallas and he said she'd already sailed."

I gave a nod. Then I knew it was about time I was going, and I got to my feet.

5

PETERING OUT

"DON'T go yet," Pantling said. "Do have another drink."

I said I was an abstemious sort of cove. And I hadn't been back in England much more than four hours and my wife would be expecting me.

"Give her a ring," Irene Pantling said. "Do stay a few more minutes. It's like being in Bandol again."

The telephone was in the hall. As I was hanging up, Irene appeared. She said she would ring her sister, who might have heard something about Dallas's American address. I went back to the lounge. Pantling poured us each another drink.

"Ashman leave Dallas much in his will?" he said.

"Well, that's rather confidential," I told him. "What do you think yourself?"

He gave an understanding nod.

"They were *very* affectionate, I think you said?"

"Lord, yes. Plain as the nose on your face. And why not?"

"Why not, indeed. It's a free country. Or should I say that France was?"

"She was all my wife told you," he said. "A dam' smart woman. But something just a little bit too hard for me."

"The business side of her," I suggested. "Just as you said."

Irene came back. Pamela didn't know a thing about Dallas, she said, but she'd been quite excited to hear about my call.

"Another spot of something?" her husband said.

She wouldn't have another, and we settled down to a good gossip. Whether that extra time would be worth while I didn't know, but I'd already heard so much—and some of it startling—that I had every reason to hope. It was about Bandol that we mostly talked. I passed on fictitious messages from M. Bourgues and Max, and I was a kind of purveyor of dreams, with the Pantlings living all over again that holiday in the sun. Irene said she daren't think of it and Ashman too because it always made her cry. Then we talked about the book—Irene said she hadn't really read it, but I was sure she had—and the money Ashman and his heirs and assigns would get and the legal methods of frustrating the Commissioners of Inland Revenue, and before you could hardly say knife it was almost ten o'clock, and I was getting up, really, this time, to go. Irene said we must certainly meet again. Pantling went out with me to my car, and we agreed to lunch together in some near future.

The streets were clear, but I didn't drive fast. That call on the Pantlings had turned out to be very much of a facer, and there was I in the middle of a mental see-saw. One piece of evidence was in perfect alignment with the inquest. Ashman *had* mastered that phobia and he might really have bathed in that river. A sultry night might have brought back Bandol and given an urge to get again into the water. A bit high-flown, that, but where human motives and impulses are concerned you can't tell what's high-flown and what isn't.

So much for one end of the see-saw. At the other had been another piece of evidence that had raised serious doubts, but that was a matter that might possibly be cleared up by what Hallows might have learned in Sussex. Maybe I was a drowning man myself and clutching at a straw. Maybe I was hating the thought of having to tell Maurice Ashman that that hunch of his had better be forgotten.

But there were two other things that were intriguing me. In the months that had passed I had forgotten the face of that girl in the Café Rond, and yet the last hour or two had brought it back to me, if in a hazy kind of way. Irene Pantling had the very figure of that girl; and had her hair been blonde, then—or so I vaguely felt—she might have been that girl herself. Her voice hadn't been exactly an echo of the girl's voice, but I had heard it under vastly differing conditions, and yet I couldn't help feeling that each voice had had something of the same timbre.

I'm a quick thinker: far too quick, as I've said, and I've an agile, far too imaginative sort of mind. It wasn't hard for me, as I drove slowly towards home, to imagine Irene Pantling and Robert Ashman as friends. I could see him arranging that holiday in Bandol to fit in with her own, and the delicious little drama when at that first arranged meeting on the boat, the two had had to act as strangers. But there was something wrong about all that, as I suddenly saw. Would Irene Pantling have tolerated the presence of Dallas Malone—the attractive brunette who had the next room to Ashman's own?

But I didn't wholly discard that theory, even if the thought of Dallas made me momentarily switch to her. Ashman hadn't left her anything in his will, and maybe because he hadn't expected anything remotely like death. As for that Hollywood yarn, I didn't, frankly, believe it. Consider the situation. Everyone wanted to keep in touch; go to each other's houses, have meetings in town, shopping expeditions, doing shows and all the rest of it. But Dallas had shied violently aside. She didn't want that holiday to extend to England. If she had an address she didn't want it known. Hence the Hollywood story—plausible but fictitious: a story with which Ashman was conversant and which he had repeated to Pantling when that dinner at Briarwood was being fixed up.

But when I thought that, I was in the inner suburbs and I had to keep my mind on the road. As soon as I was in the flat I rang Norris at his home address.

"What's Hallows's news?" I was wanting to know.

He said it wasn't too good from our point of view. I told him he could say the same about my own. In the morning, I said, I'd run through Hallows's reports.

"No need, unless you like," he told me. "He came back tonight. He'll be along in the morning, so you can talk to him direct."

"Bad as that, is it?"

"Don't know," he said in his slow way. "He's always a bit of a pessimist. You ought to know that."

I said I'd be along at nine o'clock. When I got to bed that night I ought to have slept like a dead man, but it took me a full hour before I dozed off. Thoughts were a kaleidoscope, but the one thing to which I kept coming back was a striving to see the face of that blonde in the Café Rond: to see it in profile as when I had looked round casually from my stool and had caught a glimpse of her as she made for Clement Foorde. Before I slept I'd have willingly given a ten-pound note to have known if that blonde were really Irene Pantling.

In the cool, clear morning light things looked vastly different. That Irene Pantling theory had more than a flimsy look, and I was seeing myself rather like someone who had taken just one too many for the road and driven the homeward car with far too little thought. Mine had been the mental car. I'd had that longish plane journey, and then, instead of spending a domestic evening, I'd rushed off to the Pantlings, and a couple of powerful whiskies, even spread over the evening, hadn't been an aid to thought. Irene Pantling, I could now tell myself, was a happily married woman with a small daughter, and, except for that natural nervousness when I'd rung her, every word and gesture should have told me that the relationship between her and Ashman was what she had indicated it was, and no more.

But that didn't say that the evening had been wasted. In many ways it had been intriguing, and I was anxious to get to work comparing notes with Hallows. That was why I was early at the office; but even so, Norris and Hallows were well before me. I had said that I would look through Hallows's reports, but I preferred things straight from the horse's mouth.

"I ought to tell you," Hallows began, "that I went down there with what I thought was the right idea—that that inquest verdict was all wrong and my job was to find out what had really happened. At any rate I made myself known to Mr. Grainger, who was really helpful, and he introduced me to the police surgeon. He was a youngish chap—"

"Just a minute," cut in Norris. "Youngish, you say. Any hint in that that he was inexperienced?"

"Oh no. He was keen and he certainly knew his job. I'd call him a first-class man. A real live wire."

"What was their mortuary like?" I wanted to know. "Nothing wrong with that either," Hallows told me bluntly. "One of the best I've ever seen. Just like a hospital: all white tiles and refrigerator system: bang up to date. A very nice chap too—name of Mellett—and he happened to be a detective-story fan like myself. That's why I slung everything at him: everything I'd ever read about faked drownings."

He got out his notebook.

"Things like this. Could Ashman have been murdered? Yes, if someone were swimming with him and had managed to get him under water by holding his ankles or something like that. Any marks to indicate such a thing? Never a one. Any bruises or abrasions to hint that he might have been knocked out and then dumped in the water? Never a one. Any hypodermic marks to indicate drugging before drowning? Never a one. Any traces whatever of drugs in the stomach content? Never a trace. No indication either that Ashman had ever been addicted to drugs? Anything wrong about the water in the lungs? Nothing at all. Fresh river water. No trace of salt as there might have been if he'd been drowned at sea and then dumped in the river? No salt whatever.

"And," went on Hallows dryly, "he even threw one of his own at me. There wasn't a trace of soap to hint that he'd been drowned in someone's bath."

"Pretty conclusive," I said.

"Yes, but wait a minute, sir. There was more to it than that. When our client expressed his doubts to Mr. Grainger, Mellett went over the whole bag of tricks again."

"They didn't call in a Home Office pathologist?" Norris wanted to know.

"Now, now," Hallows told him reprovingly. "If the Home Office were called in for every case of drowning, there'd be a nice how-d'you-do. Mellett's keen and he's good. He was satisfied and his Chief was satisfied."

"A rather dispiriting start from your point of view," I said. "What came next?"

"I had a look at the scene, and one of Grainger's men went with me. That meadow, by the by, where Ashman was drowned is long and narrow and shaped rather like a sausage. There's only a couple of acres of it and only thirty yards in places between the lane and the river. All the same, I thought a car might have been driven in: that's working on the theory, of course, that someone brought the body there in Ashman's own car and dumped it. So we went over that meadow with a microscope, and never a hope. The grass had been cut and cleared just before the drowning, and ever since it'd been growing like blazes. And you know the kind of August we had. That meadow was as hard as a rock underneath. And there'd been some sheep on it."

"Not so good," I said. "And then what?"

"I went to the Foxhounds at Pettiforth, and stayed there a night. Only picked up one thing which might have been useful if I hadn't been to Seahurst first. Just another detective-story favourite. *Suppose it wasn't Ashman who telephoned reserving that room.*"

My eyebrows lifted. Norris shuffled in his chair.

"Yes, it was a good idea," Hallows said ruefully, "only nothing came of it. Everything went pat at first. Whoever rang, if Ashman didn't, had been there before and he knew the run of things. He knew that Keeper, like every publican, likes his afternoons to himself. Generally has a nap to make up for late nights. What I'm getting at is that whoever rang guessed that it wouldn't be Keeper who answered the telephone. It ought to be someone less familiar with his voice. And it was. It was Keeper's daughter. And whoever rang had an enormous bit of luck, because she hadn't been back in the village very long and had never clapped eyes on Ashman. I asked her what the voice was like, and all I could get out of her was that it was a gentleman's voice. And it was very indistinct, she said, because the line was bad. Not her end—the other end. She could only just hear. All of which was nicely in keeping with the idea that someone at that other end was faking Ashman's voice."

"Pretty good, that," I said. "And what happened?"

"I traced the call and it was a London one. From a call-box. That wasn't so good."

"And then?"

He shrugged his shoulders.

"That's all, sir. What else could I do?"

He was right. There was nothing else he could do. That Ashman had never rung that inn was an excellent idea, but one incapable of further proof.

"Then yesterday I went back to Wenhurst," he told us, "and I saw that farmer who'd found the clothes. He was pretty busy and sick of the whole thing, but what I did get from him didn't help that theory about the car driving through the gate and depositing the body. I asked if he saw any tyre marks in the meadow. He said it was all tyre marks from the tractor and trailer that had carted the hay. I said what about dew, and he said what about it. There'd been the usual August heavy dew, but *after* any possible car had driven in. So that was a dead end."

"Well, there's no need for any of us to be lugubrious," I told him. "You did a very good job, and this isn't the first impossibility we've been asked to tackle and it won't be the last. Everything I picked up myself, by the way, tallied with what you did or didn't find out. For instance, Ashman had beaten that phobia of his. He'd begun to swim again."

I told them all about it.

"And, don't you see," I added, "it makes that inquest verdict absolutely water-tight, and from now on it loses us a client. Ashman did swim—on the face of things. He'd have sunk like a stone if he was out of his depth. That's not an isolated case. I've known two or three people just the same. They lose their nerve entirely as soon as they don't touch bottom. And Ashman couldn't suspect that that river was deep just where it was. He stepped in, and that was that. Like stepping on a stair that wasn't there."

George Wharton—Chief-Superintendent Wharton to you— with whom I've worked at odd times for twenty years and more on murder cases, likes to stage a dramatic curtain. I wasn't trying to spring that kind of melodramatic surprise. All I wanted was to produce one little torch-flash in the general gloom.

"There's just one little thing left," I said. "Before I get to it, what about the fingerprints on that bag in Ashman's car?"

"His, and plenty of them," Hallows said. "No one else's."

"Naturally he'd handled it when he packed it," Norris put in.

"Agreed," I said. "And if anybody else opened it, it was with gloves on. The normal assumption is that Ashman opened it to get out his bathing trunks. From what I read at the inquest report, those trunks were the common or garden dark-blue variety."

"That's right," Hallow said. "They still had them down there. And they were new."

"Then what about this?" I said, and told them about those French ones Ashman had bought in Bandol.

"There's just the possibility that Ashman left those light- and dark-blue French ones behind," I said. "We can telephone the Bon Accueil Hotel and find out. But will it get us anywhere if the answer's negative? He still might have left them behind somewhere. But if we could prove that he didn't, then we could arrive at this. Why should Ashman buy new trunks when he had an excellent pair? Even if the ones he was found drowned in weren't new, they couldn't have been a pair he'd had before his holiday. He hadn't swum for years. And if he'd used them for sun-bathing, then they'd have been bleached."

You couldn't quarrel with that argument, and in a minute or two the meeting was adjourned. I looked up the Bon Accueil number in the Michelin Guide, asked for it and then settled down to wait. And I'd given Hallows a job of work.

If Ashman's body *had* been brought to Wenhurst in his car—and however fantastic the theory we at least had to test it—then the one who drove that car had to get back to where he or she came from. The car had had to be left, so how was that return journey made? If the person was local or reasonably so, then by foot. If not, the answer surely was by train.

What, then, about times? The body, even if that lane was little more than a track and unfrequented, would have had to be deposited at dusk or after. If that job had been completed by nine o'clock, then how did trains fit in? There was a local line running through Wenhurst. To the south it joined a junction just short of Seahurst. To the north it joined another and main-line track to London.

Hallows had the answers before I had mine. There was no train to Seahurst that fitted. But there was one to London. The Wenhurst slow train left at twenty-past nine and it evidently was timed to fit in with the main-line train to Town, for there was only a ten-minute wait at the junction. From the junction the main-line train was a fast one. It reached Town at half-past ten. But that still didn't prove a thing. All it proved was that, subject to a whole series of hypotheses, a certain thing *might* conceivably have been done in a certain way.

Ten minutes later I was speaking to the bureau at the Bon Accueil. It took a minute to get M. Bourgues, and that left me a bare two minutes. He remembered me well enough, and I got him to write down the office telephone number. Then I asked him to discover by hook or crook if Ashman had left behind him a pair of bathing trunks, light blue in colour and with a dark-blue stripe at the sides. I begged him to call us back and said we'd contrive, in spite of currency hindrance, to pay his full charges. He agreed to do what he could.

I had some coffee, smoked a pipe or two and read the newspapers. I daren't leave that telephone; and I was just about to ask for a lunch to be brought for me, when the telephone rang. It was the call from Bandol: Bourgues speaking.

"I am happy to give you what you asked for," he told me. "M. Ashman did take those bathing trunks. I spoke to the porter who brought down his luggage, and so many bathing things have been left behind on the drying lines that we have formed a habit of asking at the last moment. And M. Ashman was very annoyed because he had forgotten the trunks. The porter fetched them from the line and they were put in a bag. That, I think, is what you wanted."

I thanked him profusely. I said his charges would be paid and he must send a bill. He said gallantly that it was nothing at all, and I could pay him when I came again to Bandol. Then the time was up, and that was that. Norris had gone to lunch, and when he came back Hallows and I had a hurried meal. Then we carried on with that adjourned conference.

Ten minutes later we knew there was only one thing to do—to get hold of Maurice Ashman and have him ring the manager of the flats at Everdale Court to get us permission to search Ashman's room. It was late afternoon before that had been done, and a search of the rooms was successful in a couple of minutes. In almost the first drawer we opened we found them underneath some shirts: trunks such as Irene Pantling had described, and still in them traces of sand from the fine shingle of Bandol beach. We left them where they were.

We went back to the office—Hallows and I—and had yet another quick conference. Again there was nothing to do but ring Grainger. He was out, so I asked for my private number to be rung later. With that we adjourned till the following morning. But I got Grainger's call just when I was having dinner. I told him everything was too involved for the telephone, but, if he didn't consider it beneath his dignity, we'd be glad to see him at Broad Street at any convenient time. He said I could expect him in the morning at about eleven o'clock.

He was on time and his Chief-Inspector was with him. All our cards went on the table. The final result was this.

"Interesting," he said, "and good of you people to tell us everything you have. There's the chance that Ashman regarded those trunks as special ones and didn't want to use them at home. Or he might have looked only casually for them and missed them under those shirts. All the same, we'll take over from now on."

"And what are we to tell the client?"

He made a wry face.

"Hard to advise you. You've gone as far as you can, so why not drop the whole thing?"

That seemed the best thing to do, and that, in fact, was what we did. Maurice Ashman wasn't too dissatisfied with the way things had turned out, if only because he had the satisfaction of knowing that someone besides himself had found a thing or two at least unusual about his brother's death. And, of course, he'd been mightily surprised to hear about that Bandol swimming and the collapse of his main plank for enquiry.

Grainger had promised to let us have a hint if anything came out of that new, official resumption, but a week went by and I heard nothing from him. I ventured to ring up, and he told me there were no developments. A week later he rang me one night and said that everything was again being shelved. The fullest enquiries had produced nothing new, and he was pretty confident that we were all barking up a non-existent tree.

And that was the end of the Ashman Case. Again there was one faint reverberation. Irene Pantling rang me and said the Leishmans would be in town on a certain day and would like to meet me, so would I lunch with them and her husband and herself. I said I'd be delighted.

Bernice had been asked too, but preferred not to make it. It was a good lunch, with all the old nostalgic talk of France and Bandol. That was about all, except that nobody had heard a word from Dallas Malone. I had to do some skilful lying about my not hearing either.

And so, as I've said, the Ashman Case petered out. I was pretty sure after that lunch in town that Irene Pantling hadn't, after all, had bleached hair at the time of the Café Rond affair, for I had brought the conversation round to women's changes of hair colour and she had been quite contemptuous about artificial blondes. It was true she had high cheekbones and the right walk, but it was the hair that settled things. In any case I soon forgot all about the whole thing.

And I wasn't to remember it all again till that extraordinary morning in November. That was when I had that chance meeting with Clement Foorde.

PART II

DEATH BY STRANGLING

6

UNEXPECTED COMMISSION

I WENT into the bar at the club that morning and I practically stumbled over Godram, the composer. His wife is a close friend of Bernice, which makes him and me something more than acquaintances. As he leaned back from his chair and presented a hand for me to shake, I saw that his *vis-à-vis* was no other than Clement Foorde.

"Sit down," Godram said. "Never saw a fellow like you for rushing about. Foorde, you know Ludovic Travers?"

"I've seen Mr. Travers from time to time," Foorde said in that suave voice of his. I was surprised at the strength of his grip when we shook hands.

"What'll you drink?" Godram said. "We're having sherry, as you see."

I said I always was something of a vulgarian, so I'd have my usual beer. A club tankard.

"Pint or half-pint?"

"Since it's free, a pint," I said. "A Philistine like myself has to live by spoiling the Egyptians."

Godram nipped across to the bar.

"Highly unpleasant weather, Mr. Travers," Foorde told me.

"Most unpleasant, sir," I said.

Now why did that *sir* pop out? All sorts of reasons, I think. At the back of my mind was what I might call the literary importance of the man. And he was older than myself: sixty-five, in fact. It was the first time I had really spoken to him.

And there was the rather overpowering and immediate presence of the man himself.

I hope I haven't given the impression that he was either small or senile. Clement Foorde would have made a magnificent Roman emperor, for he was almost six foot, broad, and he had the profile. The incongruity would have been that shock of white, swept-back hair. But I must say it suited him in a most uncanny way. It made him an impresario. It somehow explained and made equally congruous the black velvet jacket and the wide bow tie above the almost Vandyke collar.

Godram nipped back and my tankard with him. He leaned forward somewhat mischievously.

"You may not know it, Foorde, but Travers is a detective."

The glass stayed halfway to Foorde's mouth. His eyes wrinkled.

"A detective?" he said, and then he smiled. "He's a great puller of legs, Mr. Travers."

"I assure you it's true," Godram said. "He's even been known to work for Scotland Yard."

"Really?" He gave me a quick look as if to hear me disagree.

"Remarkable," he said. "And what do you detect, Mr. Travers?"

It was a quizzical, quite friendly sort of question.

"At the moment merely that we're talking about a comparative nonentity like myself," I told him. "I'd rather be hearing about people like you two. You yourself haven't been in the club much lately?"

"I've been abroad most of the summer," he said.

"Only July and August, surely," Godram said.

"My dear fellow, doesn't that constitute a summer?"

"And the winter of the English stage?" I ventured.

"Very happily put," he graciously told me. "Not that the stage of our day isn't in its perpetual winter. Or should I say fall?"

I didn't catch that abstruse allusion and he had to add that *fall* was the American for autumn. I gathered then that he was referring to one of the bees in his bonnet—the Americanisation of our stage. I don't think he was too pleased at my denseness, because he began talking to Godram about a place near Paris where he had spent that summer, at a villa owned, I gathered, by Henri Vitrelle, the Académicien.

"You write at all, Mr. Travers?" he suddenly asked.

I said in my callow days I'd written some rather flippant books on criminology.

"No need to be ashamed of one's youth," he said. "And flippancy is not the peculiar perquisite of any age. Our friend Godram here is an almost living disproof of that. For which I ought to ask him to have another sherry."

He hoisted his bulk out of the chair. Again don't get me wrong. He wasn't a Chesterton: it was the chair itself that was so low and deep that a kind of hoisting was the only means of emergence, and suddenly I was seeing him again as he rose from that chair in the Café Rond. Only then he had been wearing over the velvet coat that voluminous cape without which he was never seen abroad.

I hadn't finished that pint tankard, and in any case I didn't want to attach myself to them. Godram said he'd be seeing me some time, and Foorde gave me a nod and a smile, with a wave of the hand like a cardinal's blessing. Lunch had begun, but I sat on for a few minutes. No particular friend of mine was in, so I had my meal alone. Then I had coffee in the library.

I was reading some periodical or other when a steward approached me.

"Mr. Foorde's compliments, sir, and could you see him for a minute in the small lounge."

I finished my coffee and went at once. I found Foorde alone in the room, and he was standing not far inside as if he wanted a word with me and no more. His smile was graciousness itself.

"So sorry to trouble you, my dear fellow, but I want to ask a favour. Will you dine with me tonight?"

I thought quickly.

"I think I'd be delighted to."

"At seven, shall we say? My flat, as you probably know, is in Marston Square. And please don't dress. A perfectly informal affair. Just you and I."

"Splendid," I said. "I'll be there at seven."

His smile was almost a grimace. A wave of the hand and a happy little bow and he was making for the door. After he'd gone I stood there for a minute or two, and I found myself polishing my glasses. That's a nervous trick of mine when the unusual happens suddenly to pop up. What I was furiously wondering was why I had been chosen for so signal an honour as a private dinner at the famous Marston Square flat. It couldn't have been my *beaux yeux*. Or that I was likely to be an epigrammatic mine.

And then I suddenly thought of something. It couldn't have arisen out of Godram's jocular remark that I was a detective? Surely the great Clement Foorde was not angling to be a client of the Broad Street Detective Agency? I shrugged that one away. Amusing, but too absurd. And I had only to wait four more hours to have some of the answers.

So at seven o'clock that night I was in a room which had become in many ways as well-known by name as Shaw's at the Adelphi. That block of flats known as Marston Square was old-fashioned enough, but with the grace of a well-kept if aged dowager. One expected to hear from its windows the clip-clop of cab-horses and to see the gas-lights and their little pools of light beneath the trees. I didn't see its one innovation—the restaurant from which our meal was brought up.

But first we had sherry in what one thought of as the salon. I had read *First Curtain*, as I've told you, and I knew that room well: its superb chandelier, its Aubusson carpet, its twin Chippendale bookcases, its *sang-de-boeuf* vases on the Adam mantelpiece, and the portrait by Georges Clairon of Bernhardt as Magda in Sudermann's play. A faint air, part musk, part cigar-smoke, seemed to hang tenuously about that room. Merely to look around it was to be momentarily part of the past: to have, however evanescently, a feeling of personal insignificance. It was the cheerful fire, the tray of drinks on the low table and the comfortable brocaded chairs that snapped one back to the present.

Foorde was a charming host, and in that room was no obtrusion of self. In the dining-room, with its handsome Empire furniture, we were both somewhat dwarfed, and yet the meal contrived to be friendly and intimate. It was an excellent meal. The partridge was particularly good, and we had a bottle of a famous French wine—Tavel—which I do not remember to have drunk before in England.

Coffee and cigars were in the salon. I enjoyed that chat we had before the fire, even if it consisted largely of his drawing out of me my own recollections of the theatre. There was no striving for epigrams: indeed, he made only one remark which I still remember, and which, at the time, struck me as amusing. It happened that the conversation had got round to Godram and modern music, and so, somehow, to the popular craze for Tchaikovsky.

"I just faintly remember his death," he said. "I remember my father mentioning it. I must have been a very small boy."

Then he smiled in rather an impish way, if such immense features could ever be really puckish or impish.

"Of course he never really died, you know. At least, not in Russia."

"Didn't die!"

"Well, that's my theory. I think he disappeared on account of some Tsarist oppression or other and reappeared in America as John Philip Sousa."

I did laugh at that, and I remember it so well because it was then that the talk had a sudden, dramatic change.

"You'll forgive me, my dear fellow, if I become a little personal. I'll be frank. There's something I want you to do for me. It occurred to me only this evening when I recalled that remark of Godram's about your being a detective."

I think I must rather have stammered that I'd be happy to do anything.

"I have your word that what I say will be very confidential?"

"Most certainly," I told him. "If, as bluntly, you wish to become a client, then you can talk as freely as you would to your doctor."

He leaned back in the famous pose: feet well out, finger-tips together.

"This summer I've been heavily employed. I've completed the second volume of an autobiography and it's in my publishers' hands. I've already begun what may well be the third and final volume."

"Not necessarily," I told him. "I'm not flattering you when I say you have more than a volume in front of you yet."

It didn't displease him.

"Well, be that as it may. I have hit on a certain keynote, shall I call it, for that volume on which I'm at present engaged. I'm intending to begin it—for certain reasons which it would take far too long to explain—at a certain unsavoury episode which occurred one night this year in the Café Rond. I take it you know to what I refer."

"Incredible as you may find it," I said, "I happened to be there."

The hands fell to his knees.

"But how amazing! You actually saw the young person?"

"Fairly plainly."

"Amazing," he said again. "Perhaps it will simplify things. But to get back to my book. And to that episode. I have my own ideas about it. I believe it, in spite of Ashman's disclaimer, to have been a deliberate and planned attempt to publicize that novel of his. But that doesn't matter at the moment. What matters is that there was a great deal of vulgar publicity, in the face of which I could only maintain a certain dignity by ignoring the whole thing. Now I propose to resurrect it."

"Uh-huh?" I went, and maybe because there was nothing I could say.

"Let me be devil's advocate," he went on, and the finger-tips were together again. "You may think a resurrection unwise. You may think it cowardly, seeing that the unfortunate Ashman is now dead: a death, I should tell you, of which I was unaware till some time after it occurred, since I was in France at the time. You may even"—he smiled—"talk about a detraction from one's stature. And all I can say is that I see that episode as very necessary for the opening of that third volume of mine. You must accept that statement. I'm afraid I can't amplify it."

"That's as you think fit," I said. "A client's wishes are invariably respected."

"Well, I wish to become a client," he said. "In fact, *I* want you to discover that young woman."

I must have stared. I think I gave what I call a Whartonian grunt.

"I see. You want her name and address."

"More than that," he said. "I want her life-history."

"A tall order," I said. "The Press never ran her to earth as far as I know. We start merely at one night in the Café Rond with someone no one knew and who was there for perhaps three minutes and then disappeared." I shook a warning head. "I ought to tell you it may be a very long job. Possibly an expensive one."

He waved an indifferent hand.

"I accept that. But not the time. I want that information within a week. You look surprised. Possibly you won't understand why I need it within that time."

He leaned forward.

"Perhaps you don't know the urge and grip of creative impulse. It's something one must never neglect." His huge hands vibrated with the feeling he wanted to convey. "That book is there. Not in the thin air. Written already in my brain. I have to get it on paper. Even a week is too long to wait."

"I understand that," I told him. "And you can be sure we'll do our best. We're concerned with what you want and when, not why you want it."

"Then you'll do your best?"

"We always do our best," I told him. "But I would like to know—when you spoke of a life-history, for example—the kind of thing you'd like to receive."

His forehead furrowed. I thought I'd annoyed him in some way. Then he shrugged his massive shoulders.

"Say, if you like, that I'm vindictive. That I hope you'll unearth something—well, not entirely creditable."

He got to his feet. The French clock on the Sheraton table was almost at eleven o'clock.

"You'd like reports—when there's anything to report?"

"Yes," he said. "I think I would."

"And the contract," I said. "That had better be signed tomorrow. When can I have it sent round?"

Any time before twelve o'clock would suit him, he said, and that was about all. To ask him for a retainer would have been unthinkable, or, indeed, to mention in that room anything so vulgar as terms. It was only when I was out in the damp night air that I realized we should have to mention them in the contract.

I was early at the office to get that contract drawn, and Bertha Munney—our warhorse of a secretary—was personally to take it to Foorde. And why was I in such a hurry to get things done? Not, I think, because of the time limit. Not because of Foorde himself, for we'd had clients even more important. And certainly not the money. Ten pounds a day, with expenses, for six days, plus a bonus of twenty-five pounds if successful, was chicken-feed compared with the retainers we held from one or two companies. The reason was that Ludovic Travers was for six days employing Ludovic Travers at the expense of Clement Foorde to discover what the said Ludovic Travers had had an itch to discover ever since that night in the Café Rond. Had Foorde known those facts, they must have appealed to his feeling for irony.

It was a stiff assignment that I'd undertaken, but not so stiff as I'd lugubriously made out to Foorde. I could see three sources of possible information and I was proposing to take a day to exhaust them: a kind of surveying of an old-time battlefield before determining the vital line of action. I'd rung Maurice Ashman's Manchester number, and it was he I got first.

I was careful to say at the outset that the information had nothing to do with the case we'd undertaken for him, even if, on the face of it, there seemed a connection. I wanted, in fact, two things. Had he ever met or heard of any special lady friend?

No special one, he said. Robert hadn't been the marrying sort. On the few occasions he'd met him in Town there had been nobody with him.

"Then none was certainly mentioned in the will?"

"None at all," he said. "It was an oldish will. My idea is he'd have altered it if he'd lived."

"The other thing's this," I said. "Have you his papers?" He said he had a small case full. When I mentioned getting them to me, he said he'd be glad of an excuse to come to Town, and he'd see I had them in the late afternoon.

"Bring everything," I said. "Any scrap of paper you happened to keep."

It was then only about half-past nine, so I drove to Everdale Court. I handed over a card at the bureau and in less than no time was in Cobell's office. He was at the same desk doing apparently the same things. Maybe he hadn't budged since I saw him last.

"Hallo, sir," he said. "You here again?"

"Been a longish time," I said. "August, wasn't it?"

"Beginning of September," he said, which showed he hadn't let everything slip from his mind. "But there're no Ashman things here now. His flat's sub-let."

I said I didn't want his things or his flat. I'd come to redeem a promise. He gave me a quick, rather furtive look. "Remember your advice about finding the lady? Well, we're still hunting. That's why I wasn't able to tell you anything worth while."

"Then how did you know she was blackmailing him?"

"Ways and means," I said. "Cheque-book stubs: unusual payments that can't be otherwise accounted for: the sudden need for a man to raise money: the man himself and how people say he was pretty worried at some particular time that fits in with everything else. It's been a regular jig-saw puzzle. Now that we're absolutely sure of certain things, we're really after the lady."

There used to be times when I blushed to utter the whitest of lies in the sacred name even of justice. Years of association with George Wharton have cured me of that. I acquired the sense to know that detection is largely a battle of wits with those to whom lying is a main defence, so why deprive oneself of the very same weapon. There are times now when I can actually admire the brilliance of my own efforts. Virtue can be a tedious thing. Lying—for strictly business purposes—lets loose the imagination. That's why one sometimes calls a lie romance.

"I'd like you to be in on this," I told Cobell. "When everything gets out it's going to be a highly interesting story. It's still strictly confidential, of course; but, from the way we've managed to put two and two together, we know that the lady must have come here from time to time. In fact there were two ladies, but we won't jump that far yet. I'm still looking for a willowy blonde who was in Ashman's life for a certainty last March."

"I still don't know her," he told me. "He never was with her here, not that any of us saw. I know. I made enquiries after he was dead."

"Right," I said. "Let's shift to another possible lady. Still tallish and willowy, but this time a slinky brunette with dark eyes and dark hair drawn up on top of her head."

"Yes," he said slowly, and licked his lips. "I've seen her once or twice with him."

"When?"

"Don't rush me. This takes some thinking out."

He scowled, rubbed his chin, growled a few things to himself and then sat up.

"I think the first time was over a year ago. I was in the hall and she was there. Didn't notice her till Ashman came down and took her arm, and out they went together."

"Fine," I said. "And more recently?"

"Just before he went away for his holiday. He drew up outside in his car and they had a word or two together, and then she got out and walked off."

"In a huff?"

"Oh no. Quite friendly. Just as if he'd given her a lift so far."

"And you haven't the faintest suspicion of her name?"

"Never an idea."

"When he went for his holiday, he left here alone in his car?"

He didn't know, but if I could wait for ten minutes he might find out. As it happened, it didn't take him half the time.

"Yes," he said, "he left alone, so the man said who brought his bags down. And he drove back along the Embankment." I frowned. I found myself happy to tell him that I thought he'd given me a clue. In a week's time I ought to have something for him. Even after we'd shaken hands I was still smiling mysteriously.

But not when I got in my car again. All I'd discovered was what I already knew—that there was such a person as Dallas Malone who did not live at Everdale Court. But the time had at any rate gone nicely by. When I stopped at a telephone kiosk and rang his newspaper, I found that Breck was already there.

"It's Travers, Breck," I said. "I'm chasing a new story which is a variant of a certain old one we once talked about. Can I meet you anywhere, in, say, ten minutes, for coffee?"

He suggested the Cafeta. Five minutes later I was waiting for him. It's a big place and it wasn't so full that morning.

"What's this story?" he wanted to know.

I put just a few of my cards on the table, but I didn't guarantee they were from the same pack. Just a hint of blackmail and a harking back to the blonde. I said we had to find her.

"You've bitten yourself off quite a lump," he told me. "We never found her. We didn't even get a whiff of her."

"Depends how hard you tried," I told him.

"We tried all right. We didn't go as far as you suggested at the time. The story wasn't worth it unless we had her within twenty-four hours and got her to talk."

"Well, that's that," I said, and picked my cards up again. "It was worth a try. What we'll have to rely on now looks pretty hopeless. Try to run across her from a description. Looking for a needle in a haystack, and we don't even know what stack."

"I know," he said. "Makes me cry in my coffee. Only one thing I can tell you, and that's something you know already. She wasn't a real blonde. She was strictly synthetic."

"Yes," I said, and as if I wasn't mighty glad to hear him be so sure. "But you had a pretty good look at her."

"You didn't need much of a look," he said. "There's a lack of silkiness. A sort of brittle quality. You know how it's done?"

I knew well enough, but it's a bad thing to stop a man talking.

"It takes up to four hours," he said. "Depends on the time it takes to break down the original pigment of the hair. Peroxide of ammonia plus pure ammonia is the stuff they use, and the strength can be varied. That bleaches the hair, and then you can tinge it any particular tint you like—platinum or ash or golden—with the special kind of wash. It holds for about a fortnight, then the new roots give it away and it has to be touched up." He smiled to himself amusedly. "I once wrote an article on the whole thing."

That was about all. He had to get back to his paper, and I said I ought to be at the office. As we parted outside I told him I'd give him a first look at anything really good that might happen to turn up. I didn't look too optimistic as I said it.

I wasn't optimistic. Also I didn't go to the office. I went along to the Café Rond and had a tankard with the fond, deluding hope that its atmosphere might bring a something back. But at that time of day it just didn't have any atmosphere. It was too quiet and its air too clear and it had an elusive odour of disinfectant.

I sat moodily in one of the easy chairs casting my thoughts almost frantically around. I tried unavailingly to be back in that room on a March evening. I went to Bandol. I went to Enfield and I had lunch with the Pantlings and Leishmans. I dwelt for a minute on Irene Pantling and how I had wondered if she could have been that blonde—if, in that March, her hair had indeed been bleached. And then suddenly something popped up clean under my nose and I found my fingers at my glasses.

7

SURVEYING THE FIELD

DALLAS Malone, *I told myself, might reasonably have been the blonde of the Café Rond.*

According to Cobell, she had been in Ashman's life well before the Foorde incident. If that were a publicity stunt, then it would have had to be worked out. At all costs the kicker of shins would have had to have no possible traceable connection with Ashman. Very well then—the brunette had to become a blonde. The change would have been startling. The French look which the Pantlings and Leishmans had so much admired would have altogether gone. A nice adjustment of make-up and her own sister wouldn't have recognised her. But afterwards, from the moment she got into that waiting taxi, she would have to lie doggo till the hair became dark again. Then she could appear in public, as on that July morning when Cobell saw her in Ashman's car.

Where would she lie doggo? I didn't know. Maybe where she lived, and that was very likely in some flat or maisonette where Ashman might have installed her. And that didn't much help. In fact the whole theory, now I came to regard it in cold blood, didn't much help. Or did it? I wasn't looking now for an absolutely unknown. I was looking for a creature of flesh and blood about whom I knew a considerable deal. I knew, in fact, the kind of needle I wanted: all that was left was to find a likely haystack.

Then I thought of something else and I rang the flat. Bernice hadn't been expecting me for lunch and my call just caught her. She was just ready to go out, she said, so I made a lunch rendezvous for half-past twelve and said I'd book the table. It wasn't difficult. We were going to eat at the Café Rond.

Bernice is admirably discreet. Life would be unbearable were she otherwise: I mean if she insisted on being told the whys and wherefores of my necessary absences and prying into cases. But she's long since learned to differentiate between a husband and an enquiry agent. She never asks questions, and, if it's policy to take her into one's confidence, she does the job in hand or supplies the information requested and doesn't ask for the outcome.

Over that lunch I told her about the job in hand. There were no names: just that we urgently wanted a blonde of March who'd been a brunette before and after.

"How long after?"

"Say three good months."

"Not long enough," she said. "Was her hair long before she had it bleached?"

I was pretty sure it was.

"Then it couldn't have grown in three months," she said. "She could have had it tinted, of course, like the original colour, otherwise it would have been a horrid sight. The old hair blonde, and the new hair dark."

"Yes," I said. "But she was in the company of women in the July who didn't notice her hair was tinted. Or I don't think so."

"How did she wear her hair then?"

I told her, and she laughed.

"That's simple. She wore the pompadour because it was the most economical way to use the new dark hair, and she probably eked it out with a rat—"

"A what!"

"A rat," she said. "A sort of pad to draw your own hair over. Or it might have been a tail."

"I see it," I said. "And so she needn't have had the old hair tinted; she could have had it carefully snipped off."

"Exactly," she said. "It's quite reassuring, darling, to find you so ill-informed."

I think it was because I was wondering if that were a compliment or a warning that I lost touch with two other questions that had been in my mind. And one doesn't buy a dog and do one's own barking. I'd asked for advice and I took it—at least till we'd gone our separate ways. Then it struck me that if Dallas Malone had used that rat or tail affair to make her back hair longer, then the two other women must have noticed it. But at that lunch in town they'd neither of them mentioned it when we'd been talking about women's hair. Maybe women were clannish in such things.

But I wasn't too happy about it. There was also, or so it seemed to me, the question of that hair when she bathed. A bathing cap, of course, would have kept it in place, but my observation of Bandol beach had shown scarcely a bathing cap, even among the English. It was something that had particularly struck me at the time.

Then I wondered if a little deft manipulation of the truth could tell me what I wanted to know. And I was cocksure enough to think that I could produce a theory to account for the shortness of Dallas Malone's back hair. So I rang Irene Pantling. We had a minute or so of polite conversation.

"I really rang you," I said, "to tell you of a coincidence. I've just run into a man who knew that Miss Malone who was with you at Bandol."

"But how interesting!"

"He hadn't seen her since the spring. And he had some extraordinary yarn about something happening to her hair. She was singeing it or something and it caught fire and she had to have it cut."

"Not singeing," she said. "That's hopelessly out of date. She was drying it in front of the fire."

"But how frightening," I said. "How did the poor soul make out?"

"There are ways," she told me with a coy sort of reticence. "But you yourself haven't got into touch with Dallas yet?"

"Keep it to yourself," I said, "but we're hoping to in a matter of days."

As I drove to Broad Street I was feeling on remarkably good terms with myself. When I talked things over with Norris we were of the same mind. Dallas Malone was the woman whom we had to find. Neither of us had any doubt. Or that the attack on Foorde had been a carefully organised stunt. And that wasn't out of keeping with what I knew about the late Robert Ashman. Observation and information had indicated that he was unreliable. And he had been playing for big stakes. He and his publishers thought he had a winner, but he had wanted to make sure. Not, I hope, that I was feeling too smugly hypocritical about that side of it. Walpole wasn't far out when he said every man had his price. Maybe I've got my own price. I don't know. I do know that no one yet has happened to bid high enough.

At any rate we were in a position to get to work. We had an excellent youngish operative named Dryland who was of the man-about-town type and we gave him a thorough briefing. His would be the theatre side of the enquiry: to get into touch with the stage manager of the Maryland and with the members of the cast of that play of Ashman's that had had a few weeks' run. When he left the office he knew precisely the kind of person for whom he had to look, and he'd been given something of the general background.

Maurice Ashman dropped in shortly afterwards and he brought that collection of papers. As his taxi was waiting, he didn't stay long. I waited till Hallows came in. He was doing a routine job in town and I asked him if he could put in an evening's overtime at the flat. So we had a quick cup of tea and by the time we were home he knew as much about Dallas Malone as any of us.

We dumped the contents of the case on the table in my little room and made a central pool from which we were to help ourselves. Hallows was to tackle the financial side and I the rest. Before I'd been working ten minutes I came on something that made me bring in Hallows.

"Wicklands",

Gatsworth,

Surrey

Tel. Gatsworth 229

March 3rd, 1951

My dear Ashman,

I feel I ought to tell you that the couple you so warmly recommended have turned out more than admirably. Runlet puts his hand to anything and his wife is a better than adequate cook. I hope to see you in Town when I am less busy.

Meanwhile my very best thanks,

Yours,

CLEMENT FOORDE

"Looks like a married couple recommended to him by Ashman," Hallows said. "Anything wrong with it?"

I said there was nothing wrong. The letter bore out what I'd been told, that Foorde had been graciously pleased to be friendly with a very inexperienced young playwright and that playwright had tried to do him a good turn. Later, of course, the younger man had somehow deeply offended the older and they had ceased to be even on nodding terms. The giving of such an offence wasn't out of keeping with the free-and-easy make-up of Ashman.

"If Ashman had happened to go down there some time, he wouldn't have mentioned that girl," Hallows said. "I suppose Foorde could always be asked though."

I didn't think so. It wasn't good policy to refer back to a client. And if Foorde had known about any young woman in whom Ashman had been interested he'd have mentioned the fact, especially in that particular context when he'd been of the opinion that the whole regrettable affair had been organised by Ashman himself.

We settled once more to our jobs. I was amassing a queer and utterly useless collection of notes, bills, memoranda and letters. Few were left, and I was aware that what we had was fragmentary and gappy. My guess was that things had been retrieved from all sorts of odd drawers where they had been forgotten: that what we had were the flotsam and jetsam of a considerable correspondence which must from time to time have had a kind of spring-cleaning and been largely destroyed. Hallows seemed to be doing better with his selections and he was jotting things down on his memo pad.

Just after seven o'clock Bernice called us to the evening meal and it was half an hour before we got back to work. And almost the first thing I drew out of the diminishing heap made me open my eyes.

Thursday

Darling,

Here's what you want. Hope it will pass muster. Looking forward to tomorrow. Lovely to think of *us*.

F.

"Have a look at this," I said to Hallows.

"Some other girl he had in tow," he said. "Pity there isn't a date."

"Not so simple," I said. "In fact, I don't like the look of it. Nor will you when I say this is Dallas Malone's writing."

I hadn't a doubt. I'd seen her writing on that card of hers in the office of the *Police d'État* at Bandol and I hadn't the faintest doubt.

"Then why's it signed F.?"

"Don't know," I said, "but I don't like it. It's Dallas's writing, and I'd say that on oath. There can't have been *two* women?"

"Wait a minute," he said. "How old's this paper, do you think?"

It was plain paper, obviously—and hurriedly—torn from a pad. In the white one could just discern a yellow. There was a mark as if the paper had been beneath something rectangular, and that exposed, yellowing part was slightly brittle.

"Over a year old," I said.

"Quite that," he told me. "So if I got everything right about the Dallas woman, Ashman never flaunted her around. And she was remarkably secretive about giving away any address to those people at Bandol. Don't you think that could be reconciled with this idea? That she wasn't always Dallas Malone? That her Christian name at the time of this letter began with an F.?"

I had to smile, and largely with relief.

"You've got it," I said. "There always was something phony about that Dallas Malone. It's just too romantic. The sort of name a woman like that would pick for herself."

"Well, if I may say so, sir, there's no point in reading into it what isn't there."

"Why not?" I said. "What might be there?"

He smiled a little lamely.

"Well, I could make a penny novelette of it. Let's call her Fanny. Fanny's met Ashman and they've just begun a big affair. Or it's going to start on the tomorrow. And she's going to change her name to Dallas."

"Why?"

He grinned.

"Wouldn't she rather be Dallas than Fanny? Or, to go on with the novelette, she changed it because she wanted a new identity. There was a husband or something in the background."

"Then what was the something she sent him in the letter? Something she hoped would pass muster. It couldn't have been money."

Now, he said, I was drawing him out of his depth. I was out of my own depth too, but I did put that letter carefully in an envelope and in a bureau drawer. It represented for me almost a part of the woman herself. It was the first personal contact I had made since that far-off evening in the Café Rond. Ten minutes later there wasn't a central pool. I slipped my various categories into different envelopes and wrote what they were. I took out that letter of Foorde's and put it with the F. letter. Hallows seemed to be totting up figures, so I fetched a couple of bottles of beer. By the time I'd filled the glasses he was ready for me.

"A pretty hopeless game," he told me, and waved a hand at the letter pile. "Those don't matter. They're just receipts and so on. All personal. But not a quarter of the old cheque-books and only about a dozen bank statements."

"Nothing coherent at all?"

"Well, there's this," he said, and showed the memo pad. "Just over a year ago we get two payments of £87 10s. made at a three-months interval. The same thing pops up again last June."

Something struck a bell.

"On quarter-days?"

"Yes," he said. "I wondered if it might be rent. At the rate of £350 a year." He passed me a stub. "Nothing to show what it was for. Just that little squiggley mark."

"I think you're right," I said. "£350 as the rent of a flat. Anything else?"

"Only that on March 7th of this year he drew out the biggest sum I've found—£250 to be exact."

Our eyes met.

"Well?" I said.

He shrugged his shoulders.

"Might have been her fee for that shin-kicking business."

"You're a thought reader," I told him. "But wouldn't that have been a stiff payment? Considering she was the lady friend?"

He shrugged his shoulders again.

"Don't know. Everything's hypothesis."

"Then what's your idea of his general financial position?"

"Everything's recent," he said. "Not a thing over two years. But it fits in with what his brother said. He was mighty low down a year ago."

He showed me a bank statement. I said that wasn't necessarily a guide. His balance might be low, but we didn't know about his investments.

"If he had any, then the dividends weren't paid through this bank," he said. "No statement shows any record."

"Right," I said, and pushed across some of the big envelopes. "Let's call it a night as far as these are concerned. I'll send them back in a day or so and advise the brother not to destroy—just in case. So let's think about how we stand. See if we can plan the next moves."

What we arrived at was largely pity. It was a pity Ashman hadn't put the name of the flat—if flat it was—on the stubs of the £87 10s. cheques. It was a pity he hadn't made a note under the *Cash* of the £250 cheque. It was a pity we couldn't have a heart-to-heart talk at his bank, and that we weren't the Yard. It was a pity we hadn't enough men to enquire at all the £350 flats in or near Town; and even if we had, the job would have to have the devil's own luck to be done within five days. And the same applied to ration-card enquiries.

"Wait a minute," he said. "What about an ad.? A lost ration book in the name of Dallas Malone. Mightn't a tradesman come forward?"

I didn't see why. A *found* ration book, perhaps, which some tradesman might think she had lost. And Dallas Malone herself might see the advertisement. It might scare her and set her on the run.

Then I thought I had it.

"Why not all the local suburban papers?"

Superficially it was a good idea. Dallas Malone wasn't likely to read a local paper. But when we tried drafting an advertisement we were up against the impossible. A ration book would be stamped by the issuing office, and a finder would return it there. So we gave the whole thing up.

"Nothing likely to be her in the telephone directory?" Hallows said.

I checked it again, but there wasn't a Dallas Malone or a Miss D. Malone. That she would be on the telephone seemed more than likely, but her number certainly wasn't on call.

So we decided to make it a day. Hallows left, but I sat on for a minute or two trying to assess that first day's work, and it was striking me that things had gone better than I could ever have dared to hope. A kind of background pattern had begun to emerge and Dallas Malone herself was taking shape. But I was worried as to how to extend the enquiry. At the moment only Dryland—our man-about-town specialist—was working an angle. But there ought to be other angles of approach. I thought about that bleached hair, then discarded that angle at once. Too many men and too much time would be needed to try hairdressing salons and beauty parlours for brunettes who'd decided in the middle of March to try a metamorphosis to the blonde.

But as I was finally telling myself that the night would bring counsel I did think of a couple of things. There was a theatrical agent whom I might see. Ashman, for all we knew, might have tried to insinuate Dallas into the theatre and that possible change of name had been to a stage name. There was also a line of approach which had been unaccountably neglected.

What of Lanyer and Pope, publishers of *The Silken Petticoat*? If anyone knew Ashman's affairs it would surely be his publishers. And wouldn't Ashman have had a literary agent? I could get his name from the publishers. In fact, when I at last rejoined Bernice in the lounge I was feeling optimistic. It was only when I woke in the morning that the November chill made things less roseate. Foorde didn't merely want the name and address of Dallas Malone; he wanted a biography. A biography, mind you, of a woman whom only an optimist would hope ever to find—at least within five days.

But there was some cheering news at the office. Dryland had seen the stage-manager of the Maryland, who had seen Ashman with a brunette who was certainly Dallas Malone. But he had never been introduced and therefore didn't know her name. His wife also had seen that brunette, and just a week ago she had come home from a West End shopping trip.

"You know that smart girl we saw once with poor Bobby Ashman? I almost ran clean into her this afternoon in Swan and Edgar's. I was as near to her as I am to you now."

If that were credited, as it had to be, then we were right about that Hollywood talk being an excuse for Dallas to avoid any London contact with the Pantlings or Leishmans. It helped to sharpen the outlines of what we still only vaguely knew. And it gave me a kind of confidence when I moved on to 7 Rudyard Street, the offices of Lanyer and Pope.

Rudyard Street lies north of the Strand and just clear of Covent Garden. No. 7 was an old-fashioned building wedged uncomfortably between two larger ones, and inside it was rather like a rabbit warren. An elderly, mousey woman was in the ground-floor enquiry office. I gave her my private card and asked to see one of the principals.

"There's only Mr. Lanyer now," she said, "and I think he's busy. Mr. Pope died last year."

There had been a hesitation before that word *died*, and I wondered why.

"Tell Mr. Lanyer it's very urgent," I said. "Also assure him I shan't keep him more than two minutes."

She rang. A high-pitched voice was audible from where I sat. It said, apparently, that I'd have to wait. And I did have to wait, a good ten minutes. Then the buzzer went and I was told to go up. First floor, first door on right.

I knocked on the frosted glass, heard a something, and went in. Arthur Lanyer was working at a desk, cigarette in one hand and a flying pencil in the other. He was a man of sixty: florid, full-lipped, double-chinned. He merely waved a hand at the sight of me.

"Sit down, will you. I shan't be a moment."

A couple of minutes and he was leaning back. A smile spread across the face.

"Now, my dear sir, what can I do for you?"

"I'm not selling you anything and I've not brought a manuscript," I said. "My name's Travers. Mr. Maurice Ashman can verify anything I tell you. I'm chairman of the Broad Street Detective Agency. Mr. Ashman employed us on a matter concerned with his brother's estate."

"Yes?" he said, and the smile wasn't there. There was a quiet in the room, and Lanyer might almost have been listening for a something to happen.

"Nothing whatever to do with you people," I said. "I merely mention it as part of the credentials. What I've come to you for is to see if you could give us some information on quite another matter. We're anxious to find a Miss Dallas Malone, who we've every reason to believe was a friend of Robert Ashman. Did you ever hear her name?"

"Never," he said, and there was quite an emphasis.

I gave a description. I also imagined a blonde sister whom I christened Florence. He'd seen neither.

"Well, another dead end," I said with a gesture of resignation. "Only one other person to see, and that's his agent."

"Mr. Ashman had no agent," he told me. "We acted as his agent."

"The devil you did," I said. "A terrific job, isn't it? I mean, in addition to your ordinary work as publishers? All those foreign rights and film rights and heaven knows what."

"An organisation like this is always equipped to dispose of foreign rights," he told me reprovingly. "And we have the accounting staff."

"Yes," I said. "I really ought to congratulate you. The book still alive?"

"A firm five thousand a week," he told me with a certain complacence. "In America it's over the two hundred thousand mark."

"Fine," I said. "And there ought to be a further boost when the film appears."

"You can never be sure," he said cautiously.

"And," I said quizzically as I got to my feet, "you never even offered me a cigar."

He stared.

"Just a little joke," I said. "But you're working now, I take it, as agent for Maurice Ashman."

He spread his palms.

"Yes, but chiefly for the Commissioners of Inland Revenue."

"I know," I told him heavily. "But how do you find Maurice Ashman? I find him personally an extraordinarily nice fellow."

"He is indeed," he said, as he opened the door for me. "A very charming man. A good business man too."

"I'm sure of it," I said. "And thank you very much for letting me bother you like this."

"It's been a pleasure," he told me. "No trouble at all."

I made my way down the narrow stairs and out by the long, narrow passage. I turned towards Drury Lane and took a street that brought me out near the Cafeta. Breck wasn't there. I didn't want him. For once I preferred my coffee alone.

8

RUN TO EARTH

THE devil—as we were instructed from our youth up, and in spite of the claims of politicians—is still the biggest cause of mass employment. As I sipped that scalding coffee or smoked my pipe I was unemployed. I had learned nothing from Lanyer about Dallas Malone, but the devil—or something less sulphurous—was setting my brain to work.

I thought about Arthur Lanyer and Robert Ashman: the money both had made and Lanyer's consequent rake-off. I thought of Maurice Ashman, now entirely in the hands of Lanyer. No intermediary of a literary agent to check receipts or verify new sales. I thought, above all, of the face of Arthur Lanyer when I had said that I was from the Broad Street Detective Agency—the way the eyes had suddenly opened, the stillness of the man, the expectancy and perhaps the fear.

That was why I had reassured him. And yet he oughtn't to have been reassured. There oughtn't to have been a look of relief, if, that is, his conscience was clear. And yet I didn't know. Suppose that Lanyer was feathering his nest at the expense of the estate, would that be possible in view of the hand in things that the Commissioners of Inland Revenue were taking? Or had he quoted them *at* me as a kind of proof that everything was above-board?

Again I didn't know. But by then I had the bit well between my teeth, and in a minute or two I was at the Cafeta telephone. I rang Arthur Lanyer. The mousey receptionist answered, but in a minute I heard his voice.

"This is Travers worrying you again, Mr. Lanyer," I said. "Not business this time, but don't you live in North London? I think I've heard a friend of mine mention the name."

"Oh no," he said. "I'm out in the country—comparatively. At Caterby. Must have been someone else of the same name."

"Sorry to have been a nuisance," I said. "Very nice to have seen you this morning."

I ordered another coffee, and because Lanyer lived at Caterby. At the time of that enquiry on behalf of Maurice Ashman I had wondered just why Robert had told the Foxhounds he would be late. What would make him late? All sorts of things, of course, beyond my knowledge, and yet Ashman had been a man with no set absorbing job to do. And now here was Lanyer living at Caterby! Ashman might have gone through Caterby. The way would have been as direct as any. And why shouldn't an author be going to have tea, say, with his publisher?

The idea got hold of me. I even pushed it to its logical conclusion. Suppose, I told myself, that Lanyer was financially, and very immediately, up against things: mightn't he have wondered if working with an executor mightn't be a solution which working with someone so astute as Ashman could never produce? If—and I was ready to call it a very big *if*—Ashman's death was not accidental, then who had profited most? Surely Lanyer had been in a position to profit more than anyone.

And then, if only because I'd finished the now tepid coffee, I came back to the present. Ashman's death, in spite of minor discrepancies of evidence, had been accidental, so why should I be worrying my wits over Arthur Lanyer? My job was to find Dallas Malone, and the sooner I pushed along to that theatrical agency the better. So I paid my bill and began walking towards Trafalgar Square. And then I happened to look up, and there I was passing my old publishers.

I went in. The girls in the reception office didn't know me, but I had the entrée inside five minutes. Clare—let's call him that—was glad to see me, or so he said.

"Shan't keep you a minute," I told him as I accepted a cigarette. "It's about a friend of mine who thinks he's written a goodish book. I advised him to send the manuscript to you, but someone else has told him to give it to Lanyer and Pope. So tell me, in the strictest confidence, just what you think of them."

"There's only Lanyer now," he said. "Pope, quite a nice chap in a dreamy sort of way, shot himself just over a year ago."

"Financial troubles?"

"I think so," he said. "Rumours were going around. Then Lanyer got a backer and they had a hit or two and weathered the storm. And now this *Silken Petticoat* pops up."

"Yes," I said. "The firm must be making a packet. And won't this *Silken Petticoat* furore attract other authors like my friend?"

"You never can tell. Publishing's a queer business. Up and down, down and up. It's the constant level that counts, not one terrifically good seller. Not that I wouldn't mind one myself."

"I'll see what I can do," I told him.

He knew me too well to take me seriously. All the same, it's good to keep on joking terms with a publisher. Life's full of surprises, and, after all, one never knows.

By the time I'd left Clare it was too late to begin another job, so I treated myself to lunch. And once more, instead of concentrating my wits on Dallas Malone, I kept thinking about Robert Ashman—and his publisher. I think by that time I'd deluded myself into almost believing that the finding of Dallas Malone was somehow bound up with Ashman's death, but at that particular moment, with the morning still vivid in my mind, I could have made myself believe anything. And it's gratifying to one's ego to have even a fairly obvious deduction proved irrefutably true. That mousey receptionist at Rudyard Street *had* hesitated at the word *died*, and there had been something in the hesitation. Lanyer and Pope had been in Queer Street and Lanyer himself had had a lucky escape.

You see how easy it is to build up what one wishes to be a logical sequence? Lanyer had had an escape, I told myself, and with Pope's death on his mind he didn't want another experience of the kind. Maybe then he was using *The Silken Petticoat* to build up a private reserve. But maybe Ashman hadn't been quite satisfied about the way things were going. He might even have discovered something more or less fishy. Or he might have discovered too late that he'd signed a contract that gave Lanyer too much control and had threatened to get the contract broken. Motives everywhere, reason after reason why Lanyer might have wished Ashman dead. And when I found one objection—

that Lanyer wouldn't have killed the goose that was sure to lay even more golden eggs—I had the answer in the same breath. If Ashman had threatened to leave Lanyer, then what matter what eggs he laid?

When lunch was over I came down to earth, if only because I had a job to do that left Ashman himself largely out of account. And I was probably realising that all those fine theories about Ashman were weeks out of date. I should have found them when we were working for Maurice. Now that inquest verdict was more impregnably right than ever. Robert Ashman had been accidentally drowned, and I'd be several kinds of a fool to try to prove otherwise. Besides, it was none of my business.

So I cast one last lingering look behind and went along to the theatrical agency. It was Tom Holberg's: the best agency in town; and if Tom had never heard of Dallas Malone in any connection whatever with the theatre, then no one had. But he didn't leave it at that: he rang a couple of other agencies, and the answer was still that there wasn't a Dallas Malone. So that was that, and I wasn't too happy as I made my way back to Broad Street. Nothing had happened there, so I mooned around for a time, and just as I was thinking of going, a taxi drew up and Dryland got out. He was in such a hurry that he didn't glance into Bertha's room as he hurtled along the corridor. I went after him.

"Here you are, sir," he said, and he was panting a bit. "Had the devil of a rush to get here, but I think I'm on to something. Just listen to this."

In the cast of Ashman's play, *The Twisted Dial*, had been a daughter, played by Angela Norton, and an aunt, played by Margaret Allison. It was Angela Norton whom Dryland had seen, and she had never heard of a Dallas Malone. But Dryland had been almost importunate and the following information had emerged. At the end of the play's run Margaret Allison and her husband, Walter Huskin, had gone to Hollywood, and that meant giving up their maisonette in St. John's Wood. Ashman had bought from them the rest of the lease—Angela believed there were three years to run—saying he wanted it urgently for a widowed sister. He had acquired it furnished.

"And where *is* this maisonette?" I was wanting to know.

"She thought it was in Tarrant Road. That was the sound of it: she didn't know the spelling."

Norris buzzed through to Bertha to check with the local directory.

"There's something not quite right in Miss Norton's story," I said. "What he paid down for that furnished maisonette must have been a kind of key money: otherwise he wouldn't have gone on paying rent to Margaret Allison's agents. Or giving Dallas the money to pay it. Not that it matters all that much."

Bertha rang through. There was a Tarrant Road within five minutes' walk of the Tube station.

"Right," I told Dryland. "Get along there at the double. Enquire along the road, and if no one knows her name give a description. Soon as you've identified the house, ring back here. I'll come along in the car."

I took a taxi to St. Martin's and got my car. Back at the agency I had another man stand by. It was a misty night that chilled one to the bone, but to me it was as bright and sunny as Bandol. By six o'clock I was getting a bit impatient.

By seven I was anxious. At a quarter past the call came. The maisonette was No. 7, and I'd better come in by Giles Avenue, second on the left past the Tube station.

It took us half an hour to get there, and as I drew into the road Dryland came up.

"The other side," he told me. "The fourth place from here."

We went slowly past it and on to the end of the road, then reversed. Dryland joined us again opposite No. 7. I got out and had a look, and the first thing I knew was that in the windows was never a chink of light. And I could see practically nothing of the house itself, so I quietly opened the gate and stepped off the hard path to the grass.

That so-called maisonette was really a smallish detached house, set back some twenty yards from the road. At the end of that path, which I now knew to be crazy paving, was the front door, and on each side of it were modernised windows. I moved quietly to my right and came up against a tall fence against which was a kind of shrubbery. I turned back the other way, and there, at the side of the house, was the tradesmen's entrance. Something white caught my eye. On the step by the door was a pint bottle of milk.

I went carefully back to the gate, listened for steps in the road and crossed to the car.

"Looks as if she's been out all day," I said. "You two arrange your own reliefs, but keep a lookout till one in the morning. If she comes in soon, just watch the place till midnight. If anyone comes to call, tail him or her when they leave. If she comes back and goes out again, tail her too, and stay with her till she gets home again. Don't ring the office unless anything happens. In the morning report in any case at the office at eight. Is that clear?"

I left them the car. I rang the office from the flat and asked to be called if there was news. Nothing came, but I went to bed with never a care. In the morning I'd contrive to have my first real look at Dallas Malone. That little matter of a life-history didn't worry me in the least. All I could tell myself in the few minutes while I waited for sleep was that Dallas Malone had been found.

I was at the office before eight o'clock. Everything had been quiet, Dryland said, and they'd left at one.

"Better get back then," I said. "The mixture as before. If anyone calls, follow him when he leaves; and if you want help, ring for it. When she leaves, follow her, and report here when she's static again. If you have to split up, then split up. Park the car if you have to. If she hasn't shown signs of life by lunch-time—say at two o'clock—report it."

I came back at about ten, but nothing had come in. I stayed put from then on, and I even had lunch brought in. My guess was that Dallas would go out to lunch, but when one o'clock had gone I was once more anxious. I grabbed the telephone pretty impatiently when the call came.

"Dryland here, sir. She hasn't made a move. And there're a couple of milk bottles on the back step. And a newspaper sticking in the front letter-slit."

"Damnation!" I said. "She must have gone away for a day or two." I clicked my tongue. "Almost as bad as not finding her at all."

"You don't think something else, sir?" Dryland's voice came suggestively.

The whole world, including my heart, suddenly stood still.

"You know more about things than I do, sir," he was going on. "Whether or not she might be in someone's way."

Suddenly, and without reason, I was hating that smooth voice of his. Then I shook myself, like a dog coming out of the water.

"I'll be along right away."

It took me quite a time to halt a taxi, and an age to get to St. John's Wood.

"Nothing happened?" I asked Dryland.

"Nothing at all, sir. You notice the front curtains are all drawn, sir. So are some at the side and back."

"You rang?"

"Yes, sir. With an excuse all ready."

"About the bottles and paper. She might have been in a hurry when she left. Forgot to notify people."

He shrugged his shoulders.

"She might, sir. And she might not."

I wasn't in the mood for hair-splitting.

"Reverse the car and draw up about fifty yards along," I told him. "I'll be back in a quarter of an hour. You don't know me and I don't know you."

The taxi took me to the local police headquarters. I knew it well. It wasn't the first time I'd operated—with George Wharton—in that neighbourhood. I paid the taxi off and went in.

"Chief-Inspector Boone about?" I asked the station sergeant.

"He's left, sir. Gone to G Division."

"Anyone else about?"

"Well, if you'll tell me your business, sir . . ."

"This is urgent," I told him. "My name may convey nothing to you, but it's Travers—Ludovic Travers—and I'd—"

"I know your name, sir," he told me, and got busy.

An Inspector Zoller came in. Luckily for me, he'd also heard my name. I told him about the agency and how we'd had an urgent call from a prospective client. I'd gone to the house to keep an appointment and found it ostensibly empty. But two bottles of milk were on the step and at least one newspaper hadn't been taken in.

"No one answered the knock or the bell?"

"No one."

He scratched his ear.

"What do you suggest we do, sir?"

"Make an entry."

"Now, sir, you know as well as I do—"

I told him I'd take full responsibility. If necessary, I'd write him a chit beforehand. If the client was out, then I could explain to her, and I was sure she'd accept my explanations. If she was in, then she must have had a fit or something, and an entry ought to be made in any case. I talked and I talked, and I talked him round.

"Wait here a minute, sir, and I'll fetch a car."

We drew up outside No. 7. We got out and he had a long look round. We marched up to the front door and he rang the bell. He rang it again. We went to the back door and he rang the bell. He rang it three times. He looked round for an unfastened window.

"Have a look round the back," I said. "What the eye doesn't see the heart won't grieve over."

It was a patent lock, and if you know the knack of it it's as easy as tackling a tin of sardines. And I'm never without a hairpin in my waistcoat pocket.

"There we are," I said. "The door might have been open all the time."

He gave me a look. But he walked in.

We were in a none-too-tidy kitchen. We went through to a short passage and into a dining-room as cold and bleak and unromantic as the six o'clock News. We went to the other door, and as he opened it I saw an easy chair and knew it was the Jounge. Then I was bumping into his back. He was suddenly stock still, and I looked over his shoulder. Dryland had been right.

She lay on her back, one outflung arm resting against a chesterfield, and the other with palm upwards from the beige carpet. She was wearing what looked to me like a house-coat, and in the part shadow of the electric light it looked like velvet and wine-coloured.

Zoller's hand motioned me back. He went forward, circling carefully. His long legs straddled the body. A moment or two and he was springing back.

"What was it?"

"Strangled," he told me. "There's a cord round her neck."

He circled back to the door.

"What's now, sir?"

"That's up to you," I told him. "I'm only a kind of witness. But if I were you I'd short-circuit. Ring the Yard first. And mention my name. Drive it home that I thought there might be a body."

We'd left the light on in the passage angle where the telephone stood on a corner table. I went back to the kitchen while he rang the Yard. All the downstairs lights were now on, but it wasn't we who had drawn the curtains of kitchen and lounge or drawn back the curtains of the dining-room.

Zoller had finished telephoning. I hoped the mention of my name would push that murder clean under the nose of George Wharton, but Zoller didn't mention names. He said they'd be coming.

"You any ideas about when it happened, sir?"

The passage opened out to a little hall. On the mat lay a newspaper. Another was protruding through the letter-box.

"These and the milk look like the answer," I said. "I'd say she was killed the night before last."

"What was she? A pro.?"

"Don't think so," I said. "I've learned quite a bit about her, but it doesn't include that."

I stood at the door of the lounge and had a look round. Zoller squeezed in beside me.

"That walnut bureau in the corner," I said. "Someone's been through it. The drawers aren't properly shut."

"We'll soon know," he said. "Better have a look upstairs. Not that there'll be anybody there."

He switched on the light and we went up to the landing. The first door he tried opened on what had to be her bedroom. It didn't have the look of a love-nest, and maybe because the furnishings had been taken with the house. But we weren't interested in the handsome double bed or the dressing-table set.

"Drawers open, wardrobe open," Zoller said. "Someone's been through the room. Let's have a look in the others."

There were two others. Their furniture was covered with dust-sheets and the curtains were undrawn.

"Used just the one room," he said, "and that's curious when you come to think of it. Wonder what the bathroom's like." It was a well-fitted bathroom and that was all. The bath itself had a slight high-water mark as if the person who had last used it had done so hurriedly and had had no time to wash it round. In my mind a picture was slowly beginning to evolve. Zoller was suddenly pricking an ear.

"Sounds like them, sir. Better get downstairs." Wharton wasn't there. Chief-Inspector Jewle came through the door and Sergeant Matthews with him. I'd worked plenty of times with the pair of them.

"Hallo, sir?" Jewle couldn't help giving a grin. "Got yourself overtaken at last, eh?"

"The long arm of the law," I told him. I shook hands with him and Matthews. It's funny how the worthiest of people love shaking hands.

"This is Inspector Zoller," I said. "I induced him to make the entry."

"In here, sir," Zoller said, and in the three of them went. I didn't go in. That enquiry at the moment was no business of mine. I went to the kitchen. When they wanted me for question-ing they'd soon find me, and there was a story which I'd have to get ready. An agency has no rights. You may talk to a client about his confidences being secret as the grave, but that's true just so far. The law could demand his business and your own, and you'd no more so-called rights than the man in the street. And the last thing I wanted was to divulge Foorde's name.

Just as I thought I had a way out Jewle gave me a call. I heard Matthews and the circus trooping in through the front door. Jewle and I went back to the kitchen.

"A nice clean job," he told me. "Anders"—the police-surgeon—"isn't here yet, but everything's pretty clear. A crack on the back of the skull and then strangled. Zoller says you think it was the night before last."

"Milk bottles, newspapers, the drawn curtains—everything points that way," I said.

"You've no suspicions about who did it?"

"No more than yourself," I told him. "I do think that whoever did it was some sort of friend. Zoller may have told you she had a quick bath and then put that house-coat on. She didn't doll herself up."

"Yes," he said. "And she was a client of yours?"

"That's what I told Zoller," I said. "I don't blurt out my business to divisional officers unless I'm forced. She wasn't a client of mine. I was about to keep her under observation on behalf of a client. I'd just located her. That's all."

"I see," he said, and rubbed his chin. He gave a nod. "Right-ho then, sir. We needn't keep you. But I would like you to go home so that we can get in touch. It might have to be later tonight. I don't know."

He offered me a police car to the Tube station, but I said I'd rather walk. So I walked past my own car, and in a minute it was overtaking me just round the corner. I told Dryland he'd been right.

"You get me home quick," I said, "and then get on to the office. They have Maurice Ashman's number, so call him at once. This is what you tell him."

At the flat I found Bernice out, and I remembered she was doing a theatre with a friend. That was all to the good. I rang Clement Foorde and knew I could talk freely. But there was no reply.

I found that letter which Foorde had written to Robert Ashman. I asked for the Gatsworth number and in a couple of minutes I had it. But the voice wasn't Foorde's.

"Mr. Foorde in?"

"I'll see, sir. Who's speaking, please?"

"Travers. Mr. Ludovic Travers."

"Mr. Ludovic Travers. Thank you, sir."

An elderly man. I could imagine him repeating the name to himself while he went to find Foorde. The man Runlet, probably, whom Ashman had recommended.

I heard steps and a slight clearing of a throat. There was the rattle of a receiver.

"Mr. Travers? This is Clement Foorde."

"Listen carefully, Mr. Foorde," I said. "I located your wanted person tonight. She was dead. You'll probably see it in your newspaper tomorrow."

"Dead?" he said. "You mean there was something peculiar about it?"

"Yes. She was strangled."

"My God, no!"

"The thing is this," I said, "and I ask you again to listen carefully. I found the body and I had to call the police. I'm a witness and I'm going to be asked why I was there. You don't want your name brought in?"

"My dear sir, it's the last thing I want."

"Very well then. I'll see it isn't brought in. But you must realise that you're no longer a client. From this very moment we have to cease working for you. So calculate what you think you owe us and send a cheque at your own convenience."

"I will," he said. "And I'm most grateful. Some time later we must—"

"Yes, yes," I said. "But at the moment I've got my hands full, as you can imagine. Just one other thing. You'd better forget the existence of the Broad Street Detective Agency."

"I understand," he said. "I've never even heard of you."

"Fine," I said. "As for anything else that might have been found out, I guess you'll be reading that in the newspapers too."

9

OFFICIAL ENQUIRY

I RANG down for a service dinner, though whether or not I'd have time to eat it I didn't know. What was in the wind was pretty plain. Heaven knows I'm no superman, but to guess what was about to happen was little more than adding two and two.

Jewle hadn't wanted me at No. 7. He'd wanted me away so that he could make a preliminary report to Wharton. A Chief-Superintendent doesn't take over a murder case unless there's both importance and urgency. My name had been mentioned to Wharton, and Wharton had wondered and he'd make up his mind according to what Jewle reported back. I was to stay at home in case Wharton—not Jewle—should want to question me. If Wharton didn't want me after all, then Jewle would do his own questioning later.

That may sound involved to you, but it didn't to me. My ears were on the alert, but it wasn't till the meal was over and I was almost through *The Times* crossword that the telephone went.

"That you, Travers? George Wharton here."

There he was, cooing like a sucking dove.

"How are you, George?"

"Can't grumble," he said. "But Jewle has just told me you've got yourself involved in a bit of bother."

My chuckle was very audible.

"Don't you believe it. Jewle didn't even ask me if I knew her name."

"And what *is* her name?"

"Dallas Malone."

The old liar! Jewle hadn't *just* rung. And Jewle must have found that name in all sorts of places.

He gave a grunt.

"Look, would you mind slipping along to the Yard and telling me what you do know?"

I said I'd love to. I'd be with him in a quarter of an hour. I actually made it in ten minutes.

You know George Wharton's room; that is, if you've seen the Yard depicted on the screen. It's a biggish room that can be all sorts of things according to who you are and the way you look at it. Nowadays I never even notice the officialdom of files and cupboards and safe and typewriters and all the rest of it. That room's just George Wharton and me: our own chairs, the smell of ink and tobacco, the fug on a winter night, and tea on a tray. Or it's George doing tricks with those fake spectacles of his, and myself watching the face of someone in the toils of George's specious questioning.

I tapped at the door, walked in and began hanging up my coat as if the room were my own. I honestly didn't know I was doing it. I passed it off as a joke.

"Thought this might be a long session. George. You're nice and snug here?"

George regards detective agencies much as the director of the National Gallery probably regards a pavement artist operating against his very walls. He forgets that if he hadn't been induced not to retire after all he'd have been my partner. I could have laughed at the pained look when I mentioned the agency.

"It's very simple," I said, "the way I got involved in all this. If you care to ring Grainger at Seahurst he'll tell you that Robert Ashman's brother Maurice—"

"Just a minute," he said, and as if he didn't know. "Robert Ashman was that author who was drowned down his way."

"Exactly. And Maurice wasn't satisfied the death was accidental."

I told him why. I told him what the agency had done and how fair and above-board everything had been. I even told him about Bandol and the Pantlings. I admitted that we'd had to tell Maurice Ashman that the inquest verdict had been right, and that was that.

"I can give you Ashman's number if you'd like it—"

"Now, now, now," he told me almost coyly. "Anyone'd think I thought you were telling me a pack of lies."

"Well, you might like to make it official just the same," I said. "But here's where tonight's business comes in. We hate a dissatisfied client, and I didn't think Maurice Ashman was too happy about the way we'd handled things. He may tell you so. But, disregarding that, I wasn't too happy myself. I kept that case in my mind. I began thinking about that Dallas Malone who'd been with Robert Ashman at Bandol. I got her so much on my mind that I had a word with the Pantlings and found out she was supposed to be going to America, and it sounded suspiciously as if she didn't want to keep up the acquaintanceship when that holiday was over. So I kept my eye on the case. Then I happened to hear that Robert Ashman had been anxious to acquire a house from an actress who'd been in a play of his and who was suddenly going to Hollywood with her husband. That was just a day or so ago. I had a look at the house. I put a man on and he found the occupant was Dallas Malone. I went round there this afternoon to try to get an interview with her. I didn't like the milk bottles and the newspaper in the door. That's all."

"I see." He frowned for a minute and gave a nod or two to mark time. "But just why did you go to the expense and trouble? Maurice Ashman was no longer your client."

"Two reasons," I said. "You know me, or you ought to by this time. I like to know the whys and wherefores, and I'm prepared to spend my own money—which is what it amounts to—to have answers. Also, as I said, I hate an unsatisfied client. I wanted to be in a position to go to Maurice Ashman and tell him we might have something that might be worth a reopening of the case, if he felt so disposed. But things didn't pan out that way."

"Well, that's fair enough," he said, and began filling his pouch. I was watching him like a hawk, and he probably knew it. He pursed his lips and the walrus moustache blew out like an awning.

"Tell me," he said. "It might be better for all concerned if you came in with us. You're free?"

"As the air," I said. "As for coming in, I'll even do so without a fee. That shows how keen I am on getting at the truth. Honestly, George, I regard myself as personally involved."

"Right," he said. "I think you can regard yourself as on the pay-roll from now on. I'm slipping along to Jewle. You write down everything you've been telling me about the woman. Don't be afraid of length. Unless you hear to the contrary, you might be back there at eight, say, in the morning."

He pressed the buzzer and asked for a stenographer.

"If you want tea or anything, you know what to do," he told me largely, and made for the hat-stand.

I helped him on with his overcoat: the coat I'd known for years with its faded velvet collar. I almost asked him if he'd remembered his glasses.

Half an hour later the stenographer had gone, and while I waited for a proof I went down and out and telephoned Norris from a call-box. I put him *au courant* and told him to give Dryland a new briefing. I went back to the Yard and ran an eye over the proof and added a final touch or two. I walked home and with never a care. I even felt the least bit chirpy: like Blondin, perhaps, when he'd finally crossed Niagara Falls. I'd crossed my own Niagara Falls by keeping Foorde's name out of things.

In the morning I drove my own car to Tarrent Road and found only a couple of men on duty. Wharton turned up ten minutes late and blamed the fog.

We went into the lounge and he turned on the electric fire. I wondered what would have happened if there'd been a power cut. He said he'd tell me how far Jewle had got.

Her name, he said, was definitely Dallas Malone. Her ration book said so, and her passport, but an identity card hadn't been found. There were receipts and so on made out to that name.

The time of death was when I thought, but couldn't be placed nearer than between six and eight o'clock that night. It depended on when she had tea, and the unwashed plate and cup in the kitchen sink showed she had had tea. If she had it at four o'clock, then the stomach content showed death at six-thirty. If she had tea earlier or later, one could calculate accordingly.

She had been struck down and then strangled with a length of cord which the murderer had apparently brought with him. It had presumably been done in that room, for there was no sign of dragging on a floor or carpet. No great strength had been needed and the murderer might be man or woman. But whoever it was had come for something. Rooms had been searched, but there was no means of knowing if what was wanted—and wanted so urgently as to make murder necessary—had been found. There were no prints but hers and those of an unknown woman, probably a woman who did the house.

The murderer was known to Dallas Malone. After that bath she hadn't troubled to dress with any care. She had put on that house-coat, but she had no stockings, and the underwear lacked a brassiere. And the murderer had been admitted to the lounge.

There were no footprints discernible on the carpet, or the stair carpet or the bedroom carpet or floor. But a vacuum had been run over them all—not that there were any great hopes of anything from that.

"That's about all," he said. "Any ideas of your own?"

"Her nails?"

"Nothing," he said. "She didn't have a chance to scratch, or defend herself."

"The woman who cleans here. You're hoping she'll see the afternoon paper and come forward?"

"One of the neighbours had an idea," he said. "Matthews is trying to find the woman now."

"Get anything else from the neighbours?"

"Only that everyone was only on smiling terms. She didn't use the back garden, for instance, and gossip over the fence. Kept herself strictly to herself."

"Callers?"

"Only a man who's already been identified as your Robert Ashman. No callers noticed since his death."

"And her prints?"

"We've nothing on her," he said regretfully. "We're put-ting a photograph out."

He took one out of his wallet and gave it to me.

"Keep that to be going on with. Everything'll be in the afternoon papers. The *Police Gazette* will have everything already."

"Seems comprehensive," I said. "Anything particular you'd like me to do?"

"I'm a bit muddled," he told me. "I can see fifty things to do. Ashman's our only real point of contact, and he's dead as mutton."

"There're the Pantlings," I said. "They were in her company for that Bandol three weeks."

"You covered them carefully?"

"Not on an official visit. Mine was exploratory and friendly, so to speak. No authority behind me."

"You get along there now," he told me. "I'm going through any correspondence we can find. If there's time I'll see the agents who handled this place. Maurice Ashman'll be at the Yard in the afternoon."

"I'd like to be there," I said, and he gave me a quick look.

"Nothing like that," I said. "It's only that I did that job for him and I might think of one or two things to prod his memory."

As I drove towards Enfield I was feeling a considerable relief. While I might explain away to Wharton that blackmail hint I'd given to the Pantlings and the matter of a legacy for Dallas Malone, the last thing I wanted Wharton to know was that matter of a change of hair. That mention of a temporary blonde might bring things somehow to Clement Foorde. Some bright lad would remember the newspapers and that scene in the Café Rond.

I could tell myself, and honestly, that I was more than justified in keeping Foorde's name out of things. I owed a duty to a client, and I knew that Foorde, at that moment in the Café Rond, had never in his life clapped eyes on Dallas Malone. I had gone carefully into things with Breck. One so intimate with the theatre, as he had said, might be expected to be something of an actor himself, but no one could have simulated that look of utter surprise at the moment of the kick. Up to then, and even when she had mentioned Ashman, he had regarded her with no more than a faint and quizzical amusement.

Foorde—and events were to prove me right—had never known Dallas Malone. Afterwards, of course, he had had his suspicions about a connection with Ashman, but that was all. And he had commissioned the agency to find her.

There was no need, then, to tell Wharton about the Café Rond. If I did tell him, then I should have broken a trust unnecessarily. Foorde would know it, and a man with his influence could do the agency considerable harm. And telling things to Wharton might do Foorde considerable harm. Some other bright boy of the popular Press might get hold of the yarn, and Foorde's name would be connected in heaven knew what ways with that of Dallas Malone. When a man has put himself on a pedestal there's plenty of satisfaction in kicking him off. Wharton of course, might promise discretion, but even then I couldn't be sure. There's just a touch of the salacious about George, and an unguarded hint or joke might put some nose on the scent.

Irene Pantling was in, and mightily surprised to see me at that hour. I thought she'd have been shocked at my news, but, if anything, she was frightened.

"Not one of those men who come to the door and then attack women?"

"Nothing like that," I told her. "She was murdered by someone she definitely let into the house. I don't want to do any smearing now she's dead, but I ought to tell you that Hollywood story was bunkum. She's never been out of London since she got back from Bandol."

She saw the implications.

"Well," she said, "I always did think there was something wrong about her. You know—secretive."

I got her to sign a formal statement about Bandol and assured her she wouldn't be troubled again by the police. There was never a word in it about hair: in fact she'd forgotten the whole thing. There'd been no thin ice over which to slide, and as I drove back to the Yard I was a reasonably happy man. And a lucky one. No sooner had Foorde ceased to pay us than I was being paid by the tax-payer to enquire into something which had intrigued me more than most things in the course of a pretty long life.

Wharton was in his room, and Matthews with him. The rent of that furnished house was £350 a year, he told me, and an examination of the cheque stubs and paying-in book showed that Ashman had really paid it. It also looked as if the Malone balance at her bank was pretty low, but Jewle was looking into it.

"What're the bags?" I said. There were two medium-sized travelling cases, one bulging and the other less full.

"These were in the wardrobe of her room," he told me. "Full of men's clothes. We're just going to have a thorough look."

Those bags held the equivalent of three complete changes of clothes—suits, shirts of all sorts, vests, socks and ties. One was a dress suit with all the appurtenances.

"Someone had been through them," George said. "They'd been bunged back anyhow. And I rather think someone helped himself to some of 'em."

"No prints on the bags?"

"No prints. Let's try 'em for size."

He held a pair of trousers against Matthews. A coat was tried on, or, rather, an attempt was made. Matthews would have split the seams. So we laid a suit on the floor and did some calculation. The owner, we reckoned, would be about five feet seven or eight. Wharton sent down for a clerk. The suit he tried fitted as well as could be, and he was five feet seven in his socks.

"What about Ashman?"

"As big as Matthews," I said.

"Don't like it," he said. "Why should she keep a man's clothes for him?"

I reminded him about that name of hers and how it didn't ring true. I gave him Irene Pantling's statement, which included that Hollywood lie.

"She had plenty to conceal," I said. "A husband in the background was my original idea. But tell me something, Did these two cases look as if they'd just been put in the wardrobe?"

"I'd say they'd been there the devil of a time," he said. "They were in a corner at the bottom."

"Dust underneath them," Matthews said.

"Then there's a new problem," I said. "It's a certainty that Ashman slept from time to time in that room."

Wharton pounced on it. Ashman must have looked in that wardrobe and seen those two bags. He must have known what was in them. It followed that he knew who the owner was.

"A rum set-up, wasn't it?" Wharton had to add. "A woman keeping another man's clothes and Ashman knowing all about it?"

"And all the tabs cut off the back of the coats," Matthews said.

I hadn't noticed that, but that was how it was. Impossible, on the face of it, to find out where any of those articles of clothing had been acquired. It baffled the three of us. We could theorise, but no more.

"No need to be impatient," Wharton said. "We haven't begun this case yet. And it's gone one o'clock."

The bags were repacked and sent to the back-room boys. Wharton went with them. Matthews and I adjourned for lunch. I liked Matthews. He was a tall, black-haired chap with a dry sense of humour. Many's the quiet wink he's given me behind Wharton's back. And if a man can work unruffledly with George Wharton, and satisfy him into the bargain, then he's a mighty long way from a fool.

But the two of us didn't get very far when we chewed over things with our meal. The back-room boys might find prints. They might reconstruct the owner of the clothes and unearth his occupation, but he'd still have to be found. A lot of words had gone down the drain when we got back to George's room. He wasn't there, but a message said Maurice Ashman would be in soon after three o'clock.

He was on time, and Wharton came in with him. The rather odd pressure of his hand told me he'd understood my message; not that he knew a thing about those two letters which were in my bureau drawer. I noticed Maurice was carrying that same case in which he'd brought those odd papers of his brother to us at the agency. Wharton told me what the case contained.

"I know this was to do with an enquiry into the unfortunate death of your brother," he told Maurice, "but we're hoping for some reference or other to this woman with whom he was friendly. And about that enquiry. Mr. Travers has told me about it, but I'd like to hear your version, just for the records."

That suited me. I took that case, and while Maurice was talking I looked through the contents. My fingerprints would be all over everything, and it was just as well to account for them if the papers were tested. Hallow's prints wouldn't matter.

I didn't hear much of what was being said, but I can tell you that if Maurice Ashman had sent that case of oddments by registered post and had stayed in Manchester it would have been of just as much help to Wharton. So Maurice left, with Wharton fluttering round with thanks. Matthews and I dumped the case's contents on a table.

"We'll look at all that later," Wharton said. He glanced up at the clock, and I knew he was thinking about a pot of tea. He gave a little sigh as he changed his mind.

"What to do next," he said. "That's the thing. Got any ideas?"

"Not at the moment," I said.

"Funny for you," he told me, as if I was going slow at the tax-payer's expense. "There ought to be a lead somewhere if we could only hit on it."

That was George to the life: at one moment counselling patience and the next expecting miracles. But George likes to be the tycoon: a telephone in each hand and talking into a third: the vital centre of a web with a whole army of beaters to flush the flies in. He probably had a dozen lines of enquiry in operation if I'd only known it.

"I think we should give things another day to see if anything promising emerges," I said, and he'd just given a snort and was opening his mouth when the buzzer went. I merely had a glare as he picked up the receiver.

"Who? . . . What's he got to do with it? . . . Oh, I see. Well, what're you waiting for? Put him through."

A minute and his tone was unctuous. The unseen was being greeted with a cheer. He'd grabbed a pad and was grunting away as he wrote this and that down, and he didn't give away a word to Matthews and myself. All we heard were *yes's* and *good's*. Then he did say something.

"Describe him, will you?"

More grunts, more writing on the pad, then another coherency.

"That's fine. We're very grateful. I'll send a man down at once. Two men. You might book a couple of single rooms at a hotel. Ring me when everything's okay. Ring in any case. . . . Right. Thanks again. Goodbye."

He gave himself a little congratulatory nod as he swivelled his chair towards us.

"Well, something out of the blue. That was Harwich."

George, as I've said, loves a curtain. Already he'd said too much. We were the stooges. We had to feed him.

I don't give a cuss for George. I give him my best, but that doesn't make me take his antics seriously.

"Fine," I said. "When do we sail?"

He gave an excellent imitation of a chuckle.

"We don't," he said. "I'll give you fifty goes for a new hat that you'll never guess what that was."

"Nothing doing," I told him. When I win, George always forgets to pay.

He leaned forward impressively.

"Suppose I told you I know who Dallas Malone is?"

The raising of my eyebrows must have encouraged him.

"And who owns the suits?"

"Carry on," I said.

"And why she kept them?"

Then suddenly a look of something like horror came over his face. He jabbed a finger at the buzzer and had the receiver in his hand almost before the answer came.

"Get me Dartenford—quick. . . . Good God, no! The jail!"

He clicked his tongue annoyedly as he leaned back. His fingers tapped restlessly on the desk flap till the call at last came.

"Wharton here. You still have a Captain Grey on the books? . . . What! Three days ago? . . . I see. . . . Wait a minute, though. I've a couple of men coming through shortly. I'll get them to see you. . . . Right. Goodbye."

That walrus moustache shot out almost at right angles as he let out a breath. He pulled out that huge red handkerchief of his and wiped his forehead. The room was fuggy, but not so fuggy as that.

"It's the very devil."

His mouth opened in a gape.

"Or isn't it."

Apparently it wasn't. He was beaming as he swivelled round again.

"Do you know what I think? I think this case is as good as over. I'm ready to bet that inside twenty-four hours we'll have our hands on the man we want."

10

WHARTON GUESSES WRONG?

IT HAD to come out: in fact he was bursting to get it out. And, on the face of it, what he had to tell made almost a certainty that prediction about an early arrest. I wasn't happy. I hate damp squibs and being inveigled—or inveigling myself—into an investigation of a mystery which is no mystery at all. Not that I wasn't anxious to hear all the answers.

Put into proper sequence, what Wharton had learned in the last half hour was this. The woman whom we knew as Dallas Malone had been recognised as the wife of a Captain Grey who'd been apprehended at Parkeston in the February of 1951 while smuggling nylons. In the March he had received a two-years' sentence. The wife had been taken into custody but released for lack of evidence. Grey, with a full allowance for good conduct, had just been released.

"What's the woman's full name?" I asked.

Wharton consulted his notes.

"Freda. Freda Grey. The husband's a Patrick Grey."

I'd guessed right. Freda was the F. of that letter in my bureau.

"Everything looks fairly cut and dried to me, George," I said. "How do you work it out yourself?"

"It hits you clean in the eye," he told us. "He comes out and finds his wife's been carrying on with Ashman. He'd expected to find the nice faithful little woman who'd been keeping his personal possessions for him and writing him loving letters. She'd probably had some of his money too. So he did her in, got a change of clothing and whatever else he wanted and did a bolt."

There were flaws enough in that presentation, but I didn't point out even one of them. In any case Wharton wanted action, not words. Matthews and I would go to Harwich at once. The assignment was to glean every possible bit of news about Grey and his wife. As soon as anything sufficiently important turned up it would be rushed through to him. In the meanwhile he was changing his mind. He'd go to the jail at once and get the latest description of Grey, and he'd have the papers in that smuggling case sent to the Yard.

An hour later Matthews and I were on the road. I'd rather drive by night than day and we made good time. It was still short of eleven o'clock at journey's end. A Detective-Inspector Crew was waiting for us. We settled down to a pot of tea and sandwiches. The hotel wasn't a stone's throw away and it didn't matter what time we turned in.

First we were told all about Patrick Grey. He was of very good family. His parents had been killed in an earthquake in Japan while he was still at public school, and he had been brought up by a great-aunt, the widow of the rector of Thoraby, near Colchester. Crew said she had made an utter fool of the boy. There'd been complete lack of discipline and the boy had been astute enough to take full advantage of it. On leaving school he'd expressed a wish to be a doctor, and that had turned out to be an excuse to get to London and have a good time. Before long he had forged his aunt's name to a sizeable cheque, but that was hushed up. Next he was in trouble for passing dud cheques, but the aunt paid up.

"They tell me he had the most wonderful gift of the gab," Crew said. "Charming manners, of course. The sort who'd have made a first-class con. man. Then the war broke out and he joined up. Got a commission naturally and ended up as a captain."

But in the meanwhile two things had happened. When he came of age he inherited about £30,000. In the second year of the war his aunt was killed in a bombing raid and he came in for another £20,000.

"You can guess what happened when the war was over," Crewe said. "He bought Thoraby Hall and cut a rare dash. Went in for motor racing and the devil knows what and used to entertain on a big scale and so on. Then the crash came. The Hall was sold and Grey as good as disappeared. When he turned up next he was married, and he came to Dykeham—that's about six miles from here, along the river towards Ipswich—and took a furnished house, belonging to a Colonel Uplake. He had the gift of the gab, as I said, and his wife was a smart piece, and they were soon in with all the local nobs. Then in the February of last year this nylon business happened."

He went across to a filing cabinet and came back with the portfolio of the case. He looked through it and jabbed his finger at something.

"What d'you think of that?"

That was an anonymous letter—neatly printed capitals on plain white paper.

CAPTAIN GREY OF DYKEHAM IS ON A HOLIDAY IN BELGIUM WITH HIS CAR. IT MIGHT BE WORTH WHILE TO TEST THAT CAR WHEN HE COMES BACK. A WORD TO THE WISE. REWARD WILL BE CLAIMED LATER.

"No prints, as you see," Crew said, "and that's one reason why we took it seriously. No need to tell you gentlemen what we did, but we made a pretty thorough investigation into Captain Grey. One of the ports had had suspicions but hadn't got him with anything, and, of course, we managed to get hold of that early record of his. So when he landed we held the car. Of course he was highly indignant. Reckoned he had friends in high places and all that, but we're used to that kind of thing. And where do you think the stuff was? In the back seat. The springs had been shortened to half depth and underneath were a couple of thousand pairs of nylons! No one ever came forward, by the by, to claim a reward."

"Wasn't two years pretty stiff for virtually a first offence?" I said.

"Not if you knew him," Crew said. "He couldn't pay the fine, for one thing, but he did his own case in. He was so glib anyone could see he was dangerous. It's all in here if you want to read it. Sending it to the Yard first thing in the morning."

"And what about the woman?"

"Ah, her," Crew said. "We went very thoroughly into her too. She wasn't with him on that holiday because she went down with flu just before he was starting. She was the daughter of a ranker major who was killed in the war. She didn't come in for much. She was a hospital nurse and got the push for carrying on with one of the patients. Then she switched into the hair-dressing line and was in some posh salon, as they call it, in Town. That's where she ran across Grey."

"You said she was smart."

"She was," he said. "A real slap-up piece. Not off the top shelf, mind you, though you didn't rumble that till you got underneath the crust. We found some more nylons in the house when we did a search, and she swore blind she didn't know a thing. But the Chief and I were dead certain she did know something." He shrugged his shoulders. "But there you are. Suspicion isn't evidence."

It was getting late and we had enough stomach content for that night's rumination. But I did tell Crew what our assignment was, and I asked his advice about likely spots for further enquiry.

"Dykeham's your best spot," he said. "Everything's still pretty fresh down there. And you bet your life everyone'll be talking when they see her picture in tomorrow's papers."

I did take that portfolio and promised to return it early. Matthews and I went through it in my room at the hotel and it was two in the morning when we went to bed.

I was up at seven and dictated a report for Wharton at the Yard. I took a short walk and bought a couple of morning papers, and from the front page of each there stared at me the face of the woman whom I couldn't help calling Dallas Malone. But about that name. Her maiden name was Malone. I suppose she chose the Dallas because it went well with it, and to English ears it had something of the exotic.

There was something else in those papers. *The police are anxious, in connection with the murder of Freda Grey, to interview . . .*

Grey's description followed. It was interesting to note that he was five feet eight as he stood. And he was slim in build, military in bearing and with dark brown hair just beginning to go on top. There wasn't any doubt to my mind, with regard to that height, that it was his clothes that had been in those two cases. I also thought it wouldn't do any harm if we tried at Dykeham to get a photograph.

Matthews and I timed our arrival at Dykeham for eleven o'clock, and we were going to the Prince of Wales. A pub, to my mind, is often too crowded at night for selective conversation. In the earlyish morning there's rarely more than a sprinkling of the regulars and an infinitely finer chance to get into talk. And that pub, as it happened, was just a bit superior. It had quite a nice little saloon with easy chairs and plenty of low tables. That was where I went. Matthews had the ordinary bar.

There was a beautiful fire in the saloon and I had the room to myself. The landlord, a competent-looking youngish man, was dividing his time between saloon and bar, and in the latter I could just hear voices. I took my pint over to the fire and awaited developments. I was almost through that pint when they came. A middle-aged man walked in, gave me just a glance, tapped impatiently and gave me another look. The landlord appeared.

"Mornin', sir. The usual?"

The usual was a stout. The man himself was middle-aged and had the ramrod back of an ex-army man. He turned out to be a Major Matson.

He took a pull at his stout and gave me yet another look.

"Not a bad morning for the time of year?"

I said it was quite a good morning for November. He came a bit nearer.

"You're a stranger here?"

"Not to this part of the world," I said. "I'm actually a Suffolk man. I was born near Stowmarket."

There are times when one has to ape the snob, and this was one. When he heard that my father was a Colonel Travers, and a gunner, I was accepted, and in a couple of minutes we were by that fire and hobnobbing like two cronies. And so to the five-bob question preceded by a glance at my newspaper.

"Funny I should see the name of this place in the paper this morning," I said. "I was really passing through and that's what made me pull up."

"You mean that Grey woman," he said. "Looks as if that blackguard of a husband of hers did her in."

"A blackguard, was he?"

I was soon gathering that Grey had once been among the elite of Dykeham and that Matson had been among those taken in by the glibness of the man and the deliberate unpretentiousness of the life he led in the village. I listened again to that smuggling case. Freda Grey, and it was plain that Matson had had a sneaking sympathy for her and even something of regard, had disappeared after sentence had been passed on her husband.

"She was taken in by him too," he said. "That chap would have deceived the very elect, if you know what I mean. Wouldn't be surprised if he was never in the army at all. You'll have another drink?"

I had a modest half-tankard. He had a second stout.

"Talking of the wife," he said. "I think she'd got the wool well down over his eyes. That's the worst of these clever fellows. They think they know all, but they dam' well don't. I saw things myself."

What he meant I didn't know. It was sheer Siamese to me.

"Not that I blame her. Pity she didn't leave the feller altogether."

"She was running a racket of her own?"

"Good lord no, sir! Carrying on with another man. He got it in the end, poor devil, too. Read about it in *The Times*."

"A local man?"

"No, sir. A London man. Supposed to have served in the war with Grey. Now what the devil was his name?" His face took on strange shapes, but the effort produced nothing.

"Dammit, never was one for names. Not that it matters. But I saw them in here once or twice when Grey was away. And I saw them once when they didn't see me. Regular couple of love-birds."

He was enjoying it. I kept my mouth shut except to stick in it the cigarette he offered me.

"Between you and me, that's where she went when she left here. Up to London with him. Nice chap, rather. A good spender. Rare one to talk."

He looked round as the landlord's steps were heard. "Oh, Frank, what was the name of that chap who used to stay down here a lot with the Greys? You know the chap. Used to come in quite a lot."

"Ashman," he said. "Major Ashman. You remember, sir, we heard about him being drowned."

I couldn't say a word. I suppose I ought to have guessed, but I'd been too interested in the wood to see one particular tree.

"Yes," I said at last. "I seem to remember something about that. He was an author, wasn't he?"

"Yes, wrote that book, *The Silken Petticoat*. You read it?" It was almost with a leer that he went straight on. "Dam' good book. Bit near the knuckle, of course, but none the worse for that."

"I must read it."

He gave me a wink.

"Keep it out of the way of your wife. You're married?"

I said I was.

"Lost mine just over a year ago," he said, and the shake of his head was meant to be sad. "Thirty years of married life. Met her in Simla. . . ."

A quarter of an hour later I'd had a conducted tour of British India, and practically with lantern slides. It was folly to try to bring the talk back to the Greys, even if I'd had the chance to talk at all. So I aped a reluctance and got to my feet. The Major hoped he'd be seeing me again, and I said that was an idea. If I was that way in the evening I'd drop in on my way from Ipswich.

I moved the car on towards Ipswich and the rendezvous, and in a quarter of an hour Matthews joined me. He had learned little more than what Crew had told us. His eyes popped when I told him about Ashman. Not that he knew Ashman as more than something vaguely at the back of things.

"Bet you a fiver, sir, it was him who wrote that anonymous letter!"

"Why?"

"Well, to break up the happy home and get the girl himself."

There was something in that, but it didn't help to solve a murder case. Ashman was dead. He didn't kill Freda Grey. And something else. If Ashman's death wasn't accidental after all, then Grey didn't kill him, however strong the motive. At the time of Ashman's death, Grey had been safely tucked away in jail.

"We'll go back to that pub tonight," I said. "I've already hinted at it. This time you concentrate on the Grey household. What the Greys did and so on. Something might pop out."

I turned the car into a side road and so towards Harwich. We had a fairish lunch at the hotel and I sent another verbal report to the Yard. Then we went back along the main London road towards Colchester. We turned off towards Thoraby and spent the afternoon there. Matthews picked up a listener or two, and I had an excellent one when I ran into the local parson leaving the church. Between us we got a good idea of the three years or more that Grey had spent at the Hall. What we learned was only an amplification of what Crew told us, with one real difference. The village didn't regard Grey as a scoundrel. He had not owed money locally, and between him and the present owner of the

Hall the village would have had no difficulty in making a choice. Thoraby had never been so prosperous as in Grey's time.

It was well after dark when we left there, so we went to Colchester and had a late tea to pass the time till the Dykeham pub should be opened. Matthews had been telling me about Dallas Malone's daily woman—I still can't help slipping back to that name—and how she had gone into hospital for a major operation only the week-end before the murder, and then he suddenly said he'd been thinking.

"Thinking what?"

"I don't know," he said. "When the Old General"—Wharton's Yard nickname had slipped out, but he grinned and let it pass—"was giving his idea of what happened it was in that room of his at the Yard. Things seem different now we're down here."

"How do you mean?"

"Well, it's a kind of hunch. A sort of feeling you get. I can't see this Grey as murdering anybody, for instance. Everything I've heard about him makes him a free-and-easy sort of chap who was let run loose when he was a boy and never grew out of it. He chucked money about as if it was confetti, and he had to have money, so he worked that nylon stunt. But I can't get into my head that he was a murderer. He's the sort who'd want to go on living."

"But what if he found his wife wrote that anonymous letter?"

"But he didn't," he said. "Crew told us no one but the police knew about it. It wasn't mentioned in court or anywhere."

I had to agree.

"And another thing," he said. "Suppose he did do his wife in. The way I see it, he'd have given himself up to the police. He must have known they'd get on his tail."

"Don't know," I said. "Human nature's a queer thing. You don't make laws about human behaviour or predict certain reactions to events. We're all a law unto ourselves. All the same, there's one thing I'd like you to do tonight. That carrying on with Ashman is the main motive for murder, so try and find out just how much Grey was still in love with his wife."

He said he'd certainly try. But there was still something on his mind, and I asked him what it was.

"Well," he said, "are you sure Ashman was carrying on with her? Grey and he were pals in the war, so why shouldn't they have been nothing but pals?"

I saw his point. Ashman was the natural friend to whom to turn after Grey was in trouble. But there was something else.

"Ashman wanted two rooms with a communicating door when he wrote to that Bandol hotel," I said. "As I see it, Ashman had to do that because he couldn't pretend the woman was his wife. The two passports queered that pitch. So he did the next best thing. To me it's unquestionable evidence that he was living with her."

"All right, sir," he said. "Then let's take it he was. But he must have seen those two bags some time or other. So why didn't he sling them out? If she was now his woman, why let her go on keeping her husband's things?"

I couldn't say anything, except quote once more the queer twists in human minds.

"Something else, sir," he was going on. "There wasn't any money in her handbag, so he probably took that—if he murdered her. But why didn't he take the money that was in a bureau drawer? There was over twenty-five quid there just for the picking up. And he had all the time in the world."

I hadn't known about the money. When we're on a case Wharton tells me just so much and no more: enough, shall we say, for the particular and dove-tailing job in hand. Not that he isn't also a bit secretive.

"Well, you may be right," I said. "Plenty of time yet to find the answers. Grey hasn't got wings. Every port and airport's on the look-out for him."

It was almost six o'clock. The waitress was giving us a dirty look, so I paid the bill and off we went. We took it easy, and it was about half-past seven when we went into the Prince of Wales. The saloon was fairly full, but Matson wasn't there. I was still eking out my pint when the talk in my vicinity got round to the Grey murder. It wasn't hard to join in, especially when I'd created a sensation by saying I knew some people who'd known Freda Grey quite recently.

I suppose there were a dozen of us in that saloon, and quite a gregarious party we were, but never a one was of the Matson class. It was not that they were less articulate: what they lacked was the inner knowledge one gets from close acquaintanceship with those of one's own circle. I couldn't gather, for instance, if Grey had been in love with his wife, and I certainly didn't gather that he'd been so madly in love that he'd killed her for infidelity. What I did get was that Matson had given me one wrong impression. Mrs. Grey and Ashman had not always been a dual turn in the saloon of the Prince of Wales. Far more often there had been the trio, and quite often enough the duo of husband and wife.

But I do think that if husband and wife had been what the room would have called a couple of love-birds I should have been told it. Nobody made any bones whatever about sympathies over that smuggling business. Personal moralities are curious things. The poachers of my Suffolk youth, even if caught and convicted, were never social outcasts. Far from it. A man will try to swindle a railway ticket collector or the Commissioners of Inland Revenue with a perfectly clear conscience, and then find a pound note and take it to the police.

On the whole, mine wasn't too profitable an evening. The one thing of which I was sure was that in the eyes of the farming-tradesmen-soldiers-on-leave stratum of Dykeham, Grey was quite a good fellow, and that, if he'd killed his wife, then he'd had a good reason. There were even those who, in the security of improbability, had declared themselves capable of the same thing. But at about half-past nine I thought it time to be going. As I shouldn't be coming again to the Prince of Wales, I made no bones about looking into the bar. Matthews wasn't there.

We'd parked the car on the open space in front of the pub, but he wasn't there either. I got in out of the cold. In five minutes he turned up, and he was coming from the direction of the village. He slid in alongside me, and I moved the car off.

"Been along with a chap to get an address," he said. "Had a stroke of luck tonight. A young fellow called Harris who's the nephew of a chap who worked for the Greys while they were here. He told me a whole lot."

"What about the two Greys?"

"This uncle hated the sight of Mrs. G.," he said. "He reckoned she was the biggest bitch unhung. The way she and Ashman carried on behind Grey's back was something wicked, and Grey never seemed to see it. He reckoned—this uncle did—that she was behind all that smuggling racket and she was the one who ought to've been jailed. He even reckoned—I know this sounds a bit cheap—that she wasn't fit to live."

"Sounds interesting," I said. "And was the uncle the one whose address you were getting."

"That's right, sir. A chap by the name of Runlet. He and his wife were what they call a married couple."

11

A STEP FORWARD

I THINK the car must have swerved a bit. I know my hand went tentatively to my glasses.

"And what's their present address?" I said, and my voice seemed to be coming from heaven knows how far away. "Got it here, sir."

He leaned towards the dashboard lights.

"Wicklands, Gatsworth, Surrey. Care of a Mr. Foorde."

"Good work," I told him. "Just keep quiet for a minute, there's a good fellow. Something I want to think over."

The poet mentions the tangled web awaiting those who practise to deceive, and when Matthews had suddenly come out of the blue with that name *Runlet* I had felt the meshes of that web and there'd been a moment's panic. Wharton would have to be informed and Runlet would have to be found. And there would be I knowing where the Runlets were, and having to keep my mouth shut in case Foorde should be involved. And now I'd been saved by a virtual miracle. Matthews had the Runlets' address. Wharton had every reason to interview them and the reasons would be ones that Foorde himself would understand. He would know, in fact, that events had moved too unexpectedly for both of us, and that there'd been no betrayal of my word.

That was why, if you'll permit me to run on a bit, I rang Gatsworth the next morning before I sent my report to the Yard. It was Runlet who answered.

"No, sir," he said. "Mr. Foorde is in Town. He was attending a first night at the Betterton. You may be able to get him at his flat."

It took a quarter of an hour to get him.

"This is Travers, Mr. Foorde. A rather unfortunate thing has turned up with regard to the murder of Freda Grey."

I told him as much as was necessary, and how the police would now certainly have to interview the Runlets.

"There's still no need for you to be involved," I said. "You needn't necessarily be there. But I ought to warn you that murder enquiries go pretty deep. There's just the possibility that sooner or later they may rake up that Café Rond business. If so, I'd just as soon that you didn't divulge that you'd employed the agency. It might make things very awkward for myself. Also I don't see how it has the slightest bearing on her death."

He agreed. And we agreed that he could say with a perfectly clear conscience that he had no knowledge whatever of Freda Grey. He thanked me almost effusively, and that again was that.

But to get back to that drive to the hotel. I was thinking, as I said, and one thing I thought about was a letter—that *billet doux* which Freda Grey wrote to Ashman. There had been in it one incomprehensible thing, but now I thought I had the answer. She had mentioned an enclosure which she hoped would do. That enclosure, I now thought, might reasonably have been faked testimonials for the Runlets. Ashman had recommended the couple to Foorde, but that recommendation would have had to be reinforced by references and Freda had supplied them. And the date fitted. That letter was obviously written just before Freda came finally to Town and the maisonette that Ashman had so luckily secured. That would be the moment when the Runlets were out of a job.

Matthews made as if to say something, but I put him off with a "Just a minute". Something was wrong about all that. Why should Ashman and Freda Grey have been so solicitous about the Runlets? The man hated the sight of her, and she must have known at least that he didn't have any great affection for her. It was something that puzzled me even when I had a possible answer. Runlet might have brought pressure to bear on Freda Grey. He might have warned her that he knew enough to land her in jail with her husband. A new job might have been the price of silence.

They had something cold for us at the hotel, and while we were eating it I decided to open out a bit with Matthews.

"I wonder who got the Runlets that job with Foorde," I said. "He's a very important man, and it'd be a first-class job."

Of course he didn't know.

"Wait a minute," I said. "It could have been Ashman. Ashman and Foorde knew each other. They were members of the same club. In any case, how's this strike you as a theory? Suppose we discover that Ashman did recommend the Runlets to Foorde, mightn't he have done so under pressure?"

He had it in a flash.

"That's right," he said. "And Ashman and Freda Grey would have been in co. You bet your life Runlet knew some-thing."

"Let's go a bit further," I said. "Runlet knew something. He used that something to get a new job. But the new job wasn't enough. He began to blackmail Freda. When she was at the end of her tether and threatened to go to the police with the whole story, then he killed her."

"I like it," he said. "Only one little thing in the way, though. What about Grey?"

"Grey went to see his wife and found her dead," I said. "He panicked and bolted. He knew he'd be first in line for her murder."

"That's better," he said. "Ought to make the Old General's eyes pop. Bet you a fiver, though, that in a week's time he'll be letting on as if he thought of it first."

*

As I hinted, I rang the Yard the next morning after I'd spoken to Foorde. George was in and I was put through. I couldn't see his eyes, but you couldn't miss what was in his voice.

"You say this Foorde is one of the big bugs," he said.

"Think we ought to approach him about seeing the Runlets?"

"It might be as well," I said. "You'll probably find a Town address in the directory if he doesn't happen to be at that Gatsworth place."

"Right," he said. "You staying on where you are?"

"Don't see the point," I said. "I think we've squeezed everywhere dry. And we can always come back."

"That's so. Expect you here this afternoon. Suppose you don't happen to know this chap Foorde?"

I ought to say that I've a pretty wide social experience. I'm bound to have one way and another. George is often pleased to make use of it, but always with something of a sneer. Or perhaps that word's too strong. There's just the hint that I'm one of those big bugs, shall we say, at whom he consistently tilts, or that I'm at least some sort of hanger-on. And I'd caught something of that in his tone.

"Matter of fact I do," I told him. "I know him very well indeed."

The wind was only momentarily out of his sails.

"Good," he said. "I'll fix things up and we might see him together."

Things didn't turn out that way. When we got back to the Yard, Wharton, it appeared, had tried to get into touch with Foorde at Marston Square, but Foorde was already on his way to Gastworth. Later he'd rung him there and had been given *carte blanche* about questioning the Runlets.

"Sounded an interesting chap," Wharton said. "Asked me to try not to put their backs up. Married couples, he told me, were much scarcer than corpses."

Then it transpired that he wasn't going down to Gatsworth himself, and he mentioned pressure of work and how we'd had our fingers on the pulse of things, so to speak, at Dykeham and would have the right approach to the Runlets. My own idea was that if the questioning had had to be done in Town he'd have jumped at it. And as we drove down towards Gatsworth, Matthews and I agreed that, having recovered from the minor shock of our Dykeham discoveries, Wharton was still as sure as ever that Grey had murdered his wife. That made the Runlets small fry. What we might get would be supporting evidence, and no more.

It's a quick run once you're through the inner suburbs, and we got to Gatsworth just after two o'clock. It's a smallish place, as you probably know, and Wicklands, Foorde's house, was at the south end, on a minor road just through the town. I wouldn't have minded it myself, for it was quiet and yet near enough to the town: a little converted farmhouse with a rear, tiled building made into a garage and with quite a fine view from the front.

Runlet opened the door, and as soon as I saw him I knew he'd been warned of our coming. He was a tall, somewhat pompous-looking man of about sixty, heavy jowled and with deep lines that ran from the hooked nose down to the fleshy chin. A green baize apron was lying on a hall chair where he had hastily discarded it, and he had donned an alpaca coat which would have been incongruous for November if the central heating had not been going at full blast.

"The master is waiting for you, gentleman," he told us as he took our hats. "Whom shall I announce?"

I told him, and he went across the small hall to a door on the right. He tapped and we were ushered in. Foorde, in an old tweed coat, was reading by the fire of that comfortable workroom and he got to his feet.

"My dear Travers, this is a surprise. A pleasurable surprise. Your superintendent isn't here?"

I explained. I introduced Matthews and we were installed in a couple of buoyant chairs. We accepted cigarettes. We accepted an invitation to tea when the questioning was over.

"Superintendent Wharton gave me a rough idea of what this is all about," Foorde said. "Would it be in order to ask you to enlarge on it."

I told him we wanted all the information we could get about the two Greys, and with the hope, naturally, of finding the murderer.

"How'd you come to engage the Runlets?" I asked him.

He told me frankly that Ashman—poor Ashman!—had recommended them one day when he had happened to mention an urgent need in the club. He had had them on approval, so to speak, and had been more than satisfied.

"What about references?"

"That's been worrying me ever since this business cropped up. I did receive references from someone, and I'm almost sure now it was a Mrs. Grey. I'm afraid I've lost them. It's worried me, because I've obviously been wondering, ever since the name came back to me, if the person could have been—well, this Mrs. Grey. Naturally I didn't want to get involved."

"No need whatever for that," I said. "And you can trust us to handle the Runlets very gently. But now I come to think of it, did the Mrs. Grey send you the reference by post?"

His head went sideways.

"My dear fellow, I don't follow you."

I reminded him of what he must have read in the papers— that Mrs. Grey's husband had been at the time in serious trouble with the police. It wasn't the moment, in fact, for her to recommend anyone. She had been under suspicion herself.

"Wait a moment," he said, and raised a pontifical hand. "Now I come to remember, it was Ashman who gave me those references personally. It was shortly after our first conversation in the club."

"Fine," I said, and the smile, I hoped, was charming. "Just a clearing up of loose ends. Now if we might see the Runlets?"

He pushed the bell.

"I hope you'll go easy with them, if that's the right expression. Married couples, as I told the Superintendent, are not easy to come by, at least of the calibre of these."

I assured him they'd be handled as if they were Chelsea. Runlet appeared and was told to take us to the lounge.

*

Ellen Runlet was a placid-looking woman of her husband's age: short, inclined to plumpness and with grey hair fastened in an old-fashioned bun. She looked more perplexed than ill at ease. Runlet was far more watchful. I assured them that all we wanted was information about Mrs. Grey. It seemed a good key-note and the rest would follow.

"How'd you come to be employed by the Greys?" I asked Runlet.

It was a long story, as he told it, and what it amounted to was this. He had been an indoor handyman for Patrick Grey's aunt and had known Grey from boyhood. He had known the whole family and could reasonably claim to be an old retainer. His wife had been kitchen-maid at Thoraby rectory and then cook.

"Master Patrick was a good boy, sir. It was his aunt who spoiled him. I might even say she encouraged him: let him have too much money and hadn't got any control. But he was good enough at heart, sir. You couldn't help liking him. Generous as the day. If he did wrong, and he did, sir, then he didn't see anything wrong in it—if you know what I mean."

"I know. Such as putting his aunt's name on a cheque."

He gave me a quick look. It was just as well to let him know that he wasn't dealing with the totally uninformed.

"Well, yes, sir. Things like that. I suppose the way he saw it was that he was really entitled to the money. At any rate, sir, he was in a scrape or two, and then there was the war and he joined up. Did very well in it, sir. But his aunt had died and we stayed on with the people who bought the rectory. Then when the war was over and he bought the Hall we went there with him: I as butler and Ellen as housekeeper."

The crash came, as you know. The Runlets had their savings and took a tea-shop in Seahurst. They paid a stiff price for it and found they'd been swindled and with no hope of getting their money back.

"But we tried to make a go of it, sir, and we did just make it pay, what with working our fingers to the bone day and night. Then Mr. Patrick went to Dykeham and he wanted us to join him, and we were glad to, sir."

"It seemed like heaven after Seahurst, sir," Ellen Runlet told us.

"I expect it did. You liked it there?"

Her face clouded. It was Frederick Runlet who spoke.

"It was all right, sir, till this Ashman turned up. He and Mr. Patrick had been in the war together, and it wasn't long before he and Mrs. Grey were carrying on behind his back."

"You didn't tell Captain Grey?"

"It wasn't my place, sir. Once I tried to drop a hint and he asked me what the devil I was talking about."

"You were fond of him?"

"He was a gentleman, sir," he told me with dignity. "Whatever he may have done, he was a gentleman. No one could have had anyone better to work with. He treated us like friends rather than staff."

"But *she* didn't."

"She was a horrible woman, sir." That was Ellen. "Just a dressed-up madam. Everything on the surface, if you know what I mean, but underneath she was common."

"Just between ourselves," I said. "That nylon smuggling business. You think she had a hand in it?"

"Nothing's more certain, sir. I'd lay my life, sir, she was behind the whole thing. Someone had to take them off their hands, and who better, sir, than some of her low friends."

"You didn't like her."

"We hated her," Ellen said.

"Yes," he said. "And I don't care who hears me, sir, but I'm glad she's dead."

"You mention low friends," I said. "Can you tell me any?"

"No, sir," he told us promptly. "But the wife and I've talked this over, sir, and how she changed her name. And if she did, sir, how'd she get a new ration book and so on? I'm told such things are forged, sir."

"An excellent point," I said. "Undoubtedly she must have had friends. But something else. There's no catch in this question, but should I be right in adding, just as glad that Mr. Ashman was dead?"

He gave me a long, level look. It was his eyes that turned away.

"Yes, sir. I think you-might even say that."

"He was a snake in the grass, sir," Ellen said. "Ever so nice on the surface and always jolly with Mr. Patrick, and there he was trying to take his wife away from him."

"Yes," I said, and frowned puzzledly.

"But there's one thing I don't quite see. You both had reason to hate Mrs. Grey and Mr. Ashman. Yet it was they who got you your present post with Mr. Foorde?"

"Not *they*, sir," he corrected me. "It was Mr. Ashman, sir. And, if I may say so, beggars can't be choosers. We had to have a new post, sir; and much as I hated Ashman, I couldn't refuse the chance of writing to Mr. Foorde."

"You've never told Mr. Foorde of your connection with the Greys, considering what happened over that nylon business?"

"Mr. Foorde never asked us, sir, but we had nothing to conceal."

I turned to Matthews.

"Anything you'd like to ask?"

"I don't know that there is," he said, and gave his friendly grin. "No use asking Mr. Runlet if he knew Mrs. Grey was in London and had changed her name to Dallas Malone and was living in St. John's Wood."

Runlet's eyes narrowed for a quick moment. He gave Matthews a little bow.

"No, sir: I knew none of that till I read it in the newspapers."

"Then you didn't kill her?" The tone was still slightly jocular.

Ellen Runlet gave a gasp.

"No, sir," Runlet told him evenly. "But I wouldn't be ashamed to shake hands with the man who did."

"Good for you," Matthews told him, and nodded to me to carry on.

"Well, that's about all," I said, but for a moment or two I was thinking furiously. Funny that the Ashman case should have so suddenly forced itself into my mind. Runlet had hated Ashman.

"There is just one final thing," I said. "Please don't be indignant or unco-operative about it. It's just routine and means that we shan't have to bother you both again. I wonder if you'd tell me what you were doing the whole of the summer."

A look of relief came across Ellen Runlet's face.

"Why, we were here, sir—except for the holiday."

"And when was that?"

Runlet took over, and I was to wonder why.

"We really shut the place up, sir, on the 18th of August. The master went to Town—he was going to France the next day, sir—and I went to Seahurst for the week-end. Ellen had to spend the week-end with her sister at Hastings, and then she joined me on the Monday afternoon and we had a fortnight in the Isle of Wight."

"You didn't go to Hastings?"

"Well, sir,"—and he was looking a bit sheepish—"that's an old story, if you'll pardon me saying so. The sister and I, sir, never did hit it off together, as they say."

"Ah well," I said amusedly. "It takes all sorts to make a world."

"It does indeed, sir," Ellen told me. "And I must say Flo—that's my sister—isn't easy to get on with."

"Good," I said, and got to my feet. "But just one other thing, and it's still for the official records and so that you needn't be bothered again. I just have to know where you both were on the night of the 13th—the night Mrs. Grey was killed. Please don't take it the wrong way."

"Well, I was at the pictures," she said. "I met a friend, a Mrs. Woodman, and we had tea together and went in at about six in time for the big picture."

"And you got back here, when?"

"I forget," she said, and gave her husband a look. "I think it was about nine. Yes, it was just after nine. I remember now."

"Mr. Foorde was here?"

"No, sir, he was in London. He had some theatre work to do."

"The master was attending a first night, sir," Runlet told me—and her—reprovingly.

"Exactly. And you?"

"I was here, sir. The pictures, sir, have never appealed to me."

"They give him headaches too."

"Thank you, Mrs. Runlet, and you, Runlet. You've both been most helpful."

Runlet gave me a little bow and then was at the door in a couple of strides.

"Tea in the study, sir, in five minutes," he told me as he ushered us out.

It was a memorable tea: home-made tea-cake and a fruit cake that demanded a second slice. Foorde had put on his velvet coat, and I'll admit that he did seem to be trying to impress Matthews, but on the whole no one could have been more charming. He was grateful for the report we gave of the reactions of the Runlets to our questioning, but he didn't even attempt to ask what the questions had been.

When we had to go he put on his cape and an old fishing-hat and came out with us to the car. There was never a sign of fog, and he wished us a good journey and waved a courteous hand as I moved the car off.

"A nice old boy," Matthews told me. "But, by God, can't he talk! Reckon I'll try to get hold of that book of reminiscences, or whatever you call it, he was telling us about."

It was that second volume, shortly to be published, that he meant. The third volume—so Foorde had covertly informed me—was already well begun: that was why he was spending so much time at Gatsworth. I wondered what sort of an introductory chapter he had arrived at now he had been deprived—as surely he must have been—of Freda Grey and the Café Rond.

We were nicely through the little town before Matthews began talking about what we'd learned. He'd wanted to know what *I'd* learned, but I tossed the ball back.

"Well, I think we're in a position to carry on," he said. "Runlet made no bones about telling us what he thought of her, which is what he'd do as a bluff if he killed her. He was in the house alone that night, and he could have been up to Town by train and back again long before his wife was home."

"And the motive?"

I saw the quick turn of his head.

"You're kidding," he said. "He must have known Grey was due out. He didn't want that pair together again. And if he really believed it was her who should have gone to jail and not him, then he had an old score to clear off. I'll lay a fiver he'd have moved heaven and earth to get Grey started again somewhere, and he and his wife wouldn't have minded joining him."

"You're a sentimental sort of chap," I told him. "So am I, in a way. Coppers with kind hearts. Still, he certainly did, and does, idolise Grey; which means—and it's as well not to forget it—that he couldn't see his faults. No use asking him if Grey killed her. He'd have laughed at it."

"Perhaps he would and perhaps he wouldn't," Matthews told me doggedly. "Perhaps he wouldn't have been so sure. I think he'd have left a bit of doubt in our minds. He'd have had to if he did the job himself."

"Right," I said. "Let's assume he did. How'd he know the Grey woman had changed her name and where she was? She was lying doggo. Even Ashman never was seen in any high-spots with her. She had to lie low, and because she'd changed her name. If she'd been recognised as the Mrs. Grey whose husband was in jail, that'd have queered the pitch. So how did Runlet know?"

I could have added, "Think that one out." And apparently he did begin thinking it out, for it was quite a time before he said another word.

And that wasn't worrying me. I didn't want to talk. I also wanted to think something out.

12

WHARTON IS MYSTERIOUS

BELIEVE it or not, I wasn't thinking about Freda Grey. I was thinking about Robert Ashman. And I didn't delude myself with any highfalutin argument—that, for instance, Freda Grey and Ashman were closely connected, especially in the evidence of

Runlet. I just thought about Ashman and I didn't think about Freda Grey.

I suppose that at the back of my mind was not so much the failure of the agency to satisfy completely the hopes of Maurice Ashman as the fact that during the enquiry there had seemed to appear from time to time certain small things that were not consistent with that inquest verdict. On the face of it that verdict had been the only one possible, and yet, as I have said, there had been little disturbing things that had thrown the law's findings just slightly out of focus. And now something else had turned up to dull the clearness of the picture: not so much the fact that Ashman hadn't been drowned after all, as that someone had turned up who would have been happy at his death and had had also the possible chance of killing him. How that killing had been done did not for the moment matter. If there'd been no possibility of Runlet's killing Ashman, then the rest didn't matter. What had to be established was that possibility.

On that Saturday, August the 18th, Ashman had been to Pettiforth, but he got only as far as Wenhurst: that is, if the inquest verdict were right. But to get from London to Wenhurst his best way was through Caterby, and that was where Arthur Lanyer lived. South of Caterby, *and still on the same route*, was Gatsworth, and at Gatsworth was Runlet. Runlet would almost certainly have known Ashman's address and therefore his telephone number. But in any case it was the route that seemed first to matter: London-Caterby-Gatsworth-Wenhurst-Pettiforth.

And so to the next point, and it was there that Matthews interrupted me.

"I've been thinking," he said, "and I still like the idea of Runlet. He wanted money, didn't he, after losing his savings in that tea-shop? Blackmailing Freda Grey must have looked like pennies from heaven."

"Sounds good," I said, "I'm trying to work out something on the same lines myself."

That kept him quiet again. I went back to that second point about which I had to be sure.

Did Runlet know that there was any connection between Foorde and Ashman? Of course he did, I told myself. Ashman had recommended the Runlets, and Foorde must almost certainly have told them so, even though they were already aware of it. Foorde had written that letter of thanks to Ashman, and was it improbable that if Ashman met him in the club Ashman would have asked if the Runlets were still giving satisfaction? I saw it as a perfectly natural thing, and that Foorde should have said to the Runlets, "Mr. Ashman was asking after you, and I was happy to tell him I thought you'd settled down well." I could see Runlet's little bow and hear his, "Yes, indeed, sir."

But what of the later coolness between Ashman and Foorde, and the damning by Foorde of Ashman's book? Would Foorde have mentioned those to Runlet? I thought not. Foorde must consistently have assumed that Ashman liked the Runlets, and that they, so to speak, liked him. It was far from improbable, therefore, that Runlet should assume that Foorde and Ashman were still on good terms up to, say, a week before the 18th of August.

And there I had to leave things, for we were at the inner suburbs and my mind had to be on the road. Wharton was at the Yard, and I had to go over the afternoon's events. He seemed interested, but with Wharton you never can tell.

"This fellow Runlet had the chance to kill her," he told me, "and there's nothing much wrong with the motive. What I don't see is how he got in touch with her. She'd changed her name, and she was even scared that those Pantling people should see her after that Bandol holiday. Then how did Runlet find her?"

I didn't know. All I could quote was the long arm of coincidence. A chance meeting in Town, perhaps, but I knew that was footling as soon as I suggested it. The visits of the Runlets to Town would probably be rare indeed.

"If only we could pin something on him," Matthews said, "he might break down over that."

"True enough," Wharton told him blandly. "And what do you think we could pin on him?"

"Well, sir, prove he went to Town that night. A fast train'd have had him up in forty minutes."

"Yes," I said, and chiefly in support of Matthews. "If we had that evidence, and he's sworn blind he didn't leave the house, then he might crack."

"Well, no harm in trying," Wharton said.

That would be Matthew's job. What my next one would be I didn't know. After I'd given my general impressions of the interview with the Runlets and had confirmed that Runlet himself had at times been distinctly uneasy, Wharton cut clean across things with another question. It was clear he was still pinning his hopes on Grey. The fact that there was still no trace of Grey merely made him more certain.

"Uneasy, you say? Well, why shouldn't he have had a good idea of what had been going on at Dykeham. Mightn't he have thought you two were there this afternoon to rake up that nylon business?"

"After a pretty long time, wouldn't it have been?"

"The long arm of the law," he said. "Isn't that the popular idea? If a man's got a guilty conscience he doesn't chuck it off with his winter underwear."

That was about all. I had a full report to dictate, after which, as he was graciously pleased to say, I could reasonably call it a day.

It was about eight o'clock when I left the Yard, and officially I had ceased to exist. The rest of the day, as the song has it, was my own. So I made for the nearest call-box and rang the office. Norris had long since gone, so I got him at his private address. Then I took the Tube to Hendon.

Mrs. Norris had some sandwiches and coffee waiting, but we got to work at once. I was hoping, as I told him, that the breaking of the Grey case might also break the Ashman case. I told him what had been done and brought him clean up to date.

"What I'd like to do," I said, "is spend some of my own money. I think *lending's* a better word. I'm pretty sure, for instance, that if Maurice Ashman is convinced that we've never let that job of his out of our minds, then he'll cheerfully pay up if we can prove he was right. He'll be only too delighted that hunch of his wasn't sheer fancy."

Norris didn't quite see it.

"I feel in my bones," I said, "that sooner or later the Yard will hark back to the Ashman case. I'd like to be prepared, and to have something definite to tell Maurice Ashman. What I want are certain very simple enquiries made about Runlet. I'd prefer Hallows if he's available, because he wouldn't want so much briefing. Tell him what you think necessary, and be sure to stress that Runlet had the opportunity to kill Freda Grey. Then all he has to find is this:

"Mr. Foorde, as I told you, had gone to London on the morning of the 18th of August because he was going to France the next morning for a holiday. Runlet must have known all about that well beforehand, and that his own holiday would be at the same time and commencing on the same date. The house was shut up. Mrs. Runlet, as I told you, went to Hastings, and Runlet ostensibly to Seahurst. But I put two things to you. Runlet himself might have suggested that Hastings visit to his wife, and because it would be understood that he himself wouldn't be going there. The other thing is this. Why should Runlet give himself the expense of a week-end in a Seahurst hotel when he could easily have arranged to stay on in the house till the Monday morning, and then meet his wife in Seahurst and go with her from there to Portsmouth and the Isle of Wight?"

"Yes," Norris told me guardedly. "There're possibilities there."

"So we come to a tentative reconstruction of the Ashman affair," I said. "Let's rush right ahead and call it the Ashman murder. By noon on the 18th of August Runlet has the house to himself. He rings Ashman and says Mr. Foorde would very much like an urgent word with him. Could he come down in his car at, say, seven o'clock, and stay to dinner. Once Ashman has agreed, then Runlet rings Pettiforth and says he's Ashman and books a room. Then Runlet goes to Seahurst and shows himself at the hotel, but before seven o'clock he's back at Gatsworth.

"I know," I said, and raised a hand. "The theory's shot full of holes. But let's assume it isn't. On what does it all depend? On this. *Could, and did, Runlet drive a car?* How he killed Ashman doesn't matter for the moment; but if he did kill him, then he had to get him to Wenhurst. If he'd never driven a car in his life, then everything drops. It'll be just too bad, but Maurice Ashman won't hear from us again. But if Runlet did drive a car I'll have one absolute fact on which to build."

"I get you. That's the first thing Hallows has to do."

"And if Runlet did drive a car there's something to follow. I'd like to know where Foorde's car was on the 18th. The reason's this. Runlet would be operating in an area between Gatsworth and Seahurst. Nobody would know precisely where he was at any one moment. Since Foorde's house is on a side lane and right out of the town on the Seahurst side, he could get back there unobserved if he wanted to. So he might have taken Foorde's car and parked it that late afternoon handy to where Ashman's body was to be found. After dumping the body in the river from Ashman's own car he could then have gone on to Seahurst in Foorde's car and put it into a Seahurst garage and taken it back to Gatsworth next day. There'd be hundreds of strange cars put in Seahurst garages that August night and there'd be little chance of his being remembered. In any case he had all the week-end till his wife's return in which to operate."

Norris said he'd put Hallows on the job by the following afternoon at the latest.

"Absolute tact is what we want," I said. "Runlet must never have the faintest suspicion of what's going on."

"I'll mention it," Norris, said, but he gave a quick little shake of the head.

"Well, what's wrong?" I challenged him.

"Nothing," he said, and gave a bit of a grin. "The customer's always right, and you're the customer. But apart from that, and off the record, it all seems to me a bit far-fetched."

"Wasn't the Haigh Case far-fetched?" I told him. "If any author had put that acid-bath stuff into a book, wouldn't the critics have hooted at him?"

He said that maybe I was right. I didn't argue the point. I wanted my own flat and a chair and a drink, and the drowsy anticipation of bed. I got the first two, but I wasn't quite so bed-minded even when the time came, for Breck rang me just when I'd finished my meal and had settled to the chair. He wanted to see me for a moment: something too confidential for the telephone. I told him to come along to the flat.

"I think I've got a bit of a surprise for you," he said when he arrived. "That photograph of the murdered Grey woman has been intriguing me. I got our people to do some experiments with it. Do you know what I think?"

I shrugged my shoulders. I knew what he thought.

"I think she was the blonde of the Café Rond!"

That was a matter about which I hated to lie. I hoped I shouldn't have to.

"Really! How'd you arrive at it?"

"Just experiments with superimposed blonde hair. Perhaps I was closer to her than you, but I don't think there's a doubt."

"Interesting," I said, "but of course I can't talk. I'm engaged on the case, if that's any news to you."

"It got around," he told me. "But we see a story in it. I'd like you people to check and give permission to print."

I got him seated and found another bottle of beer.

"Now let's talk," I said. "What sort of a story do you want to print?"

"The old thing," he told me with a grin. "Human interest. Brunette bleaches hair for love of author. Just muck like that."

"Ashman is dead," I said. "Why smear him now?"

"No smearing."

"I know," I said. "But the devil of a lot of innuendo. But about our checking. What do you want us to do: you knowing, of course, that what I say doesn't stand for much."

"Test some blonde hair on her in the mortuary. I've already seen her there."

"Wharton's the one to see," I said, "and you'll get no such permission unless you can convince him that you'd be helping the case. Frankly, I don't see it helping to find who killed her.

Ashman, and what she might or might not have done for him, hasn't the slightest bearing. You prove it to me that it has and I'm on your side."

"Look," he said. "She vanished that evening after the Café Rond affair and we couldn't pick her up. That was a bit of a mystery. Now, if my theory's right, she turns out to be a married woman whose husband the police want to question pretty badly, and you and I know what that means. Where'd she go after that evening? She must have had friends somewhere. She must have stayed somewhere till the hair changed back to brown. And why was it necessary for her to dye her hair at all?"

"You don't expect us to publish all we know? As for dyeing her hair, she might have had her picture in some paper or other if a lucky photographer had been in the Café Rond. I've often wondered why you didn't take one with you."

"I know," he said. "I've kicked myself a hundred times. But between ourselves, what's your candid advice?"

"Get hold of Wharton and tell him about the Café Rond and all the rest of it," I said. "There's only one thing I ask. Keep me out of it. I'd rather you had the medal. What he'll do I can't begin to predict."

"You don't want Wharton to think you lost your grip about recognising her?" he told me, and he was pulling my leg.

"That's about it. Who wants to be turned adrift in a cruel world at my time of life."

"Some hopes of that," he said. "Mind if I use your phone?"

Five minutes later he was telling me that a Yard man would be with him at the mortuary. If he could swear that Freda Grey was the blonde, then Wharton himself might be coming along.

He was off at once. I was expecting Wharton to ring me, but he didn't. Maybe for once he realised I'd had a pretty long day. All the same, it took me a goodish while to get to sleep. What I couldn't help wondering was what Wharton's reactions would be, and if, in spite of all I'd done, there'd after all be a dragging in of Clement Foorde.

*

At eight o'clock I was at the Yard, and it was not till nine that Wharton came in. He was full of the Breck idea, and while he was withholding permission to print he seemed impressed with the fact that Breck was so sure. I had to tell him all I knew—ostensibly it was what I remembered from the newspaper reports—of that Café Rond business. I said he could check by the *Sentinel* files. As for any connection between the event and her death—well, I didn't honestly see it. Foorde had been the victim of a stunt, and no more. Ashman was dead—the only one who could prove it was a stunt—and I didn't see how Freda Grey could have been killed because of that stunt.

"I don't know," he told me. "There's something we may have missed. After all, you missed yourself what Breck happened to spot."

"I've heard you saying that for the last five minutes, George," I said. "But incredible as it may sound to you, there've been moments when you yourself haven't been omniscient."

"Such as when?"

"Save it," I said. "Don't anticipate your autobiography. The thing is, is there anything you want me to do?"

"Yes," he said, and he was still a bit huffed. "I think you ought to have another word with Foorde and let me have his version of the affair. Matthews is going down there, so he can go with you."

That was why in about half an hour Matthews and I were once more heading for Gatsworth. Halfway there I rang Foorde and prepared him for what was coming. He didn't like it a bit, till I assured him his name still wouldn't be published.

I dropped Matthews at the railway station and did the last mile alone. Foorde was in that same workroom. Runlet, who had let me in, seemed highly uncomfortable at the sight of me. I even saw Ellen Runlet give a startled peep round a passage corner at the sound of my voice.

"I don't know whether I'm glad to see you or not," Foorde told me. "But you'll have some coffee?"

He was wearing the same tweed coat and had evidently been working at the window table, for his typewriter was there and some sheets of manuscript. He looked curiously gigantic in that lovely old low-ceilinged room. I told him so. I said he needed the ten feet or so of a Georgian room to set him off. He seemed amused.

Ellen brought in the coffee, but she didn't give me so much as a look. There were some biscuits with it, and while we had that snack between meals I outlined what I wanted. I said it would save time if he wrote and signed a short statement, just for the files. Once the case was solved it would probably be destroyed.

Then something happened very quickly. He began giving his views. I was perhaps eight feet from the door, and all at once I moved across and whipped it open. Runlet was there. Quickly as he straightened himself I knew he'd been listening.

"I beg your pardon, sir," he told me unruffledly. "I was just coming to see if you required more coffee."

"No more," Foorde told him impatiently. Runlet closed the door. I was back in my chair.

"You must have uncommonly quick ears," Foorde told me admiringly.

"I'm told I have," I said. "I thought it was Mrs. Runlet perhaps, at the door with a tray or something. But about this brief comment."

Together we arrived at a draft, and a quarter of an hour later it was typed and signed and in my pocket. Once more he put on his cape and that old fishing hat and went out with me to the car.

"It's been a long way to come for practically nothing," I told him. "Still, the tax-payer pays."

"Yes," he said. "Don't think me personal, but with that agency of yours and one thing and another you must be doing quite well."

"I don't know," I said. "Any fool can make money these days. The trouble is to make a living."

"Yes," he said. "What an admirable way of putting things!"

As I moved the car on and he waved a farewell hand I thought his lips were moving, and I was malicious enough to wonder if he were repeating that poor quip of mine and in a minute or two would be noting it in his commonplace book. I thought of Oscar Wilde and how he complimented a friend on a witticism

and wished he'd uttered it himself, and then the friend's retort—
"You will, Oscar. You will."

I drove slowly back to the town and kept an eye out for
Hallows, and then remembered that he was not due till the afternoon. There was no sign of Matthews either, but he was staying
on in any case, so I set the car moving, and at half-past twelve I
was back at the Yard. Wharton was over his little huffiness. He
read the Foorde statement and said it was just what he wanted.

"Wanted for what?" I said.

"Just to convince that chap Breck there's nothing in that
stunt of his," he said. "And how was Mr. Foorde?"

"Majestic as ever," I said. "But it's *lèse majesté* to call him
Mr. Foorde. You wouldn't refer to the late George Bernard as
Mr. Shaw?"

He shot me a look. He said, none too sincerely, that he'd like
to meet him some time. Then I told him about Runlet listening
at the door. His eyebrows lifted.

"Runlet thought a lot of Grey, didn't he?"

"It's all in my statement," I told him.

"Of course," he said, but he wasn't really listening. He took a
little prowl round the room, looked out of the window and went
back to his desk. He filled his pipe and lighted it.

"What sort of a place has Foorde got there?"

The question was too unconcerned. Something, I knew, was
in the wind. When you've worked for twenty years with George
it's hard to let oneself be bamboozled.

"Just how do you mean?"

"Well, give me a sort of background."

I told him it was an old converted farmhouse with plenty of
oak inside and open fireplaces. The ceilings were low but the
rooms were friendly. Probably three downstair rooms and a
kitchen, and four bedrooms. A tiny circular drive and a corres-
pondingly small front garden. What the back garden was like
I didn't know, but I imagined it was fairly large. There was a
back building that was probably once a small barn, and it was
now the garage and—possibly—shed. It had a couple of dormer

windows, so the top part was probably a store-room. At the far back of the house were two or three large oaks.

"Sounds a nice little place," he said, and the tone had a curious unction. "And that's all you know?"

"That's all," I told him. "You don't want the inside furnishings, or do you?"

"Just an idea of the house," he said, and waved an indifferent hand. "You haven't had your lunch?"

I said I hadn't.

"Might as well get it," he told me. "You needn't be back much before three."

As I went out I was wondering just why he was suddenly getting rid of me. Some scheme was in his mind, there wasn't a doubt of that. It was something he was going to try out before three o'clock. If the trying out was unsuccessful or unpromising, then I'd go to my grave not knowing what it had been. On the other hand, at three o'clock I might know the answers.

At three o'clock he wasn't in his room, but there was a message for me. I was to be there at four sharp. So I went out and killed time at a news cinema. When I came back he was waiting, or at least he glanced reprovingly at the clock.

But he didn't seem in any immediate hurry. Tea came up, and when the tray was cleared he had another look at the clock. And in that half-hour he hadn't said a word about the case. What words were said, in fact, were mostly his. Then at just before five o'clock he got to his feet and made for the coat-rack.

"No rest for the wicked," he told me. "Might as well be on the move."

"You want me?"

"Of course I want you."

"Sorry," I said. "And is it in order to ask where we're going?"

"Why not?" he told me largely as I helped him on with the overcoat. "We're nipping along to Gatsworth for a word with that chap Runlet."

13
THE LOST FOUND

WE HAD our own driver, so I sat in the back with George. Just over Westminster Bridge he had the car stop and I got out and bought a selection of evening papers. I think he wanted to pretend to be reading so as to avoid much talk.

When the papers were exhausted we weren't so far from Gatsworth and he began getting me to tell him about Runlet. He knew it all, but it passed the time. Then at Gatsworth police-station he got out, but he told me he wouldn't be a minute and I stayed in the car. He was about five minutes, and then as soon as the car was almost out of the town he had it stop again. Apparently the driver already had his orders, for as Wharton and I stepped out into the pitch and chilly dark he didn't say a word. The car moved on.

"Just a minute," Wharton said. "Better get used to this damn dark."

I gave my glasses a polish and then we stepped slowly out.

"How far from the house?" he asked very quietly.

"A couple of hundred yards."

"Right," he said. "No talking from now on. Just follow me."

He halted some twenty yards from the house. A figure suddenly loomed up. It was Matthews.

"That you, sir?"

George stepped forward. He and Matthews did some whispering. Wharton reached a hand back to me, and the three of us moved on again. But only a few yards to a field gate. Matthews opened it quietly and we stepped through to a meadow.

My eyes were more used to the darkness, and I could see we were skirting a tall hedge. Quite a way along it we stopped again, and this time at a narrow white gate set in the hedge. We went through in single file.

"Gently here," Matthews whispered back.

We moved cautiously on, he in the lead, then Wharton and I. We were obviously in Foorde's garden, but where I had no means of judging. Then suddenly Matthews halted us. A dark shape was just ahead, and I guessed it was the garage.

"This way."

Matthews had craned back to whisper. We moved along a grass path to the left. I caught a glimpse of light which would be coming from the back of the house and then we were stopped again.

"Squat here, sir," Matthews whispered. "You'll be able to see both ways."

He moved off noiselessly into the darkness. Wharton grasped my arm and pulled me down. There were some dry sacks by those bushes, and we settled down there. Away to our right a distant clock chimed the half-hour.

"Half-past six," Wharton said. "We might have an hour of this yet."

"What's it all about, George?"

"Grey," he said. "We think he's in that garage."

I saw it then, and I could have kicked myself for several kinds of a fool—a garage with a second storey, probably once a chauffeur's flat. Runlet idolised Grey. Grey had bolted after killing, or not killing, his wife. He had learned from his wife where the Runlets were. Runlet had hidden him above the garage. That was why he and his wife had been nervous at my arrival that morning. Once more I had been too near the wood to see a particular tree. Wharton had seen things more objectively. He'd been the looker-on who'd seen more of the game.

It was odd, sitting there or half-reclining and whispering occasionally in the dark. There was never a star, but against the lighter darkness of sky we could see above us the tracery of an almost leafless tree. Facing us was a blackness some twenty yards away, and that was the garage. To the left was still that faint crack of light that would be coming from the kitchen window. Across our dim field of vision nothing stirred. Somewhere in that farther darkness would be men, strategically placed and ready to close in.

Now and again there were sounds. A car went by and its headlights momentarily illuminated the sky. Somewhere behind us a dog was barking, and that sound must have been coming from a mile or two away. The clock in the town chimed the three-quarters. There was the faintest movement low down beyond us, and the sight of two green eyes as a cat stood motionless for a moment and then was suddenly away. Then all at once there was a burst of light as the kitchen door opened. The man was a blackness against that light, but I knew he must be Runlet. He stepped out, and I saw him clearly as he looked up at the sky. He said something which we couldn't hear. He stepped back into the kitchen and the door closed. The night was tremendously dark again.

"A few minutes now," Wharton whispered. "He was seeing if it was raining."

Five minutes went by, and then suddenly I knew there was a difference somewhere, but it was a moment or two before I knew that the crack of light had gone. Wharton's hand closed over my arm as another light appeared—a curious bobbing, intermittent sort of light. Then I knew it was a torch, and no sooner did I know it than it disappeared.

"They're in the garage," whispered Wharton. "There's a flight of steps up."

I counted the seconds, but five minutes went by and I gave it up. Another minute or two and the wavering light suddenly appeared again, and this time it moved more quickly. There was the sound of the kitchen door gently closing. The crack of light was there again. Wharton still held my arm. A moment or two and he was getting to his feet.

He moved at a snail's pace along the grass path towards the garage. Matthews appeared from nowhere. Wharton's bulk hid me, but Matthews seemed to be leading the way. Once he made a low, hissing noise for silence as something cracked under my feet. Then we were at the garage. The door was just open, and I went through after Wharton. The door was closed behind me. Matthews flashed a torch and I saw he was in stockinged feet. He moved noiselessly through the oddments that littered the floor to the wide steps in the far corner opposite the car. He began to mount them, one slow careful step at a time. Then he began to hum something—the something maybe that Runlet had hummed as he'd gone up those steps. He waited no more than a second on the landing, then tapped at the door. We heard faint movements above us. The door opened. Wharton sprang forward towards the steps and I at his heels. We heard Matthews's voice, growling and threatening, and then we were in the room.

"It's him all right," Matthews told us.

Grey was sitting on a camp bed in the corner by the door. An oil lamp was burning on a table to our right, and there was a tray there and the chair by it where Grey had been at his meal. Matthews pulled at his arm and he got to his feet. He hand-brushed fastidiously the sleeve which Matthews had held.

That issued description had been good. He was slimly built, with a lean, handsome kind of face. The face was pale and the eyes were intensely dark. A wisp of newly growing moustache ran along the upper lip.

"You're Patrick Grey?" Wharton said.

"Yes," he said evenly, and the look was one of mild enquiry. "I'm Patrick Grey."

It was a beautiful speaking voice: the sort of voice that would cloy if you heard too much of it.

"I'm Chief-Superintendent Wharton of New Scotland Yard. There are some questions we'd like to ask you and some information you may be able to give us about the death of your wife. You're willing to go to London with us and to do what you can?"

Grey's eyes had narrowed. It was as if he'd been surprised at the words and the tone. He gave a little smile as of relief.

"I think so. You'll give me a minute to get my things together?"

He was wearing a dark-brown suit with a polka-dot brown tie. When he'd left jail he'd been wearing dark blue. From underneath the bed he produced a case. In a couple of minutes he was ready.

"You'll go with Sergeant Matthews here," Wharton told him. "Don't be alarmed if you have to wait a few minutes at the local police-station. It's a question of arranging transport."

He went down the steps and motioned for me to follow him. At the foot were a couple of plain-clothes men. Wharton produced a torch when we got outside.

"Holding him back," he whispered, "till we've seen the Runlets."

He flashed the torch along the path to the back door. He halted where the concrete path began, then stepped forward quickly and opened the door. He went through.

The Runlets were at their meal. They stared at Wharton. It was the sight of me that got Runlet to his feet. His wife made a little whimpering noise.

"Sit down!"

Runlet sat down.

"We've just seen your Captain Grey," Wharton told him. "He's going with us to London. Suppose you tell us all about it."

Ellen Runlet began to cry.

"Nothing to cry about," Wharton told her. "Not yet."

He was glaring down at Runlet. Runlet licked his lips and shook his head. A good half-minute and he still hadn't spoken. Ellen Runlet was sobbing quietly, napkin at her eyes.

"Either you talk to me or you both go to Town," Wharton said grimly. "The choice is your own."

Ellen gave a last sob.

"Tell him, Fred. . . . We've done nothing wrong."

Runlet moistened his lips again.

"No," he said. "We've done nothing wrong. The Captain came here and told us he wanted to rest for a bit. . . . We did what we could."

"He told you he'd killed his wife."

"No, no!" She almost shrieked the words. "He said she was dead and people would think he'd killed her. He was going to stay here for a bit and then go to France."

Runlet shook his head.

"All right, sir. She's given the game away. It was like she said."

Grey must have come straight down to Gatsworth that night of his wife's murder. He hadn't known how to risk getting into touch with the Runlets, and it was after midnight when he arrived, so he made an entry—an easy enough job—into the shed part of the garage and spent the night there. When Ellen Runlet came out early to feed the hens he attracted her attention. Runlet smuggled him up to the top room, which had once been a chauffeur's flat.

Grey—and it was more difficult getting that out of Runlet—had said he had gone to his wife's house and found her dead, and he knew the police would assume that no one could have killed her but himself, so he packed a few things in a bag and slipped away. The Runlets had fixed up a camp bed for him and curtained the windows and brought him his meals. In a day or two Grey had intended trying to slip across to France. Runlet had posted a letter or two for him, though what was in them he naturally didn't know. And he claimed not to have remembered the addresses.

"A good job for you Mr. Foorde was away tonight," Wharton said. "What's he going to say when he hears about all this?"

Runlet's hands lifted and fell.

"We've been out of a job before, sir. I expect we'll manage."

"Maybe you won't lose your jobs," Wharton said. "What you've told me is the absolute truth and nothing but the truth?"

"God's my witness, sir."

"You think he killed his wife?"

"No, sir. The Captain wouldn't do a thing like that, sir. Even if he had, though, sir, I wouldn't have blamed him."

"Well, I'll be seeing Mr. Foorde later tonight," Wharton told him. "You play fair with us, Runlet, and we'll play fair with you. More I can't say. And don't move from here. We might want you again tomorrow."

"What're you going to do with him, sir?"

That was Ellen Runlet. Wharton patted her shoulder.

"Depends on the truth of his story. We do nothing to innocent men."

He gave Runlet a nod and turned back to the door. As it closed behind us I heard a sound. Ellen Runlet was sobbing again.

*

There had been a handy train from Gatsworth, and Wharton had taken it alone. The rest of us came on by car, and it was almost ten o'clock when we got to the Yard. Grey was given a meal somewhere, and Matthews and I waited in Wharton's room. It was half an hour before he arrived. He'd been to see Clement Foorde. I asked why that urgency.

"Speaking a word for the Runlets," he told us. "I want that couple eating out of my hand."

"How did Foorde take it?"

His manner was magisterial as if by magic. It was plain that Foorde, in his own milieu, had been an experience.

"He took it very well," he said. "He seemed genuinely attached to the Runlets. Very surprised, of course, and a bit shocked. I assured him there'd be no publicity." He gave himself a sideways nod. "A very impressive man. And a fine place he's got there."

He let out a breath. He glanced up at the clock.

"Didn't know it was so late. Let's have him in."

Five minutes and Matthews was bringing Grey in. Everything was set. The stenographer was unobtrusively at the corner table. The fire looked cheerful. There was no sign of fuss or strain.

"Sit down, Mr. Grey," Wharton said mildly. "I think you'll find that chair comfortable."

He put on those fake spectacles of his, and there he was: the gentle, avuncular old soul who was regrettably doing an unpleasant job. Grey wasn't looking uneasy. He was dapper, if I may put it that way, through the obvious tiredness. He had had a wash and brightened himself up. Just the right amount of light-brown handkerchief showed above the breast pocket.

"I had a talk with the Runlets," Wharton went on, and he was fiddling with some papers on his desk. "Now I'd like to hear your version of things. And I'd like to say I'm being rather unusual. I'm charging you with nothing. All the same, I'd like to warn you that what you say is being taken down. So just tell us all about it. If you're perfectly willing, that is."

It might have been amusing if it hadn't been so deadly serious. Grey spoke with such an apparent indifference, and there was that charming voice of his. One might have been listening to Henry Ainley—a slightly immature Ainley—with a touch of that intimacy of A.J. Alan in the old days of the B.B.C. I could see that charm of manner: the unquestionable confidence he had given his various victims: the kind of thing that had bound the Runlets so closely to him and had left almost nothing but pleasant memories in Thoraby and Dykeham.

"You'd like everything as it happened?" he began.

"Well, yes," Wharton told him quietly.

"I thought so," he said, and paused for a moment.

"Well, it was like this. After they let me loose I met my wife in Town and we had a long talk about what we were going to do. We couldn't decide on anything. She had a little money but I hadn't any, but she had brought with her a gold cigar case and a few other valuables of mine, and I sold them that afternoon to raise the wind. I spent that night at her place, and the next afternoon I went up to Manchester to see a friend. I didn't leave him till the next evening, and it was about half-past nine when I got back to Town. I went straight to St. John's Wood—my wife had given me a key—and when I opened the door everything was dark.

"'That's queer,' I thought to myself, and then I guessed she had a headache or something and had gone to bed. Then I thought of having a drink, so I went into the lounge, and there she was. My God, I was almost stiff with fright! I think I must have panicked. I told myself I'd better get to hell out of there fast, so I got a bag and shoved some stuff in it and took what money was in her bag. Then when I got out of the house I had the hell of a scare again. About my finger-prints, you know. So I went back and let myself in again and wiped off everything I thought I'd touched. Then I made for Waterloo Station and got a train to Gatsworth."

"Yes," Wharton said non-committally. "And what made you go to the Runlets?"

"Well, I ask you," he said, and waved a hand. "My wife had told me where they were—they were one of the first people I asked about. They've known me ever since I was born. True as steel, sir: that's what they are. That's why I told them the truth. And why they believed me."

His eyes lifted with a suggestion of enquiry. Wharton gave no sign of belief or otherwise.

"To go back a bit, Mr. Grey. Is it *Mr.* or *Captain*, by the way?"

"Does it matter?" The smile was attractive. "A purely wartime rank. Not that I'm not entitled to it."

"Well, about this visit to Manchester to see a friend, and the return. You say you didn't get in till half-past nine. You can prove that?"

"Yes."

There'd been just the slightest hesitation.

"Then, pardon me, why didn't you prove it before? I'm not trying any tricks, mind you, but you may have gathered from the newspapers—you've seen the newspapers?"

"Oh yes. Runlet used to let me see them."

"Then you gathered that your wife was killed at about eight o'clock. But you still kept lying doggo at Gatsworth. Why didn't you go to the police and tell them what you've told us just now?"

"I don't think I'd like to answer that."

Wharton shrugged his massive shoulders.

"Very well. Suppose you tell us the name of anyone who can prove you took that particular train from Manchester."

Grey frowned slightly.

"I'm sorry, but I don't think I can do that either. I mean— well, I *could* do it, if you follow me, but I prefer not to."

Wharton gasped at him.

"You realise what that means?"

"Yes," he said. "But I know what you don't know. I know I didn't kill my wife, and you'll have to prove that I did."

"Captain Grey?"

He turned round to look at me.

"I wonder if I might ask a perfectly harmless question or two. Would you be prepared, for instance, to tell us the name of your Manchester friend if you were given certain guarantees?"

"That's a curious question," he said. "What made you ask it?"

"Maybe I'll tell you," I said. "But you tell me this first. You went to Manchester in what was rather a hurry. Was it to collect some money owing to you?"

His eyes narrowed for a moment. The forehead furrows might have been the ratchets of a working brain.

"Would that have been unusual?"

"In your case, not at all," I said. "Would you mind if I put something hypothetical up to you? I've been, shall we say, in the watch-smuggling racket. I get through with one load and have the necessary colleague or colleagues to take it off my hands. Not too long afterwards I try bringing in another load, but the police have suspicions—heaven knows why—and they nab me at Newhaven. I can't pay the fine and I get two years. When I come out I want money that's due to me, and there're complicated accounts still to settle. So I call on that colleague who lives at—shall we say?—Manchester."

"Very interesting," he said.

"Wait a moment. I haven't quite finished. I get out and I see that friend and we have an amicable settlement. We may even make plans for future business. Then I go back to London and find my wife murdered. I panic. Later I know I've got an alibi, but I daren't use it. I'd be incriminating that friend of mine in the watch racket and getting him inside for two years or more. I'd also be queering the pitch for future operations. He might even have some friends who'd treat me uncommonly rough when the news got out. So I decide to tell so much of the truth. After all, I didn't kill my wife, and the police will have to prove that I did. If I keep my mouth shut, that'll at least make time. I even write to my friend and put the whole thing up to him, and I get a letter back accordingly."

"Most interesting," he said. "But what was that about guarantees?"

"Well, that friend might substantiate your alibi if we didn't go too deeply into his affairs. Just enough, say, to know he was telling the truth. That the alibi hadn't been faked between you and him."

"Yes," he said. "It's something to think about."

I threw the ball to Wharton.

"Well, Captain Grey, you've heard what Mr. Travers has told you. What're you going to do?"

"Don't know," he said. "I think I'd rather think this over."

"Have your own way," Wharton told him. "We shall have to detain you as an important witness: you realise that?"

"Oh, quite." He even gave Wharton a smile. "I don't expect your beds are any harder than some I've known."

"Maybe not," Wharton said. "And how long do you think you'll be in making up your mind?"

"Probably by the morning," he told us airily. "As Mr. . . . . I didn't quite catch your name?"

"Travers."

"Of course. I'm so sorry. As Mr. Travers was saying, it might boil down to a matter of guarantees." His hands fluttered in a little apologetic gesture. "Not that I'd dream of driving a bargain. And it was Mr. Travers's suggestion."

"In the morning," Wharton told him curtly. "Take Captain Grey out, Matthews."

The door closed behind them. The stenographer opened it again and went through.

"Plausible bastard," Wharton told me. He threw the glasses on the desk top and got to his feet. "Another minute or two of *him* and I'd have had him kicked out of the room. How'd he strike you?"

"I'll own up frankly," I said. "At first I was rather attracted by him. Now I think he's a very nasty piece of work. Selfish to the core, and callous. Never a word of regret about his wife."

"I'd give something to pin it on him." Wharton's fist smote the desk. "That alibi of his. You think he rigged it up while he was holed up at Gatsworth?"

I said that wasn't really the point. Rigged or not would it stand up in the eyes of the jury? Not that we'd even got a yard on the way to bringing a murder charge.

"Pity you mentioned guarantees," he said. "It's as bad as compounding a felony."

"What else can we do? We've either to turn him loose or look into his alibi. Unless you can think of a holding charge."

"We can hold him for questioning, can't we?"

"You're the boss," I said. "But we've already questioned him about the things that really matter. What we'd have to do was think of some trick questions or get him to contradict himself."

"Leave it," he told me brusquely. "He's kept me out of my bed these last few nights, and I'm damned if he's going to do so tonight. Let him cool his heels."

I told him he'd done a fine job finding Grey at Gatsworth, and I meant it. Usually he'd have wagged his tail, but he didn't. There was something about Grey that had got right under his skin: something that might badly warp his judgment. I think he knew it. That's why he said we'd both go home. Maybe we'd have other ideas by the morning.

I was awake for a long time that night, and I was up well before my time. But the night hadn't brought counsel. I'd found no catch questions. Grey, I thought, had had a lot of time on his hands at Gatsworth. If he'd thought out a fake alibi, then he'd had time to perfect it. Not that I was too worried about that. In our time Wharton and I have busted a good few alibis that looked watertight, and one more wouldn't matter. In fact, it would be something into which to get one's teeth.

That was how I felt about things as I made my way that morning to the Yard.

14

FRESH BEGINNING

I FOUND a changed Wharton that morning: a Wharton who knew it was a question of Grey's neck, and that Grey, whatever the nausea he inspired and the unsavouriness of so-called guarantees, would have to be given his chance.

Grey was brought in. There was no need to ask him if he had had a good night. He was as neat and dapper as ever, and I thought there was a little more colour in his cheeks.

"We've decided to test that alibi of yours," Wharton told him. "Mr. Travers here will be responsible and the Manchester police will not be brought in. I think that should be sufficient guarantee of fair dealing. So if you'll give us the name or names we'll get busy."

"Yes," Grey said. "But I'm afraid it isn't so easy as that. I should want permission to telephone. My friends have to know about these guarantees."

I expected Wharton to explode, but he didn't.

"That's reasonable," he told Grey mildly. "Perhaps we'd better get that part over. Sergeant Matthews will arrange it."

"We'll be listening in?" I asked Wharton when the door had closed.

"Oh no," he said. "We'll play perfectly fair. A rigged alibi's the easier to break. It'll be up to you to judge when you get there."

"Let's say the alibi's unbreakable," I said. "Where do we go from there?"

"Fall back on Runlet," he told me. "Quite a happy situation from Runlet's point of view if he'd killed her himself and then sheltered Grey."

"The trouble is we can hold Grey for not reporting the murder, but we can't hold Runlet."

"Don't worry," he said. "Runlet wouldn't bolt. Besides, he'll never be the least bit suspicious, not the way I handle him."

A few minutes later Grey was brought back. Wharton reached for a pencil.

"A Mr. Silben," Grey said, "and a Mr. Farburn. They'll be at the station to meet the four-ten."

"Those their real names?"

Grey shrugged his shoulders.

"It's the only names I've known them by."

"Well, that's that," Wharton said. "I expect you described Mr. Travers to them. And assuming your alibi's all right, let's see if you can help us find who did kill your wife. There'll be plenty of time for Mr. Travers to catch his train."

Grey was perfectly amenable, but he didn't know he was in for an hour's gruelling. Not that Wharton was ever impatient or overbearing: he just kept quietly at Grey: worrying remorselessly as it were and giving him no chance to fabricate. He took him through the whole of that murder day. He wondered why Grey couldn't have established an alibi through contacts on the train that brought him from Manchester to London. Grey said he had had a meal before leaving, and that he hadn't left a practically empty first-class compartment. First-class, I noted, meant that Grey had raised the wind. He had had no need to save money.

Wharton made him live again every minute from the arrival at No. 7 to the final departure. How long had Mrs. Grey been dead? Why worry to remove prints since the reason for Grey's hurried departure had been the knowledge that he was bound to be connected with the murder?

Grey was unruffled. In that smooth, beautifully cushioned voice of his he talked to Wharton as if he were a small boy to whom one had to explain things in words of one syllable. He hadn't, for instance, touched his wife's body. Panic, he said: that was the keynote. Wharton, he pointed out, was asking for logic, but a man doesn't act logically in the face of a tremendous shock.

"You were in love with your wife?"

Grey's look was almost supercilious.

"That's rather old-fashioned, surely? We'd been married some years. I hate to sound indifferent, but one doesn't perpetually live in a honeymoon atmosphere. The fact that I was badly shocked shows what I thought."

"Well," said Wharton, and his tone was as near to the nasty as I'd known it, "you might conceivably have been thinking of your own skin. Your wife wrote to you regularly?"

"Yes," he said. "As far as was allowed."

"She told you all about an old friend named Ashman?"

"Why, of course," he said, and the smile was sad. "Dear old Bobby. One of the best friends a man could have."

"You knew your wife and he had a holiday together in France?"

"Oh yes. I believe they had a very good time."

"Let's be crude. You didn't ever wonder if your wife was being unfaithful to you?"

"Should I?" The eyebrows lifted delicately.

"Our information is that you had every reason," Wharton told him. "I'm not suggesting anything, but a lot of men would have had no compunction about strangling wives who'd been as friendly with men as your wife was with Ashman."

"No use trying that line, Superintendent. I haven't lived an altogether monastic life myself, so why should I expect my wife to go into a nunnery for a couple of years?"

"That night you spent together on the 11th. Did she tell you about a man named Foorde? Clement Foorde?"

"Foorde?" he said puzzledly. "Who's he?"

"You knew about Ashman's book? The money it was making for him?"

"Yes, poor devil," he said. "Tough luck that, you know. Getting a break and then that drowning business."

That was the kind of thing. They were still at it when it was time for me to go. I put a few things in a bag in case I should have to stay the night. Then I remembered something and I rang the agency.

"Anything turn up at Gatsworth?"

"Hallows is back," Norris said. "He got everything. Foorde went to the station yesterday afternoon and Runlet drove the car back. It's a pre-war Daimler, still—"

"That's all right," I said. "I happened to have a look at it myself. What about the other thing?"

"It was there in the garage all the time. Local people jacked it up on the Monday and serviced the battery and so on till Foorde himself got back."

I said that was fine. And yet I wasn't in the least degree excited. There's often the old argument about the possibility of a man's being in love with two women at the same time. I wouldn't know about that, but I do know that it's hard to be equally absorbed in two differing cases. At the moment I had Grey very much on my mind, so that information about Runlet was merely pigeon-holed.

As I came through the barrier, horn-rims well polished and eyes about me, two men came up. Both were tall and quite well dressed. The one who introduced himself as Silben might have been a police inspector off duty: fortyish, broad-shouldered, heavy browed and with a massive dark moustache. The other—Farburn—was a much younger man, and of what I might call the Grey school: unctuously mannered—he consistently called me *sir*—and with just a touch of apprehension behind the ready smile. I wouldn't have minded a heavy bet that Farburn had been at school with Grey. There was nothing of the northern about Silben's accent either: if anything it was rather south-western.

We walked a few yards to a hotel and into its lounge, where Silben ordered tea. We had the place almost to ourselves.

"So Pat Grey's got himself in a spot of bother," Silben began. "Something to do with that nasty business about his wife."

"I'm answering no questions," I told him. "I'm just here to be told things. All I can do is give our version of things."

I told them about the alibi.

"I think you'll leave here satisfied," Silben said. "In the first place you have our word that what he told you was true."

I think he noticed the rather queer look on my face.

"Give us your word and we'll put our cards on the table," he said.

"The fact that I'm here at all is as good as giving my word," I told him. "What you're getting at, I take it, is that you'd neither of you go out of your way to be cross-examined by counsel for the prosecution."

"That's rather good," Farburn said.

"It's almost too good," Silben told him. "But there it is, Mr. Travers. If Pat Grey was going to swing for want of an alibi, we'd come forward. Not that I think it'll ever happen. There's the manager here, for instance. I've told him just as much as is necessary."

A minute or two later the manager was fetched: a middle-aged man named Woodacre. I had a photograph of Grey—enlarged from one taken at that nylon period—which was still quite a good likeness. Woodacre hadn't any doubts. Grey was the man who'd had high-tea with Silben and Farburn in that very room on the late afternoon of the 13th. I asked if he'd be prepared to give evidence on oath.

"Why not, sir?" he asked me. "I've seen the police enquiries for him and read his description. It was him who was here, and there isn't a doubt about it. And the three gentlemen left here with just time for him to catch his train."

That seemed to settle things. Silben said he could, if necessary, find a man with whom Grey had spent a part of the afternoon, but he'd rather he wasn't brought in. I said I was satisfied. All that remained was for Silben and Farburn to sign a statement entirely without prejudice. There was some argument about the wording, but it was done.

"Don't know if you're going straight back, sir," Farburn said, "but there's a train in half an hour."

I said that would suit me. Everything had been a bit unexpected, as I told them. My bag showed I'd been prepared to spend the night.

"I didn't even know if I'd be blindfolded and taken to some secret hide-out," I told them.

"You've been to the pictures too often," Silben told me amusedly. "Still, you will have done just what Pat Grey did. He had tea here—a much bigger one than you've had—and he caught the same train, and we two saw him off, just as we might see you off."

"Glad if you will," I said, and I had to smile at the subtlety of it all. They wanted me out of Manchester, and they'd be on that platform till the train was out of sight. And, if I knew anything, they wouldn't go straight home.

So there was I, leaning out of the window and having a friendly chat till the train moved off. Both shook hands as the guard's whistle blew.

"Good luck, sir," Farburn said. Silben said he'd been glad to meet me. All the same, he hoped I wouldn't take it amiss if he admitted he wouldn't grieve if he never saw me again.

An interesting couple: interesting for a few minutes' speculation to pass the time in the train. But what really mattered was that Grey's alibi was good enough. Woodacre had struck me as a perfectly reliable witness whatever might have been rigged between Grey and his pals. I was supposed to be impartial, but long before I got to London I was sorry that Grey hadn't been our man. There'd been that sort of reptilian smoothness about him: the egotistical self-assurance. Grey, I felt, was more emetic than man, and the pity was that that didn't make him also a murderer.

A taxi took me to the Yard, and Wharton was there. In the train I'd written a statement.

"Seems sound enough," he told me regretfully when I'd outlined things. "Nothing to do now but turn him loose."

"Anyone on his tail?"

"No point in it," he said. "Sooner or later we'll have him for some other job. A chap like him can't change his ways."

"And who now? Runlet?"

"That's it," he said. "He'll be under our eye from now on. Wouldn't be surprised if he had a meeting with Grey somewhere."

If he had anything more up his sleeve he wasn't giving it away. Maybe the establishing of Grey's alibi had knocked some of the heart out of him. At any rate he told me I needn't hurry along in the morning.

When I turned up next morning, just before ten o'clock, Wharton still wasn't very happy. Matthews had been at Gatsworth the previous afternoon trying to find out if Runlet had taken a train to Town on that murder night. He'd just reported that Runlet was as good as unknown in Gatsworth and that any trail was far too old. No one could be expected to remember from a mere description of a virtual stranger who's taken a certain train at a busy junction.

While we were talking that over Foorde rang. I couldn't gather what was being said except that there wasn't the likelihood of the Runlets being dismissed. And that he was being told we were not detaining Grey.

"He's just going down there," Wharton told me when he'd rung off. "Seemed pretty relieved he wouldn't have to dismiss the Runlets, but I think they'll get the length of his tongue. Seemed relieved, too, that we'd turned Grey loose. Doesn't make things look so bad for the Runlets."

I loafed around for an hour or so, and I was just thinking of making a morning of it when the buzzer went. Matthews was on the line. I heard Wharton tell him to keep an eye out, and there was something about keeping on *his* tail.

"Who d'you think's popped up at Gatsworth?" he asked me.

"Not Grey?"

"Grey it is," he said. "Runlet drove to the station in the Daimler, apparently to meet Foorde, and he went straight to the refreshment room. He and Grey are chinwagging there now. Matthews daren't let himself be seen, but he's going to follow Grey if he hops a train."

We didn't get a report till the early afternoon when Matthews came in. Runlet, he said, had left the refreshment room five minutes before Foorde's train arrived. Grey had taken his time, and it was quite a while before he crossed to the up platform. Evidently he had his timings worked out, for a London train came in practically at once. At Waterloo he took a taxi to the Martindale Hotel and booked a single room under the name of P. Grey. He had told the clerk he might want the room for some days.

"Doing himself well," Wharton said. "The Martindale's pretty expensive. Think we should watch him for a couple of days?"

"A tricky job," Matthews said. "There's at least three ways of getting out, and I'll lay he's as artful as a wagon-load of monkeys."

"Any idea why he saw Runlet?"

"It might have been this. Runlet arrived with a smallish case: one of those fibre things. It wasn't heavy and it wasn't light. Grey took the case over. I'd say it had clothes in it. Things Runlet had bought for him while he was in that garage."

"Well, check at the Martindale for the next few mornings," Wharton told him, "and see if he's still there."

It was from that moment that the case began slowly to peter out. I'm not more conscientious than my neighbours, but after two or three days of doing practically nothing I suggested I should come off the payroll. There was plenty being done, mind you. Wharton had discovered in some devious way of his own that Grey had lied to us about Silben and Farburn. Those were not their real names. Both were running some kind of a soft-goods export business, which was all that Wharton told me.

That was only one thing. Tarrent Road was again being gone through with a small-toothed comb with the hope of finding someone who had seen a someone near No. 7 that murder night. Wharton went down alone, in Foorde's absence in Town, and had a long talk with the Runlets, and came back, I judged, no wiser than when he went.

Next came a conference—Commander, Crime—and I had to attend it. By the time we'd finished with the Freda Grey Case it and we were like chewed string. And no one could suggest new lines of approach. I was asked, like everyone else, but I kept my mouth shut. I did have ideas, but I also owed a loyalty to George. Later, when we were back in his room, and alone, I put something to him.

"If you think there's anything in it, George, I'd prefer it to come from you, but my idea is that the whole of the Grey-Ashman events are tied up together. I'm beginning to feel sure that if we're going to know who killed Freda Grey we'll have to go a long way back: at least as far as to that Café Rond business and the publication of Ashman's book. I think we'll have to throw the net wide and include, for instance, Ashman's publisher—an Arthur Lanyer."

He made me enlarge on it all, and I had to move over some very thin ice.

"It's that old bee in your bonnet," he told me. "That Ashman drowning business. It's stuck in your gullet because it turned out a flop."

"I rather resent that," I said. "It's all over the place, like your metaphors. It isn't a flop when you can't move the immovable. And I hadn't the authority of the Yard behind me."

I didn't press the point: I just left it with him and hoped. Later that night news came that Grey had checked out from the Martindale. By the morning the taxi-driver had been found, and he'd taken Grey to Liverpool Street Station.

"Liverpool Street," George said. "He can't be thinking of going back to that Dykeham place?"

My guess was that Grey had simply picked up his suitcases and stepped down to the Underground. Wharton put Matthews on the job of tracing him, but it was a hopeless game. Grey, as far as we were concerned, had ceased to exist.

An afternoon or two later I dropped into the club for tea, and I ran into Clement Foorde with Martin Halston, the actor.

"Like to see you in a minute or two," Foorde told me as I went by them.

Foorde hadn't been out of my mind, and because I'd been seeing quite a lot of his name. There'd been a spate of new plays, for instance, and I'd also seen the notice of publication of that second volume of the autobiography. On the same day Bernice had called my attention to a book review by Foorde—books on the theatre principally, with one novel dealing with an episode in the life of someone who could only be Bernhardt. Foorde had simply flayed it—not with a butcher's knife but a scalpel. If I'd been the wretched author my cheeks would have been more than red.

My tea was brought, and I'd just finished it when Foorde appeared. I thought he was looking overworked, and I told him so.

"Not at all," he told me impatiently. "Why must people imagine there's something lethal about work. But I have been busy. I'm afraid I've also been rather rude. The sight of you, my dear fellow, reminded me."

"Rude?" I said.

"Well, yes. I ought to have informed you and Superintendent Wharton that I've changed my mind. I find it impossible now to keep the Runlets on."

Something had happened, he said—that Grey business almost certainly—to change them from two contented people to something very different. He was seeing it in a score of ways. His small household had, in fact, been so upset that he was finding it impossible to carry on. He had given the Runlets notice and was putting Wicklands into the hands of an agent.

"I shall give the Runlets an excellent reference," he said. "They oughtn't to be very long without work. I feel a certain responsibility towards them. The whole thing has hurt me, Travers, in spite of that. But I couldn't go on. It was militating against my work."

I think he was pleased to hear that I hadn't been altogether surprised. When I enlightened him about the Grey history and told him, in confidence, that the Runlets might be besotted enough to work for him again, he was seeing the reason for the unsettled minds of his couple.

"What're you doing with Wicklands?" I asked him. "Letting it furnished?"

"No," he said. "I'm making a clean cut. Selling it, and the contents. There's very little I want to keep."

"You'll miss the place. The change from Town."

"I don't know," he said. "The country in winter can be pretty uninviting. And I'm getting past all this gadding about. Marston Square will have to contain me from now on. I hope in the near future you'll have dinner with me. This time with no intrusion of business."

I asked about the third volume of the autobiography, and he admitted he'd been unable to make any headway. At Marston Square he was hoping to settle down to a long spell of writing. That was about all. He asked me to convey—his word—his compliments to Wharton and to apologise. I said no apology was needed. He insisted there was, and then the whole thing ended in a laugh when I said we were rather like two stage Frenchmen at the swing-doors.

I felt rather sorry for him. I've known myself what it is to be torn up by the roots, and I had the idea he'd liked those days he'd spent at Gatsworth. And, in spite of his denials, I did think he'd been looking very unwell. One was more aware of his fleshiness, so to speak, and the eyes had been heavy. The gestures had been mechanical and the talk had been so utilitarian, and unilluminated with a single flash of the Foorde wit.

It was no use ringing Wharton from the club, for he had hinted at another conference: one at which I should apparently not be needed. So I went home instead, and it was about that conference that I began thinking, and the suggestions I might or might not have made if I'd been there. I began thinking about Robert Ashman and what my hunch told me was the beginning of the Freda Grey Case. Every now and again I would lean back in the chair and look at this piece of evidence and that. I had to wonder what was and what was not an irrelevance. I hoped, too, that mere mechanical thinking might be suddenly transfigured, as occasionally had happened in the past, by some blinding flash of vision, but nothing happened. I let the thoughts have play, but no sooner did they suggest a theory than I was silencing it by some irrefutable objection. Then, when my brain was beginning to reel, the telephone went. George was on the line.

"Can you be here at about nine in the morning?"

"Why not?" I said. "Something turned up?"

"In a way, yes. You know that idea of ours"—his word—"about going right back as far as we can? I think that'll be it."

"Why not drop in here?" I said. "I'm alone and we can have a preliminary talk. I'll scratch a meal for us."

I thought he'd refuse, but he didn't. Maybe he was thinking, like Clement Foorde, that a new environment would bring ideas. At any rate he turned up, and we had a meal, smoked a lot and ruined four bottles of beer. It was after ten when he left.

He hadn't admitted as much, but he'd been preoccupied with Grey. George never attempts to defend an invalid preconception; he abandons it. George can swallow his own words in proof that they never were uttered. With a nice derangement of metaphors he did say that in Grey we'd been flogging a dead horse, and with that Grey was consigned to limbo. In fact, what emerged from two hours of talk was that I was to be given a free hand to hark back as far as I liked. If he suggested that I'd better produce something worth while, then the suggestion was more playful than menacing.

I went to bed a reasonably happy man. Matthews was to work with me, and we'd have what additional help we needed. I think it was when I was telling myself ironically that I'd almost be running the Yard that I went to sleep. I didn't even wake when Bernice came in.

PART III
DEATH BY POISON

15
BACK TRAILS

THERE had to be planning before that new and comprehensive investigation could begin. Matthews had to know as much about everything as myself, and luckily there were things which he could be told which I should have been chary of putting to Wharton.

When I was pretty sure he had a clear picture of things, we tried to find a starting-point. Ashman and the two Greys, or so it seemed, had to be picked up and followed from their first association. Grey and Ashman had been together during the war, but we could find nothing in that friendship, by itself, to have accounted for the death of either Ashman or Freda Grey.

Grey hadn't met Ashman again, or so we had to presume, till after Grey came to Town following the Thoraby crash. Then Grey married, and we were at the vital trio. What had actually happened when those three people became friends? Even if

Grey had now been on tap we could have placed no credence on the version he would have chosen to give us. We had to deduce things for ourselves.

That Grey had had very little money after that financial crash seemed a certainty. The bankruptcy proceedings showed debts of about eleven thousand pounds and assets of only eight hundred. Yet when Grey went to Dykeham he had a fine car, and he would have had to satisfy the owner of that furnished house, or his agent, as to his financial stability.

Where did the money come from? The answer seemed to be, from Ashman.

And there we came to something that had never been seen before: a piece that seemed to fit snugly into the jigsaw. Ashman at Dykeham became very friendly indeed with Freda Grey. But Grey was surely aware of it. Indeed, Grey and his wife had probably planned originally that she should be the bait to wheedle Ashman into financing that stay at Dykeham. In other words, she had designedly thrown herself at Ashman's head.

We thought that ought to be checked at once, and it took best part of a morning. But when the house agent confirmed that Ashman had been given as a reference, we knew we could go right on. The Greys had been playing a double game with Ashman. He had money—less, it might be, than they thought—and they needed it. That was why Ashman had been so frequent a visitor at Dykeham. And why Grey had pretended to Runlet that it was absurd to think of Ashman as having an affair with his wife.

When that nylon affair ended in disaster Ashman became more than ever the sheet-anchor. Grey would need money when he came out of jail, so Freda made no bones about becoming Ashman's mistress. If Ashman had not died, then our guess was that Grey would have touched him for every possible penny—with the help of a divorce threat—and then the two Greys would have disappeared, only to reappear under other names at, say, Manchester.

"Was Ashman in that nylon racket?" Matthews wanted to know.

"Don't let's jump too far," I said. "I'd say he'd no idea what was going on. Grey had a convincing tongue and he could have spun any yarn about the need to go to Dykeham. And there'd be Freda's various persuasions. On the other hand, if Ashman did tumble to it later, I'm sure he wouldn't have been shocked. He was an irresponsible, adventurous type. And you know as well as I do that a very large number of people of all classes regard smuggling as a fair risk. Certainly a long way from crime."

"I think you're right," Matthews told me. "If he had been shocked he'd have broken with Freda when things got out. But what I was trying to get at was whether he could have been killed because of that nylon racket. Because he knew too much."

"Then who killed him? Grey didn't. Those two coves I saw in Manchester didn't; because if Ashman really was murdered, then it was definitely a local job. The only one left is Freda, and why should she kill the goose that was going to lay another golden egg?"

"Mind if I go back to something?" he said. "That anonymous letter. Freda couldn't have written it."

"Crew thought she did."

"If so, then everything we've worked out so far is sheer bunkum. She didn't want her husband in jail. Ashman must have tumbled to the racket and tipped off the police because he wanted Freda to himself. And because he had the wind up. Crew said she knew something. That's what she knew—that Ashman must have written that letter."

"Then did she tell her husband?"

"Later, yes. And he'd say, 'Right. You stick with the bastard till I get out, then we'll milk him for as much as he'll stand.'"

I thought he was right. If so, it proved that Freda had had no hand whatever in Ashman's death. That being so, we moved on to the new duo of Freda and Ashman. Our first knowledge of that was the affair in the Café Rond. Freda had been prepared to work a publicity stunt on behalf of *The Silken Petticoat*.

"There's that £250 that Ashman drew out in cash," I said. "It puzzles me. Freda had been set up in Tarrent Road and was costing Ashman quite a bit. She was also his mistress. Why, then, was it necessary to pay her that additional money?"

"It mightn't have been for her," Matthews said. "It might have been for something we don't know about."

We went on arguing, but somehow I always kept getting back to that £250. That was why I arranged a call at Ashman's bank.

I saw the manager and asked to have a word with the cashier who'd handled that particular transaction early in March. It took some time to find him. When I recalled Ashman and that cheque and £250 in cash, he remembered everything.

"How'd he take it?" I wanted to know. "In fivers or pound notes?"

"In used pound notes."

"You mean he definitely requested used pound notes?"

"Yes. And there was something rather unusual, as I remember now. He asked me to put a wrapper round them: the sort of thing we have. You just lick the edges and it sticks down. Makes a neat little bundle. Then he asked me if I'd mind initialling the outside of the wrapper, so I did. I asked him what the idea was, in a joking sort of way. I forget exactly what he said, but he made a joke of it too. Something about a beautiful spy and laying a trap for her."

That was the information I brought back to Matthews. It had us baffled. If the money was for Freda, why lay a trap for her? It didn't make sense. But it did bring us to the question of who else had been deeply involved in the success of Ashman's book.

"But this Lanyer," Matthews said. "Why should Ashman give *him* money?"

"Let's say," I suggested, "that Lanyer was wise to the Café Rond stunt: that it was he, in fact, who organised it. He hadn't the available cash, so Ashman advanced it against royalties. What I mean is that Lanyer could have repaid it under the heading of an advance payment or royalties. Just a little cooking of the books."

Matthews didn't see it. For one thing he knew practically nothing about the publishing business, and he also thought such a transaction unnecessary and far too conspiratorial. I began to agree with him. Had Lanyer furnished a blonde it would have been a different matter. But that blonde had been Freda Grey.

"I'd rather like to see this Lanyer," Matthews said. "What about paying a call?"

It was rather late, but I got Lanyer on the telephone. I had to tell him it was urgent business, and official. He could come to the Yard or we'd see him at Rudyard Street. He chose the latter, and he'd sounded mightily perturbed.

As soon as we stepped into his office the defence mechanism went into operation. It was after hours and he was due elsewhere for an important interview.

"We'll try not to keep you long," I said, and showed my warrant card. "I'm sorry about that appointment. It might be as well to postpone it. So if you'd care to telephone?"

He had to hedge. He'd already postponed it.

"Well, we're here to try to get any sort of information that might lead us to the murderer of Freda Grey," I told him. "You remember that when I was here in an unofficial capacity I asked about a Dallas Malone and you'd never heard of her. Now you'll have read in your newspaper that Freda Grey was Dallas Malone. Did you ever meet Freda Grey as Freda Grey?"

"Never," he said. "It was news to me. It was an enormous shock that Mr. Ashman should have been involved with such a woman."

"A bit more news," I said. "Freda Grey was the woman who went for Clement Foorde that night in the Café Rond." He stared.

"You mean Ashman was really behind it?"

"By the look of it—yes. The question is, were you?"

He drew himself up.

"You didn't come here to insult me?"

"That's the last thing we wanted. Just forget the indignation and answer the question. We're not taking notes, as you see. At the moment everything's without prejudice."

"I knew nothing about it," he told us. "I'll swear to God I knew nothing. And Ashman assured me he knew nothing. He said the girl must be some hysterical admirer."

"I accept your word. But you were naturally keen on publicising that book to the legal limit?"

"Naturally. Everyone did everything possible from the very start. Ashman himself did."

"How do you mean?"

"He asked me to write him a letter. I have a copy of it here." He looked through a file and found it.

> Rudyard St.,
> Feb. 27th

My dear Ashman,

You ask for a frank opinion of *The Silken Petticoat* on the eve of publication. I can only repeat what I have already told you.

The Silken Petticoat has, in the opinion of our reader and everyone qualified to know, everything that makes for a best-seller. It is the most promising work that has been handled by us for at least the last ten years. If it does not sell, and sell well, we shall be grievously disappointed.

I may add that we shall continue to do everything in our power to make it the best-seller it undoubtedly deserves to be. Subscriptions, while not perhaps quite up to our expectations, are still uncommonly good.

> Yours sincerely,
> ARTHUR LANYER

"Very interesting," I said. "And did he tell you why he wanted such a letter?"

The smile was a bit sheepish.

"Well, it was his idea of publicity. He was carrying it round in his pocket and showing it to anyone—well, where he thought it would do most good."

"You can let me have a copy?"

He said we should have one first thing in the morning. I switched to Ashman himself.

"Did Ashman ever stay at your place at Caterby?"

"Never."

"He never even called on you there?"

"Never. I always saw him in Town. Here generally, or we'd lunch together."

"I see," I said. "Then I think that's about all. Except something purely for the records and strictly between ourselves. Ashman was drowned on the night of the 18th of August. Just what were you doing that afternoon and evening?"

He was about to protest, then changed his mind.

"I know what I was doing," he said. "I know because the whole of that tragic week-end has been in my mind. Naturally I didn't know it was going to be tragic. I played golf that afternoon, and when I came home I pottered a bit in the garden. I specialise in roses, you know. Then I had supper at about eight—my daughter keeps house for me—and we listened to the wireless."

"That's all I want," I said. "Shan't have to trouble you again—at least I hope not."

Then at the door I had another question. I mentioned that mysterious packet of used pound notes. Could Lanyer shed any light? He couldn't.

"Unless he was giving the money to that woman."

"Then why used notes? If she'd had new consecutively numbered notes, who would want to trace them?"

He could only shrug his shoulders. I had nothing else to ask, so we thanked him, and Matthews shook hands for both of us.

"Well, that's got us nowhere," Matthews said as we walked towards St. Martin's. "So where do we go from here?"

I said we'd go nowhere. We'd think things over and meet again in the morning at the Yard.

In the morning I'd thought of only one thing—a character, minor or otherwise, in those happenings that night at the Café Rond. Foorde had been talking to a man. Who *was* that man?

I rang Breck, and his wife told me he was still asleep. I had to say it wasn't all that urgent, but would he very definitely ring me at the Yard as soon as he woke. He actually rang at just before nine.

"Still the Freda Grey business," I told him, "and we're casting the net as wide as we know how. So that night in the Café Rond. Who was the tall, professorial sort of man Foorde was with?"

"Gustave Moraine," he said. "Paris correspondent of the *Clarion*."

"French?"

"Naturalised English," he said. "His mother was English. He's absolutely bilingual."

"He was there as Foorde's guest?"

"Oh no," he said. "It was a chance meeting. I asked Moraine about it. They ran into each other in Regent Street, and Foorde virtually asked him in."

I thanked Breck. I said I'd forgotten all about the man Foorde had been with. Just a loose end that had to be cleared up.

"There we are then," I said to Matthews. "Foorde was there that night because it was a handy place. No wonder, then, he was startled when that blonde arrived."

I asked him if he had any ideas. He had none.

"Everything we've tried so far, sir, has been a dead end. So why not get busy on Ashman and find out once and for all whether he was killed or not."

"Yes," I said. "I'd like that settled once and for all. If he was drowned, he was drowned, and we can put the whole thing behind us and look for something else. Only don't ask me what."

In an hour we were ready to go. We used my car, and we took a route that Ashman might have taken that August evening. At Caterby it took us some time to find Lanyer's house: a detached Edwardian villa with quite a big garden. The garage doors were open, but the car was there. It looked as if the daughter had taken Lanyer to the station.

It was she who opened the door at our ring: a pleasant-looking young woman who didn't look in the least like Lanyer. Hence the amusing preliminaries.

"Miss Lanyer?"

"No," she said. "I'm Mrs. Croft."

"Then is Miss Lanyer in?"

"I'm Miss Lanyer," she said. "I mean I was Miss Lanyer. My husband and I live here with my father."

That made things easier. I reeled off the usual formula about red-tape. Then it appeared that Lanyer had told her about our call on him. To cut a long story short, she confirmed everything he had said. Her father, herself and her husband had been listening to the wireless from eight o'clock onwards that night. I got her to sign a formal statement, we thanked her, and that was that.

"Lanyer's out," I told Matthews as the car moved off. And something of the first exhilaration had gone already out of the morning. It was a fine frosty morning with a healthy nip in the air, but for me it might have been misty or raining. Hallows, as I told Matthews, was a first-class man, and there we were, setting out to discover a something he—and the police—might have overlooked. To me it seemed pretty hopeless.

Matthews had no such despondencies.

"I don't know," he said. "Hallows followed on after that inquest, and he brought an open mind, as they say. Now we're following him up, so why shouldn't something strike us differently from how it struck him?"

We got to Gatsworth and drove slowly through the little town.

"Just a minute, sir! Those two bills we've just passed."

I backed the car. On a wall were several bills, and two of them referred to Foorde's house.

"I thought I saw the word Wicklands," Matthews said. "Selling the house a fortnight today. Pretty quick work that. The furniture this day week."

I hadn't gathered from Foorde that he was selling all that quickly. But it was his own business.

"What about going round that way?" Matthews said.

We had plenty of time, so I took that side lane which we both knew well. I slowed the car as we neared the house. Then we heard noises and went round to the back. Two of the auctioneer's men were already making an inventory.

"Sorry," I said. "We're looking for Mr. Runlet."

"He's gone, sir. He and her too. Went a day or two ago."

"You don't know where?"

"Sorry, sir, but I don't. It was him who gave us the keys."

We went back to the car, but I didn't move it on.

"Wonder where they've gone," I said. "Mightn't be a bad idea to get back to the police-station and have the Yard find out. Or we can do it later."

"Doesn't look too good for Runlet," Matthews said. "Maybe it wasn't Mr. Foorde who was in a hurry. Maybe it was Runlet who asked for salary in lieu of notice and cleared straight out."

"We can get him when we want him."

I moved the car on. In a few miles we left that secondary road and took the narrow lane that soon ran alongside the river. It was lovely there with the trees changing colour.

"This'll be it," I said, and drew the car up. "There's the field gate, and there's the other one almost opposite it."

We got out. There was Hallows' meadow, shaped like a sausage. The ground, yielding to the sun, was losing its frost and was springy under the feet. Thirty yards from the gate, as Hallows had said, was the river, and it didn't take us long to find the actual spot from which Ashman presumably had taken his swim. We looked at it. We looked along the river. We looked round us. We tried to look below the greenish surface of the water, and all the time there was an unreality. We were trying to read words that just weren't there.

Five minutes and we went back to the car. Someone had to break the silence.

"Nothing for us there," I said. "Any point in seeing the farmer who found the clothes?"

We'd begun with plenty of time, but now we had even more, so we went on along the lane to the little bridge. Fifty yards past it a narrower track led to the farm. We drew up by the back door of the house. All round us were buildings, open-fronted mostly, and there was a fine dutch barn.

A middle-aged woman came to the door.

"Mr. Morgan Brown in?"

"He is," she said, "but he's having his dinner."

I showed my warrant card and said we could wait. She asked us to stop where we were for a minute. When she came back she was wondering if we'd rather wait in the kitchen. I said it would suit us fine. There was a good fire.

Ten minutes later Brown came in. He was a tallish, lean man of sixty. I told him we were reopening the enquiry into the drowning of Robert Ashman.

"Thought I'd be finished with all that," he said. "And what is it you want now?"

I said I was sorry, but I'd like him to tell us in his own words what had happened on that Sunday morning. It could be just like a friendly chat.

It was a friendly chat. His wife brought in coffee and we got our pipes going, and then we listened to the story of that morning. It varied hardly a word from the evidence given at the inquest. When Matthews asked a question in the short silence that followed it, I knew it was more out of politeness than anything else.

"One of your farm horses, was it, Mr. Brown?"

"I only have the one," he said. "Just to do odd jobs when it wouldn't pay to start up a tractor, or else the tractor might happen to be busy. A quiet old nag he is. Rare troubled by the flies, though. That's why I often fetch him in during the day if he don't happen to be wanted. There he stands, his old head over the gate, stamping his feet and swishing his tail and looking right miserable."

"Tell them about finding him in that meadow," Mrs. Brown said.

"Oh, that," he said. "Reckon it was someone sort of skylarking. Let the old horse out and he sort of found his way into the opposite meadow."

"You mean he wasn't in the meadow where you put him overnight?"

"The late afternoon it was," he said. "He couldn't have got out by himself. There aren't no gaps. I looked. Reckon someone saw him leaning over that gate and let him out just for devilry."

"There were gaps in the other meadow where he could have got through?"

"He *could*," he said a bit reluctantly. "I wouldn't be surprised, though, if someone opened the opposite gate and let him in the other meadow. Thought perhaps there was more feed there."

Matthews caught my eye. I gave a quick shake of the head. It was extraordinary news, but I didn't want Brown to see the implications—not just then.

"That back lane is used much?"

"Not a lot," he said. "A courting couple or so occasionally."

"There wouldn't have been any then," his wife said. "Not in the middle o' harvest."

"Might have been some boy or other. Just for devilry." He smiled dryly. "One o' them Boy Scouts thinking he was doing his good turn for the day."

"You didn't mention that at the inquest?" I asked him, and tried to make it off-handedly.

"They never asked me. And it weren't no importance."

"Of course not," I said, and got to my feet. "Well, thank you very much, Mr. Brown, and you too, Mrs. Brown, for some excellent coffee. I hope you won't be worried again."

We reversed in the yard and drove back the way we'd come. At the meadow where the horse had been put I dropped to second gear and we looked hard at the hedge, and there was never a gap or a sign of one that had been repaired. We had to go on for a half-mile before we could reverse again, then we came back to the sausage-shaped meadow and stopped at its gate.

"Well?"

"Plain as the nose on your face," Matthews said. "Someone opened that other gate, took the old horse by the forelock and put him in here. If he hadn't done that, it might have been days before the clothes were found on the bank."

"That's the man we've got to find," I said, "which brings us where we were before. Except that whoever it was was bolstering up an alibi. Those clothes had to be found on the Sunday if possible. If not he'd probably have faked a telephone call to the farmer or the police."

"And that makes it murder."

"Yes. Unless it was a busybody or a Boy Scout."

"You don't believe that," he told me with a grin. "Not after those one or two things your man Hallows picked up."

"Maybe not," I said. "But what now? Pettiforth?"

"Why not?" he said. "Looks almost as if this is our lucky morning."

16

WATER AND WATER

IT WASN'T morning, it was afternoon. We went over the bridge to the village and tried the local pub, and had to make do with bread and cheese and beer. Inside half an hour we were on the way to Pettiforth.

As soon as we came into the village we saw the Foxhounds across the green. It was a long, low building, part of it half-timbered, and it looked superior to the ordinary run of village pubs. It had quite a big courtyard with ample back premises. We drove in. It was long after closing time. I knocked at the back door.

It was opened, after a second knock, by a girl of nineteen or twenty wearing riding breeches and a pullover. She said her father was taking a nap, and her mother too. I showed the warrant card and told her why we were there.

"Perhaps we needn't trouble your father," I said. "If you could spare us a few minutes it might do as well."

She showed us into a room she called the residents' lounge. At the moment there were only two residents and they were out. It was a comfortable room with a good fire: a room in which it was easy to talk. I'd imagined her as bucolic and slow to talk, but she was nothing of the sort. She accepted one of my cigarettes, and she was soon talking nineteen to the dozen. We heard all about that telephone call to reserve the room, and so on to the reading of the news in the Monday morning paper. She told us how her father and mother had thought a lot of Ashman. When she had nothing else to say we dragged in this and that just to make more talk. But there was never a hope. Nothing emerged that we didn't already know.

I made as if to get to my feet. She asked if we'd have a drink— on the house. I said I'd have liked one if we hadn't been on duty.

"Wouldn't mind staying here myself some time," I said, and I did get to my feet.

She told us how full they always were till the late autumn, and then again at Christmas, and how the hotel—that was what she called it—prided itself on its cooking. She was now in charge of that, after being away on a two-year course.

"I don't look like a cook, I know," she told us, and laughed, "but I'm just going out to exercise the horses. We always keep a couple of hacks. Well, ever since the fishing stopped."

"No fishing now?" I asked her as we went out to the yard.

"I was almost too young to remember it," she said, "but there hasn't been any for quite a few years."

And then she told me why.

Another minute and I was moving the car out of the yard, but I went no farther than the other side of the green. Matthews knew there was something in the wind, but he didn't know exactly what. I told him, and his eyes nearly popped out of his head.

"I'll go on to Seahurst by bus," I told him. "You get along to Gatsworth and collect a sample, and do the same at Wenhurst on your way back. Come straight to police head-quarters and I'll be there. You ought to make it easily by five."

He moved off. I enquired about a bus and found I had a half-hour's wait, so I began walking towards Seahurst. It was getting dusk when I stepped off the bus. Grainger wasn't in, or Mellett, the police-surgeon, so I left an urgent message. I treated myself to tea and was back at five. Matthews was in the small hall at the top of the steps. He had what we wanted.

We went up to Grainger's room. Mellett was there: a fair-haired, spectacled young fellow of about thirty.

"Masquerading as a copper, are you?" Grainger said, but it wasn't too genially.

"We all have to live," I said, "and don't ask me why. But it's that Ashman business again."

"Oh, my hat, not that!" he said.

"Afraid so. Just a bit of information we happened to pick up and we'd like you people to enquire into it. I suppose, Doc, you haven't actually got Ashman's lung content?"

"I haven't," he said. "There seemed no point in keeping it. But why the question?"

"Just coming to it," I said. "But you do have a record of the analysis?"

"It's downstairs in my office."

"Why shouldn't we go down there?" I said. "To be perfectly frank, I don't know just what's going to crop up."

We went downstairs and through a passage at the back. Hallows had been right about that mortuary: it was the best I'd seen in the provinces. Everywhere was white tiling, and the odour of disinfectant wasn't unpleasant. It had everything: a small chapel, a waiting-room, various store-rooms, shelves for bodies, refrigeration-room and the doctor's office and wash-room. The main room had the usual porcelain slab with drain at one end and water piping below.

"Here's the analysis," Mellett said. "It was done twice, as you know, and doesn't vary more than a tiny fraction." He read it to us.

PHYSICAL CHARACTERISTICS

Slightly turbid.   Odour nil.

CONTENT

	parts per million
Chloride	.28
Alkalinity	.35
Ammoniacal nitrogen	.035
Albumenoid nitrogen	.002
Oxygen absorbed in permanganate in 4 hrs at 80° Fahr.	.027
Iron	.003

| Lead | nil |
| Copper | nil |

"Sounds perfectly in order to me," I said. "I'd say whoever did the job would make it the same. But what I'm hoping you people will agree is that the water found in Ashman's lungs didn't come out of that stretch of the Nelder."

Grainger stared.

"Why not? He was drowned there?"

"This is our information," I said. "Just after the war a small metal works turned over to Government contracts: making special cases for tracer bullets of a new type. Those works are at Penley, between Wenhurst and Gatsworth. They're still small and still operating. But from the first there was pollution—copper probably—which killed the fish. It was war-time and the fish didn't matter. After so many years it has ceased to matter, so there hasn't been any great fuss. The upper stretches of the river aren't affected. Gatsworth gets its water from it, but after the stream leaves the reservoir the water isn't used for anything. There's no main water in those villages at all, till you come to Pettiforth, and that comes from elsewhere with the Seahurst supply."

"My God!" Grainger said. "What you're getting at is that if Ashman was drowned at Wenhurst, there should have been polluted water in his lungs."

"It's reasonable," I said. "Your analysis, Doctor, was perfect. You analysed the water that *was* in his lungs. Sergeant Matthews here has a bottle of water taken from the Nelder at the actual spot where Ashman was presumably drowned. He also has one from Gatsworth. If you, Doc, now analyse the Wenhurst water—the other can come later—and find it tallies with what you took out of Ashman's lungs, then I throw my hand in for good. My bet is that it won't. And that the Gatsworth water will correspond to the Ashman water."

I was sorry for Mellett. As I told him, there was no need to apologise or explain. He'd had no reason to test actual Nelder water against that in Ashman's lungs. He'd found almost standard fresh river water, and that was good enough.

"Better get down to it at once," Grainger told him. "But I can't understand how we missed that pollution."

"My man Hallows missed it," I said. "We'd have missed it if it hadn't arisen out of a chance conversation. And you weren't here when the pollution began. It's been going on so long that it's an accepted or forgotten thing. So let's keep it a domestic matter, so to speak. And, of course, the new analyses may prove you people right after all."

"I don't feel like doing much till I know," Grainger said. "How long will it take you, Mellett?"

About an hour for a rough metal test, he said. Full analyses could come later.

"I'd like to see you at it," Grainger told him. "You'll stay, Travers?"

I said I'd come back in an hour. What Matthews and I actually did was to go to the public library and look up water pollution. We found a couple of learned tomes with everything well over our heads, except perhaps that copper pollution was fatal to fish. Instances were quoted of a solution of .5 in a million parts killing every fish in a river.

Matthews hadn't had tea, so I kept him company, and then we went back to the mortuary. Mellett had that rough check ready. The water taken from where Ashman had been drowned had approximately a .4 copper pollution.

"It's the very devil," Grainger said. "What we can say when this gets out, I don't know."

"Say nothing," I said. "There's no need for it to get out, as you call it. I doubt if we'll even have to use it—publicly."

They promised that the full analyses should be in our possession the next day. We shook hands—Mellett had a consoling grin—and out we went to the car.

"What now, sir?" Matthews wanted to know as we drew round into the London road.

"Get hold of Runlet," I told him. "When that Gatsworth analysis comes through, I think we shall want him."

He didn't say anything for quite a time. Then he was wondering how Runlet could have killed Ashman.

"Let's worry about that when the time comes," I told him. "First thing to do is to find Runlet. I wouldn't be surprised if he told us all about it himself."

Wharton was a mightily surprised man. He, too, wanted to begin working out how Runlet had managed to kill Ashman. All I would say was that it must have been in Gatsworth water: *if* Mellett's analysis of that water tallied with what Ashman had swallowed. I admitted that would mean drowning in a bath.

"Let's get hold of Runlet," I said. "We want to know where he is and have him on tap if that analysis is what we hope."

"How're you going to do it? Ask Foorde?"

"Seems the only source," I said. "And I think I'd rather see him than talk to him over the phone."

I put it that way because I didn't exactly want him to see Clement Foorde himself. I was flattering myself, too, that I could get out of Foorde more about the Runlets than ever Wharton could. But he made no objection. I got Foorde's number and he happened to be in. In a quarter of an hour I was at Marston Square, and alone.

Foorde pooh-poohed my apologies for the lateness of the hour. He had been working, he said. His was the kind of brain, he added, that functioned best in the very late hours. He insisted on ringing down for coffee, and with it we had an excellent brandy. I told him I was accepting his hospitality under false pretences. All I wanted to know was Runlet's whereabouts. We wanted to question him about Grey again.

"You knew the Runlets had gone?"

I told him I'd happened to be that way that evening but had found the house empty.

"Perhaps I should have let you know," he said, "but I found it better to have a clean cut. I couldn't contemplate any more days as uncomfortable for all of us. Between ourselves, I added quite a respectable gratuity."

"And you don't know where they are?"

He shrugged his shoulders.

"I didn't enquire. I bade them a very good goodbye and wished them well, and they had an excellent reference, with permission to use my name." Then he frowned. "If it's any help to you, I believe she had a sister somewhere on the south coast. Where was it now?"

"Hastings."

"Of course," he said. "I was almost thinking it was at Brighton, or Eastbourne. I remember now: it was Hastings."

I asked if I might use his telephone. I rang Wharton and told him Runlet might be found at Hastings. Since he wasn't on too good terms with his sister-in-law, he was pretty certain to be out of the house if the weather was fine. I suggested observation at the main shopping centre. I added that if I wasn't needed again at the Yard I'd be going home.

"It's unpardonable of me to enquire into your affairs," Foorde said, "but do I gather that you're still interested in that man Grey?"

I said, or I had to say, we were.

"I had a letter from him today," he said, and I must have stared. "He seemed to have picked up—from somewhere—that we shared the same school. He mentioned the fact and had the effrontery to thank me—*thank* me, mind you—for what he was pleased to call my various kindnesses to the Runlets."

"Nothing surprises me about Grey," I said. "He has the impudence of the devil. Might I see the letter?"

"I threw it into the fire," he said. "I wanted nothing to do with the fellow."

"You're wise. Be absolutely ruthless if he attempts to force himself on you in any way. He's just a specious trickster. Where did he write from, by the way?"

"He didn't. That's what made me feel there was something unpleasant about the letter. That, and its glibness. I think the address was simply London, W.1. Does that correspond with any address you have?"

I said we hadn't any address. He'd been at the Martindale but had vanished from there. Then I was getting up to go, but he dissuaded me. I wasn't interrupting his work; and if I were, then it would be good for him. So we began talking generally, about furniture I think it was, and I happened to admire that Georges Clairan portrait of Bernhardt, and at once he was on his favourite topic of the theatre.

He told me that as a very small boy he had been taken by his maternal grandfather, the old Comte de Chavragnes, to Bernhardt's dressing-room on the first night of her famous Hamlet. That, he went on, was the beginning of her third, her finer, sublimated period. In the second she had done little but exploit her own personality, or Sardou had exploited it for her with a succession of melodramas. All her great parts had been designed for self-exhibition: Fedora, Theodora, La Tosca—all were Bernhardt.

He was a fascinating talker when he was in the vein, and he certainly was that night. There was a fascination merely in watching him, with his touches now of Porthos, now of the Abbé Liszt: the great bulk of him stretched out from the chair and that *mousquetaire* moustache and imperial: the mass of swept-back hair and the gentle gesture of a white hand, and with it all that precious, beautifully modulated voice.

It was after eleven o'clock when I rose to go. I refused to let him accompany me along the corridor, and as I went down the old-fashioned stairway, across the dimly lighted reception hall and out to the chill of a frosty night, I was still back at that turn of the century. When I looked hopefully round for a taxi I should not have been surprised if a hansom had clip-clopped towards me from the shadows of the trees. But there was neither taxi nor hansom, and I decided to walk home.

That night, I was thinking, had been almost a celebration of a highly successful day, and then, as I began thinking about the day, the glamour of the night began somewhat to fall apart. Foorde had gone out of his way to be extraordinarily charming to me, and I couldn't help feeling something of toadiness in myself, or a subservience. Foorde had dazzled me with experience and strung before me a score of famous names, and I must have sat gaping like a rustic on his first trip to Town. It was a queer sort of feeling and one that I couldn't analyse: the knowing, perhaps, that while I didn't like Foorde the more I liked myself even less.

And before I got back to the flat there was something else that came vaguely into my mind. About that famous salon, where I had spent that hour and a half, there had been some kind of difference, and for the life of me I couldn't think what it was. It puzzled me, but it didn't keep me from sleep, and when I woke in the morning it had gone from my mind.

When I walked into Wharton's room next morning he was at the telephone and uttering a monstrous deal of soft soap and placation. I guessed he was talking to Grainger, so I scribbled something and passed it to him.

"Grainger," he said, and cupped the receiver. "Everything's turned out as you said."

In a minute I was doing the talking.

"Morning, Grainger. I understand everything's turned out beautifully."

"For you, yes," he said, "but not for us."

"Don't you believe it," I told him. "Mellett there?"

"Hold on a minute and I'll get him."

Mellett didn't sound too happy either. He was even less so when I asked him if there'd been any traces of chloral hydrate in Ashman's stomach.

"Should there have been?"

"Not necessarily," I said. "I was wondering if someone slipped him a Mickey. You, as a detective-novel fan, will know what I mean."

That didn't cheer him. He said there hadn't been any post-mortem appearances. I said that with chloral hydrate there very rarely were unless the dose had been mighty strong. And with an ordinary Mickey it wouldn't be that. Just enough to make a man pass out, or lose his grip.

"I suppose you haven't still got any stomach content?" I asked, and more to cheer him up than anything.

"As a matter of fact I have," he said. "You see, I'm practically new to this kind of work, and the Ashman business was my first really tricky job."

I wished I could have reached out along the line and thumped him on the back.

"Marvellous!" I told him. "What're you grumbling about? Have another crack at it and see if you can find traces. And of alcohol?"

"There *was* alcohol," he said. "Only a very small quantity. No possible question of it causing unconsciousness."

"Fine," I said. "You get to work, there's a good chap, and give us a ring some time later."

As I told Wharton, we were having the devil's own luck.

If Mellett hadn't been young and keen and taking his job mighty seriously, that stomach content would long ago have been flushed down the drain. Then he told me that Matthews was on the way to Hastings. If the luck held we ought to be talking to Runlet before the day was out.

"What's your idea of how he might have worked it?"

"All sorts of way," I said, "once he'd got Ashman there. I suppose he could have spun him some yarn. If it concerned Foorde, though, Ashman ought to've been suspicious, because he and Foorde weren't on speaking terms, though Runlet wouldn't know that."

"If Runlet appeared to be speaking in perfectly good faith, mightn't Ashman have come down out of sheer curiosity?"

"Maybe," I said. "Or Runlet could have made it some personal matter between Ashman and himself. We did once have the idea, you know, that Runlet might have blackmailed Ashman about knowledge of that nylon business. Whatever it was, all Runlet had to do when Ashman arrived at Wicklands was to apologise or not for Foorde's absence—according to the circumstances— pour him a sherry or a short drink with a Mickey in it, and that was that."

He was interested to hear about that letter that Grey had written to Clement Foorde, and after that there wasn't anything for me to do, so I had the morning off. When I reported back after lunch there was still nothing doing. I lent Wharton a hand with some clerical work and we had tea. It was just after four o'clock when a call came from Matthews.

Matthews had picked up Runlet, who had been about to enter a cinema with the two women. Runlet, he said, had claimed an alibi for that Saturday night, and he was just off to Seahurst with him to check it.

"Ask him if Runlet knows where Grey is," I whispered to Wharton.

We had to wait quite a little time.

"He was a bit shy about coughing it up," Matthews said. "He's at the Bewley Hotel in Southampton Row. And he told Runlet he was coming at once into some money. It sounded to me as if he'd soaped the Runlets up so that they'd join him again."

"Runlet any hard thoughts about Foorde?"

"Good lord, no," Matthews said. "He couldn't speak too highly of him. Nothing else? Then I'll be pushing on. I'll give you a ring as soon as I've gone into that alibi. Then you can tell me whether you'd like him in Town or not."

Matthews wouldn't have too long a drive, so it wasn't worth my while to leave the Yard. Wharton and I drew up our chairs and yarned for a time and read the evening papers. It wasn't till well after six o'clock that Matthews rang.

"The alibi's O.K.," he said, "and I've got a statement. Runlet was at Seahurst all right. Spent the evening with his nephew's wife, who was staying at Seahurst with some friends. All fair and square to me. Don't think it's even worth the trouble of cross-checking with Dykeham."

Wharton clicked his tongue.

"What do you want done with him?" Matthews was wanting to know. "Take him back to Hastings or bring him to Town from here?"

"You've got the Hastings address?"

Matthews said he had.

"Then take him home," Wharton said. "He'll be on tap if we want him for anything." He added a last minatory word. "But that alibi of his had better be good."

"It's the very devil," he told me. "If Runlet's out, where are we?"

"Back at Grey," I said. "We'll have to tackle *his* alibi. It never was plumb water-tight to me."

"But Grey didn't kill Ashman?"

"I know," I said. "But he might know who did."

Wharton made a gesture of annoyance. Then the buzzer went again. Mellett was on the line. Wharton had a word and passed the receiver to me.

"Hello, Mellett. How did things turn out?"

"Well, I treated with ethyllic ether and I found a trace."

"That's all there should have been," I told him. "Good work, Mellett. We're very grateful to you. Send the official chit in due course."

"So there we are," I said to George. "Now we know that Ashman really was murdered. All we have to do is find who did it."

But we didn't even begin talking about that. Once more the buzzer went. George lifted the receiver and gave an annoyed hallo. Then he was staring.

"Who? . . . Where? . . . Right, I'll be down straightaway. See a car's there."

He flicked the receiver down and made for his hat and coat.

"The devil to pay," he told me, and he wasn't troubling about a curtain. "Grey's dead. Foorde has shot him."

17

JOURNEY'S END

Two cars were outside the door and a uniformed constable was on duty. Wharton brushed impatiently by him, and I followed across the hall and up the stairs. A plain-clothes man was at Foorde's door. We went through.

Jewle was there and Anders, the police-surgeon. Foorde was sitting unconcernedly in that tall Spanish chair of his and facing the door. He got to his feet at the sight of us. He even gave me a smile.

"Sorry you've been troubled like this, Superintendent."

"Troubled?" Wharton said, and waved a hand vaguely around. "It's my job."

Across the room, just in front of the Empire table, was Grey: on his back, feet from the table and a dark stain on the waistcoat front. Coat and overcoat were both open. A light-brown hat lay about a yard away.

Wharton frowned down, pursed his lips, then got on one knee. The waistcoat was singed. That shooting had been done at close quarters.

Anders began to speak. Wharton gestured impatiently and got to his feet.

"Now, Mr. Foorde, suppose you tell us all about it."

"Why not?" Foorde said. "Though I can't say it's altogether a pleasure. But I was sitting in that chair about twenty minutes ago when there was a tap at the door. That was unusual. Usually I'm warned if there's a strange caller for me. So I opened the door, and there was this man Grey. Before I could close the door on him he walked in.

"I can't remember the exact words he said, but he began in the vein of a letter he'd written me a day or so ago. Reference to his school and the Runlets. I told him I had nothing to say to him, and I was going to the door to show him out when he produced a gun. That gun there, by his hand. He told me to give him what money I had. I told him not to be a fool, but I didn't like the way he was holding the gun. So I went across to the table there as if to find some money, and he was right behind me. Then I suddenly whipped round and had him by the arm. We struggled a bit, and I actually had the gun in my hand when it went off."

He shrugged his shoulders.

"That's all, Superintendent. If you'd like me to put that down in black and white, I'm perfectly prepared to do so."

"Time of death coincides," Anders said quietly.

Wharton was looking down at the carpet, and from where I stood I could see the marks of the struggle.

"Yes, Mr. Foorde," Wharton said reflectively. "That seems all right. But a man of your size oughtn't to have had much of a struggle."

Once more Foorde shrugged his shoulders.

"My heart isn't all it should be. And he was like an eel. It was as much as I could do to stick to his arm and work my way to his hand."

"Anybody hear all this?"

"Yes," he said. "Old Sir Henry Ridge, who has the flat beneath. I believe the Inspector here has had a word with him."

"He confirmed everything," Jewle said.

"What do you mean—everything? He wasn't in here, was he?"

"He heard loud voices and the shot," Foorde put in gently. "He came up to see what had happened. This is what he saw. Then I rang the police."

It was a queer atmosphere in that room: Wharton brusque where he ought to have been suave, and always giving little apologetic glances towards Foorde, and the others as subdued as if we were all in church. There was Foorde himself, overwhelming at any time, but now self-invested with a kind of Olympian indifference. He wasn't even troubling to make himself out the victim of fate. Almost the least important thing seemed to be the body of Grey.

"You say you were holding the gun when it went off?" Wharton said.

"I wouldn't be sure," Foorde told him. "I think I was. I know he was twisting my wrist. But does it matter?"

"Matter? Surely you can't mean that? If you actually fired the gun, there's the question of manslaughter. If he'd fired it and you'd been killed, then it'd have been murder." He turned to Jewle.

"Make arrangements for a paraffin test. We'll have to know exactly who was holding it when it was fired."

He explained to Foorde just what the test was.

"Luckily I happen to know about that letter Grey wrote you," he said. "Everything's in keeping with what we know about him. All the same, I'd like to see that Sir Henry Ridge. I wonder if you'd ask him to come up here?"

Foorde shot a quick look. It was a long time, I guessed, since he'd been given a virtual order. But he went.

"Now," said Wharton. "Prints on the gun?"

"Everything as it should be," Jewle said. "Two confused sets."

"What *is* the gun?"

"Looks like a French or Belgian 6.35 millimetre. That'd be our .25."

"Expect you're right," Wharton said. "Grey had been in Belgium. How many in it?"

"Full. Just the one shot fired."

"What was in his pockets?"

Jewle waved at the table.

"Just the usual. About a fiver in his wallet."

"No papers?"

"No, sir. No papers. Not even a card."

Wharton went across to the body. There was something suddenly in my mind.

"What about my slipping along to Grey's room? There might be something there."

"Yes," he said. "Take a man with you. Give it a good go-through."

I took Grey's keys from the table. One of Jewle's men named Edwards went with me, and as we were going down the stairs Foorde and an elderly man were coming up. He looked like an ex-civil servant, and that should have been in capitals.

"You off?" Foorde asked me pleasantly.

"Yes," I told him. "They've discovered that room of yours is a bit too cluttered up."

*

We took a police car. The Bewley was at the Euston Road end: a newish building in reinforced concrete that looked as hospitable as a morgue. I saw the assistant manager. He tried to look as shocked as if Grey had been a bosom pal. He also made as if to go into the room with us.

Edwards turned the key in the door and we got to work. The first thing I knew was that Grey had bought himself quite a lot of new clothes, including a handsome silk dressing-gown. There was also a fine new leather case. It was in the bottom of the wardrobe, like that case that Freda Grey had kept, and it was the only thing in the room that was locked. We put it on the bed and opened it.

Inside, and each in its little cellophane wrapping, were seventy-eight pairs of nylons. There was a cheque book and a paying-in book. Only one cheque had been used, and that to pay the hotel. The paying-in book showed the account had been opened with £320, and the day after he had left the Martindale. There was also a bundle of notes: £108 in all. But there wasn't a single letter. There wasn't even a piece of paper.

Or there wasn't till Edwards noticed the inner flap which the nylons had hidden. It was a sort of tight pocket, and a couple of fingers brought something out. It was an envelope. With gloved fingers I drew out the something inside. It was a kind of wrapper, the paper buff. Suddenly I knew what it was—the paper that had wrapped those two hundred and fifty pound notes which Ashman had drawn from his bank!

But there was more. On the buff paper were fingerprints round which circles had been drawn in ink. There was also a squiggley initialing in pencil—the marks which the bank cashier had made at Ashman's request.

I put that envelope in my pocket and we finished our search of the room. We did it as thoroughly as if we'd been spies in a melodrama, but there was nothing else that we found. The clock had moved on over an hour when we got back to Marston Square.

Grey's body had gone. No one was in the room but a plain-clothes man. He told me Wharton was in the dining-room with Foorde, who was making a statement.

I asked what the paraffin test had shown.

"Mr. Foorde actually had the gun," he said. "But there were marks of the other's hand."

"And the old boy—Sir Henry Ridge: you heard what he said?"

"Yes, sir, and he bore out everything Mr. Foorde told us."

I was looking about me. In the utter stillness I all at once heard faint voices from the dining-room. I moved across the thick-piled carpet to where Grey's body had been and looked down at the chalk marks. I was thinking they were more than a desecration. And then suddenly I knew something. I knew why that room had seemed different when I had left it the previous night.

I walked slowly round that room, and when I caught the eyes of the plain-clothes man he was looking at me rather puzzledly. I looked at the Adam mantelpiece and I looked up at that Georges Clairan. I looked at that fine old Spanish chair with its tooled leather and the noble curves of arms and legs. I looked at the low, Queen Anne table with its array of periodicals and papers. On top was a *Spectator*. I folded it and put it in my pocket.

I went across to Foorde's desk and actually reached for a sheet of paper. Then I changed my mind. There was no point in writing a note to Wharton. In my own mind I was certain, but my mind wasn't Wharton's. What I had to give him was a cut-and-dried case: something with never a flaw or a loophole.

"There doesn't seem a lot doing here," I said. "I think I'll push off for the night. Tell the Chief so when he comes out, will you?"

I pushed off, but it wasn't to the flat. In Wharton's room at the Yard I opened the Freda Grey file and collected her prints. There'd be a duplicate set down below, but I wanted to make sure. I took Grey's prints too. I found a taxi and went round to the flat, where I had what I grandiloquently call my private little criminological collection, and there I found Ashman's prints, which I'd secured at the time of the Maurice Ashman enquiry. Then I got out my fingerprinting apparatus. I also had for cross-checking purposes the letter which Freda Grey had written to Ashman and the one Foorde had written about the Runlets, and that copy of the *Spectator*.

In the middle of it all Wharton rang from the Yard. I said I'd merely gone home to wait for instructions.

"Find anything at the Bewley?"

I hesitated. I decided to come clean.

"Something rather important," I told him. "I'm actually working on it now. Be with you in half an hour. That do?"

I just managed things in time. Wharton wasn't looking too happy, even if he was sampling a pot of tea.

"What's all this?" he wanted to know when I put the biggish envelope on his desk.

"Among other things, it's the wrapper that was round those two hundred and fifty used notes that Ashman drew out of his bank early last February."

"You found it in Grey's room?"

"I did."

His eyes narrowed.

"Then he got it from his wife. Ashman paid her that money after all."

I shrugged my shoulders.

"There's more to it than that," he told me. "He got it from his wife. Did she give it to him? Or did he take it?"

"After killing her?"

"Exactly. And why? What use was it to him? How did he know what it was?"

The hands went out in a gesture of annoyance.

"Everything's cock-eyed. That business this evening. Everything pat. Just as Foorde described it. But why should Grey, just out after a stretch and questioned on his wife's murder, attempt armed robbery? That's what it amounts to. Was he mad, or what?"

"Why not look inside the envelope?" I asked him. "Slip your gloves on first."

He had a look, but not at those two letters. Those were still in the bureau drawer at the flat.

"These prints with the rings round them. What's that for?"

"The rings were drawn by Ashman himself," I said. "He wanted to identify them, or be able to identify them."

"Whose are they? The cashier's?"

"No," I said. "I think the cashier's must be those I've put a little tick against. Those with a little cross are Freda Grey's. Those with the dots round them are Grey's. And you'll notice one thing. Everybody has taken care not to touch those prints with the circle round them. They're as unsmudged as the day they were made."

"Look," he said with a forced patience. "What I want to know is this. The prints with a ring round. Whose are they?"

"Foorde's," I said. "It was Foorde who committed the murders."

But it wasn't quite so cut and dried as that. Wharton had forced my hand and I had had to speak before I was sure—sure enough, that is, to satisfy a Director of Public Prosecutions. Wharton himself was sure enough, even if he did realise that he had to present the best possible case. That night there was no need to indulge in argument or slick dialectics. Everything, after that first moment of awareness, stood in sharp focus. All we had to do was make others see as clearly as ourselves.

So the next morning Wharton himself went down to see Runlet, and he was pleased with the statement he brought back. I spent well over an hour trying to get Gustave Moraine in Paris, but when I did get him the line was remarkably clear. We were into the third period of three minutes before I'd got what I wanted.

Breck, he said, had been under a misapprehension about his—Moraine's presence—in the Café Rond. It had been the previous day when the two had met in Regent Street. Foorde had suggested dinner, but Moraine had been heavily engaged. The conversation had gone something like this.

"I can't even manage lunch to-morrow. Then there's a meeting of the Amis de France at three, and tea afterwards."

"What about dinner tomorrow night?"

"Can't be done. There's a minor conference at Fleet Street at half-past seven."

"Well, your Amis de France affair is in Lower Regent Street. What about dropping in at the Café Rond at about six or so for a drink and a chat?"

That is what had been agreed. Moraine had dropped in at about a quarter past six and had found Foorde there.

So far so good. Before lunch I went round to Christie's and after it to Sotheby's. Then I called on Austin Fryer. He's the senior partner in the firm of King Street antique dealers: as knowledgeable a man as any in the trade and one for whom the Broad Street Agency had once done a highly successful job of work. He told me everything I wanted to know, and chiefly about carpets.

Wharton was back when I returned to the Yard, and we compared notes. There were still one or two things that we wanted, and one of them would require behind the enquiry the authority of the higher-ups. So we adjourned till the following morning. I did go on to the Bewley and asked about Grey's telephone calls. I wasn't so lucky. Grey hadn't used the hotel system at all. If he had done any telephoning it had been from outside. And then, when I came to consider it, it wasn't anything of a weakness after all. Grey would have been a fool if he had used a line that could be checked.

It was lunch-time before Wharton had concluded his business with the higher-ups. While he was at it a call came from Foorde. I took it.

"Oh, it's you, Travers. A most distressing business, that of the other night. But about the inquest. Did I understand it was tomorrow?"

"Tomorrow," I said. "We'll send details along to you."

"Why I asked was that this business has thrown completely out of my stride. I'd like to get away for a day or two. I shall probably have a week or so in Paris."

"No earthly reason why you shouldn't," I said.

"Then I'll probably leave after the inquest. I shall be looking forward to seeing you when I get back."

"All to the good," Wharton said when I told him. "You'd better write down what he said before you forget."

It was after four o'clock when he came back from the bank. We had a cup of tea and went into things, and at last we were satisfied. All that remained was to draft out and more or less commit to memory what would be said to Foorde. It was after six o'clock when that was done and Wharton went out for a final word with Commander, Crime.

"Tell Foorde we'd like to see him about seven," he said. "Smarm him well over."

Foorde was still at Marston Square—at least no word to the contrary had come from the two men on his tail. Two minutes after asking for his number I was talking to him.

"Sorry to bother you, but Superintendent Wharton and I will be along to see you at about seven o'clock. That suit you?"

"It's about the inquest?"

"Yes," I said, but I knew I had hesitated. There was a silence, and it was a moment or two before he broke it.

"I shall be here," he said. "But I wonder if you could tell me one thing. There was nothing about it in the papers, but did you ever find out where Grey was living?"

"Well, yes," I said. "Why did you want to know?"

"I just wondered. It'll be a relief, you know, when it's all over."

"It certainly will," I said. "At least to you."

"You mean?"

"Well, won't it?"

"Yes," he said, and the voice for once was curiously weary. "I suppose it will."

I rang off then, and I was wondering if by chance I had given anything away. It was a pity I had let that slight irony creep into my voice. Not that it mattered. Foorde couldn't stir without our knowledge. And to make a man's mind a bit uneasy was often a good policy. It put him too desperately on the defensive. And in any case we weren't going to Marston Square for a friendly chat. Foorde would know where he stood from the word go.

At a quarter to seven we were set. At five to we were getting out of the car. Matthews was with us. He'd stay outside Foorde's door.

Once more we went across the hall and up the stairs to the corridor. My heart was beginning to beat a bit quickly and I was wondering how I could stop it. Wharton rapped on the door. He opened it and we stepped inside.

18

THE LAST VOYAGE

FOORDE was in that tall chair by the fire. At his elbow was a table with a glass, a siphon and a decanter of what looked like brandy. There was also a box of cigars.

He was immaculately dressed: broad linen collar white as the first snow, the ample tie neatly spread, the black velvet jacket glistening richly in the light of the tall reading-lamp behind his head. There was a faint scent in the room as if he had only just dressed after a bath.

He made as if to rise.

"Don't get up," Wharton told him abruptly. "We'll find ourselves chairs."

"You'll have a drink? Or are you on what you call duty?"

"No drink."

"A cigar, perhaps? I can recommend them."

"Thank you, no."

"Then perhaps you'll allow me to drink by myself," Foorde said smoothly. "My heart has been troubling me today. The doctor ordered me to bed. Nothing too serious, that rest and these two-hour tablets won't put to rights. But do sit down, gentlemen. You've come about the inquest?"

"No," Wharton told him bluntly, and reached for a chair. "Something far more important. I think perhaps you know what I mean. All the same, you're entitled to try to explain a few things. Mr. Travers here is going to relate them to you. Interrupt him or not as you wish."

"I shall be most happy to listen to Mr. Travers. You'll pardon me just a moment."

He poured himself a drink and the hand was not too steady. He took a cigar, rubbed it gently between his fingers, clipped it and lighted it. I was wondering just how to begin. I couldn't tell him he had deliberately tried to bind me to him in a kind of friendship, and that I'd been so much of a fool as to take the hospitality and the graciousness at their face value. I, who'd always imagined I'd hated poseurs and snobs, had let myself be flattered. I'd have liked to tell him so, if only to deflate that ego of his, just as my own had since been deflated, but I knew there'd be no need to drag in the personal. By the time I'd finished talking he'd know the truth about both himself and me.

"Now, Mr. Travers, I'm at your service."

"Then I'll begin," I said, "and with yourself. Early this year you were financially in Queer Street. The reasons were various. Heavy expenditure over a number of years and accumulated debts which your reputation could no longer stave off, and also the failure last year of a firm in France in which the bulk of your money was invested. Last February you were being sued by your wine merchants for a debt of £300, but the case was dropped because you paid them early in March. I have to tell you where you obtained the money.

"To do that we have to think of Robert Ashman. You were his patron in a way. You may have helped him with theatrical work. I don't know. But when he wrote a book which looked like being a success—he showed you a letter from his publishers to prove it—he got you to read it and you gave your opinion. There were things about it you didn't like, and that was when the scheme came to him. He had a supreme impudence and was no respecter of persons; but how he put things to you, again I don't know. Rumours of your financial troubles had got about—I'd heard them myself—so he might have put the scheme bluntly, or jokingly, or even as a dare. But you wrote to the Press about his book and made your criticisms so strong that the book couldn't help but have a tremendous boost.

"He gave you £250 when you badly needed it. He may have thrown the bundle of notes jokingly in your lap with a kind of, 'Have a look at that', or it may have been a strictly business transaction. Also he may have promised a further percentage of royalties, but he certainly did take care to protect himself, and to be in a position to double-cross you. He kept the wrapper from the notes. It had a bank cashier's signature on it, and it also had your signature—your finger-prints."

He looked at the ash of the cigar.

"This word *may*. Isn't it rather redolent of fiction?"

"When I use the word it's only an unimportant context," I told him. "Don't be critical—yet. There'll be plenty of facts. You *may*, for instance, have pretended to Ashman to treat the whole thing as a joke, and the money as a loan. That doesn't matter. You had the money and he kept the wrapper. And you'd tacitly agreed that in public you hadn't to be on speaking terms.

"Now to that night in the Café Rond. There was a question I should have asked myself about that. If I had asked it, then both Freda Grey and her husband might have been alive today. The question was this. *How did Freda Grey know you were going to be at the Café Rond at a certain time?* You didn't know her. Only Ashman could have known, and he could have obtained the information only from yourself. Therefore you *weren't* at daggers drawn. And so on to the logical climax.

"Pardon the hypothesis, but this is what probably happened. You met Moraine in Regent Street on the Sunday. Ashman rang you that night about a meeting. You said it couldn't be till the Monday night after, say, seven o'clock, as you were meeting Moraine in the Café Rond at six or thereabouts. That was when Ashman, who had both a fertile and an unscrupulous brain, saw another publicity scheme. The next morning Freda Grey became a blonde, and the rest we know. You were furious. You knew that only Ashman himself could have been behind the affair.

"But what could you do? You could work like the devil and finish that second volume of an autobiography, and so get a publisher's advance and pay Ashman back what you'd be pleased to call a loan. But that wasn't important once Ashman had shown himself for what he was. He didn't want the money. He was making, thanks to you, as much money as he wanted. You might still be useful. I think he even had the impudence to suggest other means of publicity. But there it was; everything you had made yourself, everything you were and had, was at Ashman's mercy. One word from him and you were a ruined and discredited man. So you killed him."

"Pardon me," he said, and it was a bravado to kill that climax. He had glanced at his watch.

"I'm not being rude," he said, "and you're not boring me. It's just that I have to time my next tablet. Please carry on."

A grunt from Wharton had begun as a growl. He was finding it hard to keep his temper.

"You made a slip about that holiday of yours," I went on. "In the club you took pains to tell me you had been in France all July and August. But you hadn't. You went to France on the Sunday after Ashman's death."

I admitted we couldn't tell how he had induced Ashman to come to Wicklands, and then I told him of that miscalculation about the water in the bath. Nelder water wasn't uniformly Nelder water pure and simple. I said that after dumping the body from Ashman's own car he probably came back to Town by train. He had gone there in the morning with a return ticket but had come back in the later afternoon. Wenhurst station would be gloomy enough that night and he had only to get into the train at the last minute. And he was the easiest man in the world to disguise. The world, in fact, always knew him in the voluminous cape and the broad felt hat. Put on a bowler and an overcoat, turn up the overcoat collar to conceal the lower part of the face, and there was disguise enough.

"If proof of all that were needed," I said, "it lies in what follows. You hoped your troubles were over. You'd gone to France to put them behind you, but when you got back you had a tremendous shock. You didn't know about Freda Grey: that she was Ashman's mistress and he'd told her everything. That paper wrapper had become an heirloom: a lucrative source of money, and Freda needed money. She blackmailed you. You had to raise money at all costs. That was why you approached me, as representing the Broad Street Detective Agency."

I didn't glance round at George to see how he was taking that disclosure. I did wait a moment while Foorde once more looked at the ash of the cigar and took a sip of his drink and then another glance up at the clock.

"You didn't want Freda Grey found," I said, "because you knew where she was and who she was. You wanted us, frankly, to dig up about her all the dirt we could as a kind of counter-balance to her blackmail. But that was when you also had to raise money, just in case. The last thing on earth you'd do would be to destroy the perfection of this room about which you'd written in your autobiography and which had become an inseparable part of the legend—if you'll permit me to say so—which was yourself."

He gave me a little bow at that.

"But you sold the *sang-de-boeuf* vases at Sotheby's and the Aubusson carpet at Christie's and replaced that eighteenth-century carpet with a modern replica. But meanwhile something happened that you could never have foreseen. You didn't know she had a husband. You'd agreed to let her have the money at the end of the week, but her husband came out of jail and he heard the whole story. He wanted money at once. She telephoned you to that effect, and you agreed to bring the money. You came to the house that foggy night, and you killed her. You hunted the place for that wrapper, but it wasn't there. It wasn't there because her husband had it, and he was then coming back from Manchester.

"He'd inherited that wrapper and he proceeded to make use of it. You didn't even know he existed till he telephoned you out of the blue. I imagine you were driven almost crazy. As soon as the police hunt was over and he was let loose he put on the pressure. That was why you were selling Wicklands and its contents—to pay Grey what he demanded—and why the Runlets had to go.

"And then you had a magnificent idea. It came to you that night when I was here asking about the Runlets. You introduced Grey's name. You spoke of a letter. In other words, you prepared the way for Grey's call on you. You knew Grey would be ringing you to fix up finally about the money. You also tried that same night to get Grey's address from me, but I didn't know it. If I had known it I think you'd have killed him at his hotel. Don't ask me how."

Foorde politely stifled a yawn. He glanced again at the clock.

"But I'd swallowed that letter and the tale you told me," I went on. "Next day when Grey rang you you told him you had the money and were prepared to hand it over on receipt of the wrapper. He came here that evening, and as soon as he was inside the door you shot him at point-blank range. You made the sounds of two angry voices and stamped on the floor and carried his body to near the desk. You rubbed your wrists and scuffled the carpet, and by then your neighbour below you had come up to see what was happening. And you'd had time to go through Grey's pockets. I think he'd brought a fake wrapper which you put in the fire. But he'd double-crossed you. We have the wrapper. It was found in his room at the hotel. And something we didn't find at the hotel—*any more shells for that gun*. A man doesn't have a gun and only just six shells.

"Not that deduction was needed. Here's the wrapper, in this envelope. It tells the whole history. The cashier's prints are on it, and Ashman's, and Freda Grey's and Grey's. These ones here with the rings round them are your own. They're the hall-marks, as it were, that make the piece genuine. And that's all. I don't claim that there haven't been omissions, but the gist of everything is there."

"Yes," Wharton said. "The gist is certainly there."

His hand went to his breast pocket as if to produce the warrant, then it fell again.

"You've heard what was said. You realise the gravity of it. Any questions you'd like to put? Any explanations to give?"

Foorde put the cigar carefully on the ashtray. It must have been a fine cigar. The aroma had been superb and the ash had been even and it had still not fallen. He poured a little more brandy into the glass and squirted just a suspicion of soda. He leaned back in the chair, glass in hand.

"No," he said slowly. "I don't know that I'm prepared either to admit or disprove. The excellent Mr. Travers"—there was a slight sneer with the smile—"has told us a story which would have been hailed enthusiastically by Sardou. I trust he regards that as a compliment."

He took another sip at his drink.

"But please, gentlemen, don't think me altogether a fool. While I admit nothing, I was at least aware that it wasn't necessary for you two gentlemen to call on me here for the sole purpose of acquainting me with my role at an inquest." The ring flashed as he waved a hand.

"But that doesn't matter. What I would say is this. I've had a longish life. A full life. You're familiar with du Bellay? The sixteenth-century friend of Ronsard? There's a line of his that I've always thought superb. It has the French conciseness. The perfect patina."

He gave us a peering, quizzical sort of look.

"Perhaps even the erudite Mr. Travers doesn't know that line. It's this:

Heureux qui, comme Ulysse, a fait un beau voyage.

Which, if you'll permit me to translate, is—*Happy he who, like Ulysses, ends a great adventure.* Life, gentlemen, *has* been an adventure."

He glanced at the clock. In a minute, and far too late, we were to know that that talk of a heart and a doctor and tablets had been sheer bluff. As he was saying those last words his fingers were in his waistcoat pocket, then the capsule was in his mouth and he emptied the glass. He gave a queer shake of the head. Wharton uttered a kind of growl and went forward, and Foorde was feeling for the handkerchief in his breast pocket and wiping his mouth. He swayed in the chair, and Wharton's bulk hid him from sight till he slid from the chair to the ground.

A minute or two later Wharton was at the telephone. I stood looking down at Foorde, and all at once I picked up that white silk handkerchief and covered the horribly distorted face. Strangely enough, I was feeling no hatred; only a furtive kind of pity. *Un beau voyage*, I said to myself. And at the end of it, for all that flaunting of a panache, not a landing in a loved Ithaca but shipwreck and annihilation.

Wharton was suddenly at my elbow. I didn't even know he was no longer at the telephone.

"The hell of a way to die. Hope to God the higher-ups aren't too sore about it."

He was sniffing. I thought it was at the faint odour of cyanide, but it wasn't.

"Him and his brandy and cigars! And his French! Who did he think he was?"

He whipped that handkerchief from the face. There are times when I have almost hated George Wharton, and that was one.

"Guilty as hell. One thing I can give him credit for: he had the nerve of the devil. I've seen worse on the stage."

He felt for his pipe and began lighting it.

"What was he? Mad as a hatter?"

"At the very back of him someone like you and me," I said. "He made just the one slip, and after that the fates were riding him and he couldn't stop. All the same, it's a pity."

"A pity?" He looked as if he couldn't believe his ears.

"It always is," I said. Then Matthews peered round the door. He came over. He looked down at Foorde and he looked at me.

"Too clever for us," I said. "He had the last laugh."

"Not much of a laugh by the look of him," he said. "Don't expect he's laughing much where he is now."

"You never know," I told him; and as I put that handkerchief again over the face, I saw that Georges Clairan, and I was wondering if already in some shadowy limbo or purgatorial fields Foorde was hobnobbing with Bernhardt and Coquelin or even Molière. Telling Sardou, perhaps, of a fine new plot that had just come into his head: one just made for Bernhardt: a plot outlined to him in his earlier days by someone called—who was the fellow?—oh yes; a chap with the odd name of Ludovic Travers.

THE END

Lightning Source UK Ltd.
Milton Keynes UK
UKHW011051180820
368381UK00001B/76